JOURNALED TO DEATH

Recent titles by Heather Redmond

The Journaling mysteries

JOURNALED TO DEATH *

The Dickens of a Crime series

A TALE OF TWO MURDERS
GRAVE EXPECTATIONS

* *available from Severn House*

JOURNALED TO DEATH

Heather Redmond

For all the family who have enriched my life these past few, love-filled months. Leander, Andy, and the assorted offshoots of clan Hiestand, Ruhoff, Austin, Pruett, Perry, Johnston, Ragusin, Levy, and Stokes.

This first world edition published 2019
in Great Britain and 2020 in the USA by
SEVERN HOUSE PUBLISHERS LTD of
Eardley House, 4 Uxbridge Street, London W8 7SY.
Trade paperback edition first published
in Great Britain and the USA 2020 by
SEVERN HOUSE PUBLISHERS LTD.

British Library Cataloguing in Publication Data
A CIP catalogue record for this title is available from the British Library.

ISBN-13: 978-0-7278-8950-8 (cased)
ISBN-13: 978-1-78029-660-9 (trade paper)
ISBN-13: 978-1-4483-0358-8 (e-book)

All Severn House titles are printed on acid-free paper.

Severn House Publishers support the Forest Stewardship Council™ [FSC™],
the leading international forest certification organisation.
All our titles that are printed on FSC certified paper carry the FSC logo.

Typeset by Palimpsest Book Production Ltd.,
Falkirk, Stirlingshire, Scotland.
Printed and bound in Great Britain by
TJ International, Padstow, Cornwall.

ONE

'The usual today, Doctor O'Halloran?' Mandy Meadows couldn't hide the genuine smile that always crossed her face at the sight of the handsome surgeon. The hospital reminded her of a small town, the way she saw the same people over and over. She moved from behind the coffee bar's cash register and might have leaned forward a little.

The surgeon quirked a brow, his dark blond hair curling over his forehead. His gaze dipped down. Mandy wasn't sure if he was checking out the hint of cleavage exposed by her University of Seattle Hospital uniform's scoop-neck 'USea' T-shirt or the basket of almond biscotti next to the register.

A line had formed behind him, though, so she couldn't flirt her way into upselling his order. Next was Dr Burrell, a neonatologist, and he would be in a hurry. She guessed the men were about the same age, a couple of years older than she was but still under forty.

The surgeon's voice dipped into a sexy rumble. 'Thanks, Mandy.'

Mandy ignored the tingles racing down her spine as she rang up his quad shot. He passed his employee card across the reader and the cash register spit out his receipt.

'I'll be with you in a moment.' She flashed a slightly less flirtatious smile at Dr Burrell then turned to the espresso machine to fill Dr O'Hottie's – no, Dr O'Halloran's – order.

While she pulled shots, the counter shook. Dr O'Halloran did like to go through her snacks. Dr Burrell's phone rang but he didn't answer it. Unlike most of the hospital staff, he respected the sign that said, *No phone calls at the counter, please.*

When Mandy handed her favorite surgeon his white cup, he half-smiled before walking toward the elevators. Mandy couldn't help watching his fit, scrub-covered body as he sauntered away.

Dr Burrell cleared his throat and pushed his glasses up his nose.

Mandy's cheeks flushed. 'I am so sorry, Doctor. What would you like today?'

'My usual?' The words came out with the hint of a question.

She tilted her head. 'I do apologize. What is your usual again?'

He smiled sheepishly. 'Just checking. What are your specials today?'

Mandy pointed a perfectly manicured finger at the printed card in front of the cash register. Her daughter, Vellum, had painted black polka dots over her red nail polish. They planned to film for Mandy's lifestyle blogging accounts that evening and her fingers would be on display.

Dr Burrell let out a deep breath as he scanned the list. 'Who does all the calligraphy on your signs? It's really beautiful work.'

'I do. I teach all sorts of crafty things online. I'm a semi-professional video blogger.' Now that she was divorced, she needed her income from the coffee bar, her social media, and her tenant to keep up the mortgage on her Maple Leaf neighborhood house.

'I'll have to check that out,' Dr Burrell said with a polite curve of his lips.

Mandy laughed. She could see the reserved doctor keeping a journal, probably a beautifully bound leather edition he studiously wrote in with an old-fashioned fountain pen. But she doubted he'd like her brand of bold, primary-colored, art-focused journaling. All the rage these days, it had taken over from adult coloring books, scrapbooking and rubber stamping as the newest creative craze. It fed her artistic side and helped to build her vlogging business.

She saw two nurses exit the emergency room on the other side of the ground floor. They were coming for their drinks. She needed to move the doctor along because they could be 'witches with a B' at this time of day. Three o'clock was shift change at the hospital. 'That would be great, Doctor Burrell. How about I get a drink order started for you? Or were you looking for one of the cookies? I think the ginger thins came out really well today.'

'I'll have to have one. And a dirty chai, please. Sixteen ounces.'

'You know, it's less expensive to get a regular latte with chai syrup instead.' Mandy blushed. 'Not that you need to worry about saving money.'

'No, no, I appreciate the tip.' He grinned, taking half a decade off his narrow face. 'But I like that new chai brand Fannah ordered.'

Just then, like a ghost behind her, Mandy's co-worker Kit appeared. She glanced over Mandy's shoulder, saw the neonatologist's order and went to prepare his drink. After he moved to the delivery side of the counter, Mandy quickly rang up the nurses' orders. By the time she was finished with that, her manager had arrived with the fresh cash drawer. Fannah opened the register and swapped the drawers, then went to count the till. It was the end of Mandy's shift.

Thank God.

Noting that Kit was finished with the drinks, Mandy quickly went to the sink and washed the pitchers and spoons that had piled up during her time alone. Then she went to the back office, ready to grab her things and maybe even be home before her daughter arrived from school.

When she glanced up, Fannah was blocking the door. One look at her face told Mandy that things weren't going to go quite that smoothly today.

'What's up?' Mandy asked, twisting her fingers together.

'Your cash drawer is fifteen dollars short.' Fannah gave her a level, dead-eyed stare. She could be a lovely person, but also the opposite. 'You know our policy. It must be paid back immediately unless you want to be terminated right now.'

'All I have is fifteen dollars,' Mandy protested. 'It's Vellum's allowance. It'll ruin my whole night at home with her if I have to give you the money.'

Fannah's voice stayed level. 'Then you want to lose your job today?'

Mandy doubted Fannah wanted to fire her. She hated training new staff. 'Look. I remember being distracted by a trio of teenagers. Maybe one of them put their hand in the till while they were distracting me by asking how various flavor combinations tasted in the drinks. In fact,' Mandy said, warming to her theme, 'I think some Kind bars are missing, too. We seem a little light on them and I didn't sell that many today.'

'You need to keep an eye on that,' Fannah snapped. 'I'll have to start an inventory right away. You can have an hour of overtime to help Kit while I do it or you can be terminated. Either way, it's up to you.' Fannah's gaze remained unemotional as she held out her hand, palm up, to receive the fifteen dollars.

Mandy gritted her teeth at the injustice of it. She couldn't afford to lose her job. While her income as a lifestyle vlogger was increasing, it didn't pay the health benefits she desperately needed. That was what this hospital coffee bar job was for. She supposed Fannah was trying to meet her halfway, since the hour of overtime would cover the fifteen bucks when her paycheck came.

Slowly, she opened her wallet and withdrew the ten- and the five-dollar bill her daughter was expecting when she arrived home. She knew exactly what Vellum planned to spend it on, too. Friday night was movie night with her best friend. Mandy had exactly forty-eight hours to come up with the money or Vellum would go running to her father. The mere thought sent Mandy's blood pressure racing north.

As soon as Fannah snatched the money, Mandy texted her daughter to say she'd be late. She wanted to promise to pick up pizza on the way, but that would have to go on the credit card. As it was, she might have to withdraw cash on it to pay the allowance. Which would automatically begin collecting interest. But that was tomorrow's problem.

She turned to Fannah. 'Don't we have a security camera watching us? Couldn't we identify those teenagers? See them with their hand in the till?'

'No security in this part of the hospital,' Fannah said. 'Sorry, love.' Just like that, nice Fannah had been restored. 'Why don't you assist Kit with the drinks while I do the inventory a little early today? If we don't have many customers, you can mix up cookie dough and get it in the cooler.'

Like most hospitals, much of what they sold was packaged goods from third-party vendors, but the staff loved fresh baked cookies and were willing to pay a premium for them. They used a toaster oven and the small industrial workspace in the back to make their product.

They had a rush for fifteen minutes or so, mostly hospital staff at the end of their shift who couldn't face the Seattle commute without caffeine in their systems. Or maybe the heaters in their car couldn't keep up with the bitter February chill outside. Through the glass windows across from the coffee bar, Mandy could see it was already growing dark. Her thoughts went to the art piece she planned to create tonight, a spring scene, something with the cherry blossoms that would make Seattle so beautiful in about six weeks. She and Vellum had sketched and painted the stunning trees at the University of Washington Quad last year and she would happily incorporate those memories into her journal.

After that, Mandy mixed up a batch of dark chocolate chip cookies and one of ginger thins. She covered both bowls with plastic wrap and stuck them into the refrigerator to chill before she clocked out.

As she passed by Fannah, her boss called, 'You're right. Based on the sales data, it looks like three Kind bars are missing. Having said that, it's been a week since I did an inventory. They didn't necessarily get stolen today. But it's something to keep an eye on.'

'Can we ask for a security camera?'

'*You* probably can.' Fannah shrugged. 'Scott likes you a lot more than he likes me.'

Mandy had heard the story. Scott Nelson, their divorced hospital maintenance supervisor, had chased Fannah about six months ago. And who could blame him, given her seductive, husky voice and former fashion model body? But Fannah had shut down his constant requests for dates and Scott had barely spoken to her since.

At the end of her commute, Mandy took a left off Roosevelt Way and pulled into her long, partially paved driveway. A couple of spots of ice formed in muddy depressions. This was the perfect night to hang out with Vellum in their cozy new home art studio. She had paid her tenant, her cousin Ryan Meadows, to haul her plug-in electric fireplace from the basement into the sunroom after her ex-husband had moved out, to make it usable in all seasons.

'Mom!' Vellum called as Mandy entered through the back door of the house. Her daughter held an open soda can and a slice of toast covered with peanut butter and bananas.

Mandy kissed her daughter on the cheek and set her purse on the counter. 'Anything good in the mail?'

'No. Just bills. Why did you have to stay at work late? I thought we were filming tonight.'

Mandy made a face. 'There was a problem with my till and I had to give Fannah all the cash I had on me or lose my job.'

'That sucks.' Vellum licked peanut butter off her glossy lips.

'I know, but she gave me an hour of overtime to make it up. I'll get you your allowance. Just not tonight.'

'But by Friday, right?' Vellum asked anxiously.

'I'll figure it out. I don't want to ruin your movie night.' Mandy glanced around. 'Is there anything in the fridge? I'm starving.'

'There's some of that stir fry you made this weekend, but all the rice is gone.'

Mandy opened the refrigerator and pulled out the container. 'Is Ryan home?'

Vellum took a bite of her makeshift sandwich and spoke around it. 'I don't think so. All the leftovers would be gone if the human vacuum cleaner had been upstairs.'

'Hmm. I could call a certain teenager the same thing.' She dumped some of the mushroom, carrot, celery and tofu dish into a bowl, leaving one last serving for Ryan. It was hard to keep good boundaries where her cousin was concerned. Six years older, he'd protected her from bullies in her grade school years and they'd remained close ever since. Unfortunately, he'd developed a drinking problem about fifteen years ago. He'd managed to hold on to his job as part of the maintenance staff at the hospital, but he drank heavily outside of work hours, often with a questionable group of friends. Though he would never eat upstairs family-style, she'd long since persuaded him he was doing her a favor by eating their leftovers so she could keep meals fresh. He was very private, but she had seen him every day since he'd moved in last spring. He always responded when she texted him and scheduled a time to chat or do small projects around the house.

Mandy checked her social media on her phone while she waited for her food to heat. She and Vellum ran her 'Mandy's Plan' empire together, consisting of an online craft shop with fully monetized social media sites complete with videos, classes, and sponsors. More than a year ago, Mandy had taken a class about journaling for record-keeping and stress relief. When her marriage broke up just weeks later, her mother helped her assess any skills and interests she had that might help her earn money. Since she had dabbled in art for most of her life and had learned how to create digital art a couple of years ago, she decided to make stickers for her journal and anyone who might buy them from her. To highlight her products, she filmed herself and Vellum using them and posted the video logs online. Soon, tens of thousands of people were following her on social media and she worked hard to give them what they wanted, with fully realized monthly setups for journals as her business's cornerstone.

'What are we going to sell for April, Mom?' Vellum walked over to the large wall calendar and looked at the dates.

Mandy planned her monthly journal layouts, called spreads, at least six weeks in advance. Everything had to be done early if customers were going to design their own journals around her artwork, whether they bought her stickers or art pieces, copied her or Vellum's work directly, or used it as a jumping-off point for their own creativity. March was already in the can, even though it was only February fourth. She was starting to design her April spreads so she could go back and build up sticker sets using her iPad and some software.

'I think cherry blossoms are the way to go this year,' Mandy said. The microwave dinged. 'They'll just be starting to bloom when most people are designing their April spreads. We can do a variety of flowers for the stickers.'

'What headers are you going to do?'

'A "to do" list, of course. The month and the numbers. Mood tracker. Habit tracker.'

Vellum swallowed a mouthful of banana. 'What about your extra one?'

'I'm thinking I'll do a reading log.' Mandy liked to create one new spread idea with her stickers for each month. Last month she'd done a movie tracker.

'Is April a reading month for most people? How about a garden log instead?' Vellum put the last bite into her mouth and set her plate in the sink.

'You know, honey, that's a great idea. And it fits perfectly with my idea of different flowers for the stickers. We can do garden stake stickers too. Our customers will love that.'

Vellum smiled with satisfaction. Although she occasionally complained about working on Mandy's business, Mandy did pay her for her time. And it beat having to babysit or mow lawns. 'I'm on the clock right now?'

Mandy took her food from the microwave. 'You got thirty seconds, kid. I'm going to eat some dinner and we'll get going in a few minutes, OK?'

'Yep.' Vellum put her earbuds in her ears and fiddled with her phone. Her head started bopping to some music.

Mandy hoped some of Vellum's income went into her savings account instead of purchasing entertainment. But there were only so many important thoughts she could have in the course of one long day. She'd add talking to Vellum about money management to her goal list for the month. Cory used to manage all the money matters. In the long run, she realized it had been a mistake to let him take charge.

The basement door slammed below them. Ryan must be home from work.

After she'd eaten and done the dishes, Mandy thoroughly washed and moisturized her hands, then took a quick look through the bills while her hands dried. Utilities, mortgage, internet, divorce lawyer. 'Blech.'

She dropped the envelopes on the counter and walked through the dining room into the art studio. It was perched over an open space that held gardening tools. Cory had been the family gardener, and Mandy hadn't found the time to take over her ex's duties. Ryan had promised to mow as part of his rent as soon as the grass began to grow.

As always, her shoulders relaxed and her soul sighed with happiness as soon as she entered the space. She went around the room turning on lights, then switched on the fireplace. She couldn't afford to make any permanent upgrades like the recessed spotlights she craved, so she'd chosen a variety of tall and short lamps, which created a clear glow and a shadow-free filming area around the worktable. One thing she did to be different from the other journaling vloggers was work with Vellum in tandem. It helped her followers see that every artist had a different style, and their work didn't need to turn out just like hers. It also expanded their range, with both student- and working-mom-oriented journal spreads.

'Is the tripod set up?' Vellum asked, coming into the room.

Mandy checked her phone, the newest model, to make sure she was filming the table properly. 'Check. Hands pretty?'

Vellum waved her fingers. Her manicure was yellow with tiny cartoon stickers.

'Very cute.'

'Since your manicure isn't very mature, I figured I'd better go even sillier,' Vellum explained. She sat down at her spot on the left and pulled her journal off the windowsill.

Mandy had already taped down a piece of drawing paper the same size as the journal with some pretty pink washi tape. She added pencils and a couple of hard-tipped pens. 'Let's quickly get down a pencil sketch so we know what we're doing, then I'll start the recording.'

'Where's your sample?' Vellum asked.

Mandy opened her hard-cover sketchbook to the right page and leaned it on the wall between them.

'Nice,' Vellum said. 'When did you get that done?'

'About two a.m. when I couldn't sleep,' Mandy explained.

'Mom. You have to take better care of yourself.' Vellum used her annoyed teenager voice.

'At least I used my insomnia wisely.' She picked up her pencil and lightly sketched the image on her drawing paper. This would be the copy she'd scan and sell in her online shop. Customers could buy the image as is or she would add a small calendar on demand.

Vellum watched her, then attempted to copy the design in her own journal.

'Don't worry if it isn't perfect,' Mandy said. 'It took me at least five tries to get my sketch right.'

'What was the hardest part?'

'Making the branches look natural,' Mandy said. 'I wanted a perfect oval around the Space Needle, but still naturalistic.'

'The Space Needle looks like a spaceship. How natural is that?'

'I'm adding the mountains in the back, along with some of the skyline.'

Vellum wiggled her pencil. 'It's pretty ambitious.'

'That's why customers pay us the five bucks to get our copy,' Mandy said.

Vellum smirked. 'You're making it hard on purpose?'

'We have to make it ambitious.' Mandy defended herself. 'Or what is the point of calling ourselves experts?'

Vellum stuck her tongue out the side of her mouth as she concentrated on reproducing the sketch. Meanwhile, Mandy's pencil glided effortlessly up the middle of her paper, building her Space Needle, then filling in the tops of the mountains behind it, then back to the office buildings below before starting on her branches and cherry blossoms.

Twenty minutes later, Vellum dropped her pencil and stretched out her hands. 'I'm good.'

'OK.' Mandy cleared away the pencils, leaving just the pens. 'We'll ink on camera, then let it dry before working on the color.'

'Don't you want to check mine?'

Mandy grinned at her daughter. 'It's art, honey.' She turned around and switched on the video app on her phone. Later, she would add a voiceover and music, completely erasing the audio track from the original filming at times. They had a setup in the corner where she could record her face under proper lighting for the intros and outros, but the phone camera worked perfectly for table work.

At her nod, she and Vellum both put their hands on either side of their work and drummed their fingers on the table, displaying their manicures. 'Today we're going to work on the calendar page for our April monthly spread. I'm really excited about this image. We're Seattle girls, and I've been waiting for the chance to fit in our local landmark, the Space Needle.'

'Love it,' Vellum said encouragingly. 'But we had to add in flowers, too, because it's April!'

'You're so right,' Mandy agreed. 'We'll start with our Tombow Fudenosuke hard-tip markers. If you aren't experienced with them, I'd suggest a Micron fine-tip marker. As you can see, we've already penciled in a lot of our plans. We can erase our mistakes before they become permanent.'

Vellum laughed. 'But even if you make mistakes with ink, you can always incorporate them into your designs. If that doesn't work, cover them with a white pen. I always like—'

Vellum was drowned out by a loud noise in the house. Mandy stayed rooted to her chair, knowing she'd ruin the take if she started moving around. But the noise continued, like Bigfoot was walking down her uncarpeted basement stairs.

She frowned and turned to shut off the recording.

'What is that?' Vellum asked.

'I set the laundry basket by the basement door this morning and forgot to take the load to the washer. Maybe Ryan knocked it down the steps?'

'It didn't sound like the laundry.' Vellum bit her lip.

Mandy jumped to her feet. What if something had happened to Ryan? 'Stay here. I'll go check.'

She dashed to the basement door in the hall between the main areas and the bedrooms. The laundry basket was still by the door. Not only that, the door was closed. She heard another thump, then all went quiet.

'Ryan?' Her hands itched suddenly. She closed her fingers around her palms.

No one answered. She called her cousin's name again as she put her hand on the doorknob. 'Please be OK.'

TWO

The basement door wasn't locked. Mandy pulled it open easily. The lights were off, making it too dark to see.

'Ryan? Are you there? Hello?' she called down the steps, her voice getting increasingly frantic.

No answer. She flipped the light switch and peered into the brightened space. The stairwell went straight down for most of the distance to the basement, then turned onto a landing, blocked in from the main part of the room by a built-in bookshelf facing out.

Blinking, she started down the stairs, calling for her cousin again.

Then she saw it. A shape, pressed against the back of the book-shelf. A long shape. She put her knuckles to her mouth, unable to translate what she was seeing.

Ryan's body stretched out flat on the floor, his eyes staring up at her. She could smell the booze wafting off him. Typical, at any hour when he was off shift.

'Oh my God,' she whispered. 'Ryan.' He'd fallen down the steps. She knelt next to him, calling his name again, and tentatively put her fingers to his neck, then his wrist. No pulse pressed against her, but then she didn't really know what she was looking for. Besides, his eyes were open. Vacantly open, and partially covered by an overlong fringe of graying brown bangs. Her cousin was dead.

She moved into a crouch, surveying his body. He still wore his janitor's uniform from the hospital. His mouth hung open, his tongue protruding slightly. She put her hand on his chest but felt nothing moving. *Oh God.*

Then she saw a teal rectangle poking out from under his lower leg.

Her stomach lurched. 'No!' she cried.

She recognized the teal journal. When had she last seen it? Had he slipped on one of her discards? Had she inexplicably left it on the stairs?

She stumbled to her feet, tears blinding her. What if Ryan had fallen because of her carelessness? The walls tilted as she zig-zagged up the stairs with legs that wanted to fold into the fetal position. Her fingers poked through her pockets, trying to find her phone. *Help, she needed help.*

Then she remembered it was still on the tripod. *Vellum.* Her daughter couldn't know. But Mandy didn't have a landline. She ran into Vellum's room and grabbed her phone to call 911.

'Please state your emergency,' said a pleasant voice on the other side of the line, once Mandy's fumbling hands had made the connection.

'My cousin. He's dead,' she blurted.

'Ma'am?'

'I'm sorry. He's on the staircase landing,' she said.

'What is your name and address?'

Her thoughts seemed to be covered by fog. Slowly, she pulled them through the gray, strand by strand. 'Amanda Meadows.' She stuttered through her address.

'Is your house clearly marked?'

'Yes. I should go check on my daughter.'

'Please stay on the line,' the woman said. 'Can you identify the deceased?'

'Yes.' A sob rose from deep in her chest. Mandy pushed it back down. *Lock it in a box.* 'My cousin, he lives here.'

'His name?'

'Ryan Meadows.' Mandy realized she was breathing hard, like she'd been in a race. Black spots danced across her vision. 'He's only forty-two.'

'Mom?' Vellum appeared in her bedroom. 'What's going on? The basement door is open.'

'Shhh.' Mandy pulled her daughter completely into the room by the arm. She put her hand on Vellum's shoulder.

'Why are you using my phone?' Vellum asked, bewildered, pulling away.

'Shhh,' Mandy said more loudly.

'Ma'am?'

'Yes, I'm still here.'

'Emergency services should be there soon,' the operator said. 'You will hear the sirens.'

'Sirens?' Vellum squeaked.

'Ryan died, honey,' Mandy said.

Vellum's eyes grew wide. 'In the basement?'

Mandy nodded. She wanted to vomit.

Her daughter's lips trembled. With her lower lip pressed out, she looked eleven again. Mandy was reminded of how young her daughter was, just fifteen. Not even old enough to drive.

Just then, Mandy heard the sirens. 'I have to let the police in.' She pressed her fist against her stomach. 'We don't want them to break down the door.'

Vellum sat on her desk chair. 'I can't go out there.' She picked up her old stuffed Winnie the Pooh from her bookcase and clutched it to her chest.

'OK, honey,' Mandy said. 'Stay put.'

Mandy lifted the phone to her ear again as she walked through the hallway to the front door. Luckily, she didn't have to pass by the gaping door to the basement.

She looked through the peephole out to the front walkway. A police car, lightbar flashing, had pulled off the street next to her raised front lawn. As she watched, uniformed police officers exited the front seats. She saw the driver say something into his mic. The lightbar turned off. Another whine resounded in the cloud-covered winter sky, an ambulance signaling its approach.

The two uniformed officers rang her doorbell. She arched back in shock. Why hadn't she simply opened the door when she saw them? Her hands shook as she turned the deadbolt and opened the door.

'Ma'am?' A dark-skinned, muscular police officer twitched his lips at her. 'I'm Officer Jones. We had a report of a death?'

'Yes, Officer. My cousin. He rents from me.'

'You can terminate your call now,' said the voice in her ear.

'Oh, sorry.' Mandy disconnected and thrust the phone into the back pocket of her jeans.

'Officer Martinez, ma'am. Did you find him?' asked the second officer, a burly Hispanic female, several inches shorter than Mandy but probably matching her in weight.

'Yes, Officer. On the basement landing. We heard thumping noises, louder than normal steps.' She rubbed her roiling stomach.

'We?' asked the male officer.

'My daughter and I. The three of us live here. Me, my daughter and Ryan.'

The female officer took out a notebook. 'Ryan is the deceased?'

'Yes.' Mandy pressed her lips together. 'He drinks. I think he slipped and fell.'

'Why do you think that?' the first officer asked.

Mandy's chin trembled. 'One of my journals is under his leg. I must have left it on the steps.'

'Is that common?' the second officer asked.

Mandy shook her head. 'No, but why else would it be underneath him?'

'Did you touch the body?' the first officer asked, his voice growing kindlier.

She wiped her eyes. Tears had dripped down her cheeks without her even noticing. 'I touched his neck and his wrist. I didn't move him. My daughter didn't see him. Oh, I touched his chest, too.'

Officer Jones nodded. 'Where is your daughter?'

'Her bedroom. We were both in the art studio, and then I went into her bedroom to get her phone so I could call nine-one-one.'

'We'll need to come in now,' Martinez said. Her tone stayed aggressive.

Mandy stepped back from the door as an ambulance pulled up in front of the house.

'You're sure he's dead?' the female officer said acidly.

Mandy's voice shook as she answered. 'His eyes are open.'

'Where is this landing?' she asked.

'Down the hall. The basement door is on the right around the corner.'

'We'll take a quick peek then come back for the EMTs,' said the first officer.

The two officers came into the house, the woman hoisting her belt as she stepped in. They disappeared from view for a couple of minutes while Mandy stayed at the door, feeling like her feet were bolted to the small floral rug on the hardwood floor. She heard light footsteps, then Vellum was beside her, wrapping her arms around Mandy's waist.

'The police, the EMTs,' Mandy murmured. 'We just have to get through all this.'

Vellum said nothing, just buried her face into Mandy's neck. Mandy kissed her daughter's cheek, narrowly missing a mouthful of Vellum's thick dark blond hair. She'd inherited Cory's abundant straight hair, so unlike Mandy's fluffy dark brown curls.

Officer Martinez reappeared and walked into the living room. 'Why don't you take a seat?' She pointed to the couch.

Mandy pulled her daughter across the room while the officer went outside. Two EMTs came into the house. Mandy could hear them going down the steps. No one spoke to them for several minutes. She listened to the rain pounding on the roof and remembered she needed to repair the gutters this year. Ryan would have helped her. He liked handyman jobs. She couldn't afford to keep up the house without him.

She bent her head. A sob escaped her. Vellum leaned against her shoulder. She could feel her daughter's slim body shaking.

'We're a mess, aren't we, honey?'

Vellum sighed. Mandy closed her eyes, only opening them when more people came into her house. The patrol sergeant introduced herself and asked them to stay put for now. More time passed. A lot of time.

'Ma'am?'

Mandy glanced up at the sound of an unfamiliar voice. Since Cory had left, she hadn't seen any man as attractive as the speaker. On another day, he would have been worth a second look. He had thick dark brows about the same color as her own, above slightly narrowed eyes of a piercing light blue. A long, straight nose, jutting cheekbones covered by tanned skin. His five o'clock shadow came perilously close to a beard, but she could still see his bowed upper lip and long, full lower lip through the scruff.

The man held a badge in front of her nose, then clipped it back on his belt. A gray jacket and slacks hung over a triangular body. The shoulders of the jacket were spattered with rain. No tie, but a blue dress shirt that didn't have the intensity of his eyes. 'I'm Detective Ahola, Homicide. I'm going to take your statement, then you will have to leave the premises so the crime scene can be processed.'

Mandy frowned. Vellum's head lifted. 'It must have been an accident,' she protested. 'We heard him fall down the steps.'

'Please, Miss—'

'Vellum Moffat,' Mandy said. 'My daughter.'

'Do you mind if I record your statement?' the detective asked, pulling his phone from his belt.

'No,' Mandy said.

The detective fiddled with his phone, setting it on the trunk in front of Mandy. He spoke some preliminary information, including a code number and the date, then started asking them questions about the evening.

'It was really loud,' Vellum confirmed, when they returned to the noises they heard.

'I thought it was the laundry basket,' Mandy admitted, 'but it's still where I left it this morning.'

'Yes, ma'am. May I?' He gestured to the plush cranberry-colored recliner to the right side of the fireplace. She used to have two of them, but Cory had taken the other one when he moved out.

She nodded. He proceeded to run her through the evening's events again, taking notes along with making the recording. She answered as honestly as she could, keeping her attention focused on his expressive eyebrows. When they came together, she expanded her answers. When they tilted down, she sped up.

Abruptly, he started firing questions at Vellum. At least he hadn't attempted to question her without Mandy present. At first his questions were the same as those to Mandy, but then he asked one that Mandy knew would terrify her daughter.

'Were you or your mother apart for any length of time after she came home from work?'

Vellum gave him a patented teenage 'adults are nuts' stare. 'I went into my bedroom while she ate dinner, but my bedroom and the kitchen share a wall. She never left the room.'

'How do you know that?'

Vellum gave a bored shrug. 'It's an old house. The floors squeak.'

'What about later, when you started working on your, err, journal project?'

'She never left,' Vellum asserted.

When Vellum came to the end of her brief recitation, Mandy put up her hand, feeling more like herself now. 'What aren't you telling us? He slipped and fell, right? Why is a homicide detective questioning us?'

'Just following protocol, Mrs Meadows.'

'Ms,' she corrected. 'I went back to my maiden name after my divorce.'

'Mom,' Vellum protested.

Mandy realized that last sentence might have come off as flirting, which she wasn't attempting to do, of course not, not with her cousin dead in the house. 'Just being factual.'

'My dad moved out last year. They just signed the final papers a week ago.' Huge tears filled Vellum's large, expressive milk chocolate eyes and cascaded down her cheeks.

'Are you done?' Mandy asked. 'I'd like to take my daughter somewhere more comfortable.'

Vellum gasped in horror. 'Can I at least get my stuff?'

Detective Ahola glanced between the two of them. Then he lifted his hand and crooked two fingers at Officer Martinez, who'd been in the hallway. Mandy hadn't noticed. 'Can you supervise them while they gather a few things? Medications and such.'

'My phone?' Vellum asked.

'You can keep your phone, Miss Moffat, but your mother can't take hers. We need to take a copy of that video you were filming at the time of Mister Meadows' death.'

'No phone?' Mandy whispered. 'Can you legally take my phone?'

'I can get a warrant if you like,' Detective Ahola said. 'But I'd rather process the phone quickly and get it back to you.'

'You have nothing to hide, Mom. Just let them take it. I have all your contacts backed up on my phone.' Vellum pulled at her sleeve.

'But—' Mandy felt any power she had eroding. 'I suppose my video is too long to simply text to you, Detective.'

He nodded. 'That's my assumption. You can forward your calls to your daughter's phone. Do you know how to do that?'

'I'll figure it out.' Mandy swallowed hard. 'You'll lock up when you're done?'

'And notify you when you can re-enter,' he promised. 'By the way, how did he come into the house, if no one saw him upstairs?'

'He has his own entrance into the basement from the backyard,' Mandy explained. 'The door is underneath the mudroom off the kitchen.'

The detective nodded. 'Thanks.'

Mandy could feel Vellum's body shaking, so she rose from the sofa. Her daughter followed like a puppy. In the master bedroom, Mandy pulled an overnight bag from under her bed, then made a face at all the dust on it. When was the last time anyone had talked her into going anywhere? She slid it back under the bed and pulled a bookbag from her closet, tossing warm pajamas and a work outfit into it.

Vellum shifted from side to side, impatient, as Mandy settled toiletries into a plastic bag and threw it on top of the clothes. She desperately wanted her journal to record her thoughts and fill out all her daily trackers, but it was in the art studio. Knowing Officer Martinez wouldn't let her near that part of the house right now, she followed Vellum into her bedroom. Her daughter stuffed several items of clothing into her school backpack.

'Don't forget underwear,' Mandy reminded.

'Mom!' Vellum shrieked.

Mandy groaned at the misplaced outrage and sat down on the edge of the bed while Vellum selected socks and other items from her top drawer. Then she pushed a bunch of makeup off her dresser directly into her bag.

In a softer voice, Mandy asked, 'Do you have what you need for school tomorrow?'

'I didn't do my homework.'

She shifted on the bed, glancing around the room to see if any homework had left her daughter's backpack yet. 'You can do it at Grandma's.'

'Can't you write me a note? Extreme distress?'

'It will just pile up if I do that. You'll be miserable for the rest of the week.'

Vellum shoved her feet into heavy black boots. Though hideous, Mandy knew her daughter loved them.

Officer Martinez gave a hacking cough, indicating they were out of time.

'My purse is in the kitchen. I'll need it.'

The officer let her eyelids flicker for a moment, to express her disgust. 'I'll have to search it.'

'Ryan never came upstairs since I got home,' Vellum said.

'Sorry,' the officer said. She opened the bedroom door and shouted for someone to photograph the purse and bring it to her. After that was taken care of, she led them back through the house, where she allowed them to remove their coats and hats from the coat rack. Then she took them outside the front door and around the house to the driveway, because she didn't want them going near the basement door.

Mandy unlocked the passenger side door of her car and dumped her bags in the back seat, then slid into the driver's side. The officer tapped on her window. She opened her car door again.

'Here's a card with the information you'll need about tonight,' the officer said.

Mandy took the card. 'Thank you.' She watched as the officer went back up her steps, as if she lived there, not Mandy.

'Where are we going?' Vellum asked with a hiccup.

'Grandma's.'

'She lives across the street.'

'I know that, but I might as well park over there so I can go to work in the morning.'

'She's got that dumpster parked in her driveway and there's never room on the street at this time of the night.'

'It never ceases to amaze me how detail-oriented you are,' Mandy said. She hauled herself out of her seat and grabbed her bags. Vellum pressed up close against her as they walked gingerly down the driveway, keeping an eye out for ice.

Barbara Meadows, Mandy's widowed mother, dressed in flared yoga pants and a long sweater, had the front door open before they'd climbed up the steps from the street to her raised front yard. 'I've been wondering what's going on over there. Is everyone OK?'

Tight-lipped, Mandy shook her head. Barbara glanced at her then stepped back into the house, holding out one hand to Vellum. 'Come in, sweetie. I'll fix you some hot chocolate and you can tell Grandma all about it.'

'Non-dairy,' Vellum reminded her.

'Oh.' Barbara rolled her eyes. 'There might be some soy milk on the rack downstairs.'

'I'm not going down to the basement,' Vellum told her.

'Why not?'

Mandy took her mother's arm. 'We need to talk. Vellum, why don't you make yourself some of that tea you like?'

Mandy pulled her mother upstairs, so that Vellum couldn't hear them. She could feel the fine bones in her mother's fragile hand. The subfloors were exposed, since her mother was having the carpet replaced.

'Why didn't you come over when you heard the commotion?' Mandy asked, collapsing into Barbara's plush cream loveseat in her sewing room. She hadn't grown up in this house, but this room had been her bedroom for the last two years of high school. They'd moved south from Lynnwood after her father had received a big promotion at Boeing. He'd died suddenly last year, before Mandy's marriage collapsed. She'd often wondered what she'd missed during her grief-stricken months. All those nights over here, sitting in the kitchen with her mom, instead of staying home with Cory. He'd obviously found comfort elsewhere.

'There were so many police milling around.' Barbara shuddered and patted her short, permed blond hair. 'Then I saw that white vehicle with the words "Medical Examiner" across the back come up the street.' She shook her head. 'I just couldn't face it, Mandy. I'm sorry. You must think I'm a bad mother.'

Mandy stared at her, incredulous. 'You thought we were all dead?'

'No. I would think the entire street would be blocked off if something that bad happened.' She sighed. 'No, I thought Ryan's liver gave out, poor boy.'

'He fell down the stairs,' Mandy said flatly. 'Maybe slipped on one of my journals. Maybe murdered. I don't know.'

'Murdered?' Barbara shook her head in the negative, even before Mandy could answer her.

'Why would homicide detectives show up?' Mandy asked. 'We were questioned by an actual homicide detective.'

'Maybe they're just being thorough.'

'I used to pride myself on my intuition. That notion was shaken badly after Dad died and Cory left. But I had the sense there was something going on that the police were being secretive about.'

Barbara's nostrils flared. 'If it was murder, I suspect those strange new friends of his, Dylan or Alexis.'

Mandy opened her purse and pulled out a stick of gum. She offered her mother the package but she waved it away. 'I don't know. I mean, I don't get what the pair of them get out of their friendship with Ryan any more than you do, but Ryan is hanging out at home instead of who knows where.' She paused, then her voice hitched when she spoke again. 'I mean "was". Oh, Mom, this is horrible.'

'So complicated.' Barbara picked up a cream throw pillow and played with the fringe. 'I'm not convinced they're just friends. He's considerably older than both of them.'

'Whatever has been going on stayed in the basement,' Mandy

assured her mother. 'I've barely spoken to either Dylan or Alexis. Neither Vellum nor I have seen anything inappropriate for teenaged eyes.'

'I'm glad to hear that. You're a good mother, but teenagers see much more than we had to these days. I'll bet something was going on. Maybe Dylan didn't like Ryan's relationship with Alexis? Or were they the couple? No, Ryan only ever dated girls.'

Mandy winced and tried, not too hard, to visualize how new friends might have caused Ryan to fall down the stairs. Or why. 'You think one of them was jealous of the other's friendship with Ryan?'

'Or they were doing drugs.' Barbara always blamed drugs.

Mandy snapped to attention at that. 'Ryan didn't do drugs. He prided himself on just drinking. I remember him telling me about the slippery slope when inhibitions are lowered.' She pushed the gum into her mouth, hoping to stop grinding her teeth.

'I vote for Alexis. That Russian temperament. She's volatile.'

'I can't deny that,' Mandy admitted. 'I've heard loud fighting when they're over. That's how I learned he had these new friends. There was some kind of fight around Halloween.'

Her mother's lips turned down. 'At least that's finished. Vellum won't be exposed to any more nonsense. I know you were loyal to Ryan, but he wasn't a good man.'

'Ryan kept his distance from Vellum,' Mandy told her. 'Besides, I didn't hear either of his friends in the house tonight.' Neither of them spoke English as a first language, and their distinctive accents made their presence obvious.

'You think he slipped on a journal you left on the steps and fell?'

'Down to the landing,' Mandy confirmed. 'But I've been thinking and thinking. I don't recall seeing that teal journal in months. I only used it for a pen test then lost it somewhere in the house. My subscribers like videos where you show how pens behave in different journals, like if the ink bleeds through the paper or not.'

'I love the results of all the doodling you do,' Barbara said. She was a loyal viewer.

'Thanks. But if I didn't leave that journal on the stairs, who did?'

THREE

'You'll make sure Vellum gets to her bus stop?' Mandy asked as she set her borrowed 'Best Grandma Award' coffee cup in her mother's sink the next morning.

Barbara squeezed her shoulder. 'Of course. You don't want to be late for work.'

Mandy leaned into the hug. 'That I do not. Can Vellum come straight here after school, in case we can't go home yet?'

'Of course.' Barbara drummed her fingers on her lower lip. 'I can't be here. I have a volunteer meeting at the food bank, but I'll give her my spare key.'

'Perfect, thanks.' Mandy kissed her mother's cheek then pulled her hat down to her eyebrows and over her ears. She wished she'd remembered to bring gloves the previous night. But she hadn't, so she stuck her hands in her coat pockets as she left her mother's house and crossed the street, her purse swinging in the wind.

At least it wasn't raining. Frost tipped the grass with white, the kind of morning that looks wonderful in December with Christmas lights and lawn decorations, but not so great in February, when everyone just wants spring.

As she reached the other side of Roosevelt Way, her neighbor Linda Bhatt opened her kitchen door and walked down her side steps, arms crossed over a bulky sweater.

'What happened last night?' Linda called, coming to meet her on the street. She still wore flannel pajamas and had thrown on some Ugg boots. 'Do you have time to come in?'

'I have maybe four minutes to spare.' Mandy stopped under a large evergreen that would shelter her from the wind. 'Can you stand the cold?'

Linda nodded. 'Anything for you.' Tall and Rubenesque, she was the neighbor who'd show up with half a pan of brownies after eight at night and beg Vellum to eat them so she wouldn't. She and her husband, Dr Sanjay Bhatt, had divorced four years ago. About a decade younger than Mandy's mother, she'd been Mandy's best friend for the six years she'd lived in her house. The twenty-plus year age difference between them never seemed to matter.

'My cousin died last night,' Mandy said, hearing the choked sob in her voice. She hadn't had to say the words for several hours, hadn't even thought about a funeral yet. Would that fall to her or to Ryan's sister, Jasmine? Did he have a will? Probably not. No kids, no spouse.

'Oh, gosh.' Linda rubbed Mandy's arms vigorously with chubby, beringed fingers. 'How terrible. Did Dylan or Alexis call the police?'

'No. Why?' Mandy frowned.

'They were in your basement apartment and only left about ten minutes before I heard the sirens.' She paused. 'I was driving to the freeway when I saw the police go by.'

Mandy's mouth dropped open. 'You have to be kidding me. Are you sure?'

'Yes. I had to get cookies over to the animal shelter before five-thirty so I was keeping a close eye on the clock.' Linda supplied the local shelter with handmade cookies to keep possible pet adopters in the shelter munching while the staff tried to match them with an animal.

'I didn't hear anyone talking downstairs, much less doors closing.'

Linda shrugged and wrapped her arms around herself again. 'I'm sure of it.'

'How could I be that oblivious?' She had thought she heard every noise from downstairs.

'What were you doing? Taking a bath?'

'No, we were filming a video in the studio.' Mandy rubbed her stiff fingers against the insides of her pockets. 'I've been in a fog since I signed my divorce papers.'

'I know, kiddo.' Linda's face creased with sympathy.

'Plus, I had a bad day and had to work overtime.' She told Linda about the cash drawer. 'Not that any of it matters now.'

'You could have run over to my house to borrow the fifteen bucks,' Linda said. 'You know you could.'

'I know. But I pride myself on my independence now.'

'There's no point in upsetting Vellum,' Linda said gently. 'Not when the problem is so easy to fix. How about I drop the cash by when she gets home from school?'

Mandy shook her head. 'We don't have access to the house right now. Vellum will have to go over to Mom's after school.'

'How long will they keep you out of the house?'

'Detective Ahola said he'd let me know,' Mandy said.

'Hmmm,' Linda mused. 'I dated a cop, before Sanjay.'

'Really?' A loud truck drove down Roosevelt, drowning out part of Linda's answer.

'Yes. I had a terrible attraction to overbearing bullies,' Linda said with a laugh. 'I'm happier single.'

Mandy chuckled. 'Single, my ass. Don't think I've missed seeing George Lowry sneaking around. His house is right behind my mother's.'

Linda grinned. 'I didn't say I was going without sex.'

'Say, why haven't you talked to the police? I thought they always talked to the neighbors when things like this happened. Maybe they do know it was an accident.' Mandy shifted. Her fingers were getting really cold.

'I left about five minutes after Dylan and Alexis did,' Linda explained. 'To take the cookies to the shelter.'

'Oh right, sorry. You were gone before Ryan fell,' Mandy mused. 'At least we know Dylan and Alexis have alibis for part of the time just before he died. My mother predicted they were the killers, if he was murdered.'

'I'm sure it will turn out to have been an accident,' Linda soothed. 'It's an unexplained death, that's all.'

'Yeah, because no one else was there.' She hadn't overheard a fight, though that didn't mean the pair weren't somehow involved in whatever state Ryan had been in that caused him to fall. They didn't always fight when they were over, though she'd never thought them capable of being quiet enough for her to miss them being there. On that sour note, Mandy realized the time. 'I'd better run.' She gave Linda a quick hug then dashed across the side street.

At her house, nothing seemed to be going on. She wished she dared go in and pack up whatever was left in the refrigerator so she didn't have to buy lunch, but she didn't want to find herself in trouble with the police. Instead, she climbed into her car and got the defroster going, then took her ice scraper from the trunk and attacked the windows. When she had the front window scraped almost clear, she spotted a pair of cheap tan gloves on the front passenger seat. She squealed with pleasure and pulled the door open so she could put them on and warm up her icy fingers.

By the time she made it to work, she was only a little late for prep. Since she'd made the cookie batter the night before, it didn't matter. She worked diligently while the oven warmed, prepping iced tea and iced coffee, along with the bases for a lot of their blended drinks. Though it was freezing outside, the warm temperature in the hospital, not to mention the stress, had many people ordering ice-blended or cold drinks all year round.

About half an hour after she arrived, some of the day staff started to turn up. Fannah had been at the front counter since six. Mandy was due to take over for her at seven. At ten minutes before seven, she walked across the foyer until she reached the security-protected private staff door.

She waved hello to a number of her customers as she headed toward the maintenance office.

'Any specials today?' one of her regular nurses called.

'I mixed up a base for a white chocolate cinnamon ice-blended,' Mandy told her. 'Give it a try.' Breathing a sigh of relief when she saw the lights were on in the maintenance department, she opened the door.

'Hey, Mandy,' Scott greeted her from across the room. A little above average height, a beer gut had started to overcome his once athletic body. The weight had yet to ruin his face. He still had a firm jawline and taut features.

'Hey,' she called back. 'Glad you're in a little early.'

'Nowhere else to be. What about you?' He folded his hands over his desk blotter.

She sat down in the visitor's chair, already hating being there. No external windows, florescent lights that hummed, and walls lined with metal racks full of cleaning supplies. The only personal items were a couple of family photos. A younger Scott with a man that was probably his father, holding up a big fish; a slightly younger Scott with a kid on each side and a cat on his lap. 'Did you talk to the police yet?'

He frowned. 'Can't say I have. What's up?'

She stared at the John Wayne thermometer on the wall. 'My cousin died last night.'

Scott's eyes widened. 'You mean Ryan?'

'Yes, of course. Do you know my other cousin, his sister Jasmine?'

'I don't think I ever had the pleasure. I'm sorry, Mandy.'

'It isn't much of one right now. She turned forty this year and isn't taking the milestone well.' Mandy slumped in the chair. 'I wonder if I should have called her last night, but they barely spoke. I assume the police contacted her or her mother as next of kin.'

Scott made a sympathetic noise.

Mandy pulled a tissue from her pocket and dabbed at her eyes. 'I didn't get much sleep last night. We had to stay at my mother's.'

'Vellum OK?'

'Sort of. She didn't see the body.'

Scott leaned forward. 'Do you think it was suicide?'

The tissue dropped from Mandy's hand. 'Why?'

Scott lowered his voice, though no one else was in the room. 'He was about to be fired.'

Mandy's lips trembled. She knew how important Ryan's job was to him. He was proud of his long tenure at the hospital. 'I thought he was good at his job.'

'He did the work, but he often smelled like alcohol after his lunch break.'

Mandy squeezed her fingers together in her lap. *Oh, Ryan.* He'd never mentioned his job being in trouble. 'His drinking was that out of control?'

'You didn't notice?'

'He didn't come to the coffee bar unless we were commuting together. His car died a lot. But it's been at least a month since he had trouble.' She realized his car hadn't been in the driveway when she came home the night before. 'Is his car at the hospital? Did Dylan or Alexis pick him up?'

'Who are they?'

'Friends,' she said vaguely.

'I don't know about his car.' Scott made a note on a pad of paper. 'I'll ask Security to search for it.'

'Speaking of security,' Mandy said, catching sight of the clock over Scott's head. She needed to take over from Fannah at the coffee bar. 'That's the other reason I'm here.'

'What's that?'

'We have a thief targeting the coffee bar. Yesterday, I'm sure some teenagers stole fifteen bucks from me, and food has gone missing too.'

'How terrible,' Scott said with an edge of sarcasm.

'It is,' Mandy said stoutly. 'You know I'm a single mom now. Cory quit his job so he gets to pay almost nothing in child support, and I have to cover the mortgage by myself.'

'He's working under the table?' Scott asked blandly.

Mandy pushed the chair back. 'It doesn't surprise me that you'd be on his side. Men. I hate you all.'

Scott laughed and put up his hands. 'Calm down, Mandy. Cory's a good guy. I'm sure he's having a tough time with the divorce.'

Mandy ground her molars together before speaking. 'He's the one who cheated.'

'There's two sides to every story.'

Mandy shook her head. How could she ever have liked Scott? Men sucked. She had enough misplaced wifely guilt without having it reinforced. She stood up. 'I'd like you to put up a security camera to catch the coffee bar thief. If we had footage, we could catch them in action.'

'I'll look into it, Mandy. I'm sure you're feeling jumpy, but now we're down a guy, thanks to this.' He looked at Mandy. 'I'll get it on our list.'

Mandy's lips trembled. 'Ryan's death was an unfortunate accident. But I'm sorry to hear he was about to lose his job. I suppose he knew that?'

'Next time I caught him smelling of alcohol,' Scott said easily. 'Sorry, Mandy.'

She imagined a string pulling her head toward the ceiling and straightened her posture, then walked out of the room as regally as a queen. This was going to be a very long day if she let every comment about her sadly flawed cousin wound her.

About nine a.m., she saw Detective Ahola approach the coffee bar with another man. He had pouchy half-circles under his eyes today, but despite them, could still have modeled. Her gaze dropped south, checking for badges. It felt uncomfortable to deliberately check out a man's beltline. *Yes, Mandy, both men had badges hung on their belts.* She quickly moved her gaze back to eye level.

'Ms Meadows,' Detective Ahola said in a business-like tone.

'Yes, Detective?' She gave him her professional smile. 'What can I get you gentlemen? We have a great ice-blended drink today.'

Detective Ahola curled his upper lip, as if revolted. Given how trim the man was, she doubted he ever let sugar cross his lips.

'I'll just have a mocha,' the other man said. His physique was more, well, Russell Crowe-esque, to say the least.

'What size?'

'A large one.'

She looked to Detective Ahola for his drink.

'Black coffee.' Detective Ahola wiped his upper lip. 'Why is it so warm in here?'

'It's always like this. Most people don't keep their coats on.' She rang up the sales and went to make the drinks. Fannah appeared from the back and took over the cash register.

The detectives stepped around the counter to the wood block they used to place finished drink orders, in between the espresso machine and the blenders.

'Any news?' Mandy asked in a low voice.

'Just here to interview the deceased's supervisor, Scott Nelson, and co-workers,' Detective Ahola said. His eyes narrowed at her. 'Anyone I should pay special attention to?'

She felt pinned by that icy blue gaze. 'I didn't see Ryan much at work. He told me about the job opening, so he was partially responsible for me working here, but he didn't even drink coffee.'

The other detective picked up his drink. 'Was he generally liked around here?'

'This morning, his supervisor told me he was about to be fired.' There it was, that choking sound again. She turned her head away. 'Sorry.'

'Why?' Detective Ahola asked.

'For drinking on the job. Allegedly,' she added. She didn't know if it was true or not.

'I see.' As Detective Ahola spoke, the other detective tilted his drink and took a long, noisy gulp.

Detective Ahola cleared his throat and picked up his own drink. 'Anything else?'

'Can I go home after work?'

'I can't let you do that yet, Ms Meadows. The scene wasn't processed completely last night.'

'Oh.'

He lifted those heavy brows and waited for her to speak.

She felt forced to fill the silence. 'Did anyone speak to my neighbor, Linda Bhatt, yet?'

'Where does she live?'

'Across the side street. She said she saw my cousin's friends leave just before five-thirty, and then she left too, and missed everything.'

The detective put his hands on his hips. 'Mr Meadows was in the house shortly before his fall, along with multiple people?'

She could feel his displeasure, but she hadn't known about that when he interviewed her. 'Yes. Dylan Tran and Alexis Ivanova. But I didn't hear them.'

'No?'

She shook her head. 'Except I remembered this morning that I didn't see his car anywhere. It wasn't in the driveway and it couldn't have been in front of the house or the police cruisers wouldn't have parked there.'

'Was this a normal occurrence?'

'Not recently. He had a lot of car trouble last fall, but not in the past month or so. I asked Scott, his boss, to see if it was in the hospital garage.'

The detective pulled out a notebook and jotted down a few notes. 'Do you happen to have his license plate number?'

'No, but Scott will. It's in our employee records.'

The detective snapped his notebook shut. 'Thank you. I'll be in touch when you can return home.'

'I don't have my phone,' she reminded him.

'Your daughter's?'

'No. She'd have a fit if I took it. She's fifteen.'

The other detective grinned. 'I remember that phase.'

Fannah walked up to Mandy and handed Detective Ahola the coffee bar's card. 'You can reach her here until three p.m., Officer.'

'Detective,' Mandy corrected. 'They're homicide detectives.'

Fannah's face became very still.

'Ryan died last night. I'm sorry, I haven't had a chance to tell you.'

Her supervisor didn't speak.

'In my house,' Mandy explained.

Fannah turned away and moved rapidly into the back room. Mandy stared at her, then heard the bell ring. She had customers waiting at the cash register, including Dr O'Halloran. 'I'm sorry but I need to work.'

Detective Ahola ignored her plea. 'Was she a friend of Mr Meadows?'

'No. I mean, I don't think so.' Mandy glanced at the surgeon, who gave her a cheery wave over the fruit basket. Always rushing, he'd be annoyed if she didn't wait on him right away. 'I really have to get back to my job.'

Detective Ahola tapped the business card on the wooden block. 'You do that. We'll be in touch.'

Mandy's morning went downhill after that. Once the news about Ryan's death spread around the hospital, her whimsical notion of the USea Hospital being like a small town proved true. Some people stopped by to be kind, but others came to gossip and she was forced to listen to their casually cruel words about Ryan while she rang up their drinks.

Eventually, Fannah took pity on her and settled her at the drinks station. She didn't have to speak to people as much when she made their drinks, and the wooden block put a physical barrier between herself and the customers. All three of the weekday staff were scheduled for full shifts, so Mandy hoped to stay where she was until she was off work at three.

'What's going on?' Kit asked. She had her apron around her neck just before her shift started at noon.

'Ryan died last night,' Mandy said. How many times had she said that today? Her stomach clenched. She didn't think she'd be able to eat any lunch, though her break started in a couple of minutes.

Kit's eyes went unfocused. After a moment, her fingers scrabbled around her waist, looking for her apron ties. She looped them around her back then knotted them in front. Tiny, exquisite, her-life-ahead-of-her Kit. A dozen years younger than Mandy, she envied Kit for all the excitement still ahead. Career, boyfriends, marriage, babies. Some days she felt a lot older than thirty-six.

Mandy waited for the obligatory 'I'm-so-sorry' comment, but Kit seemed completely checked out. She had faint purple bruises under her eyes, like she hadn't slept well. 'Are you sure you should be here? Are you ill?'

Kit rubbed her nose. 'I'm fine. Just tired.' She yawned.

'Yeah, well . . .' Mandy trailed off, but still her co-worker didn't speak. 'Are you clocked in so I can go on break?'

Kit ran into the back room and put her badge under the scanner, then returned. 'I am now.'

'Thanks,' Mandy muttered, ripping off her coffee-stained apron. A couple of overenthusiastic gossips had tilted their cups while chattering away and splashed her. Neither of them visited the coffee bar regularly and apparently didn't know to keep the lids on their drinks at the counter.

Mandy's afternoon didn't get much better. As staff took their breaks, they came to gossip. Then her non-regulars, people who had family being cared for at the hospital, would start asking questions about what they'd overheard. A couple of rude elderly people were overcome with horror at the idea that she'd seen a dead body, as if people didn't die in this exact hospital every single day. They left without ordering.

Five minutes before her shift ended, the phone rang in the back room. Fannah had left for the day, so Mandy dashed into the back to answer it. 'USea coffee bar. How may I help you?'

'Ms Meadows?'

She suspected she knew this voice. 'Speaking.'

'This is Detective Ahola. We have released the scene and you can enter your home now. I suggest you call a professional death scene cleanup company and let them do their job before you enter the basement area.'

'I doubt I can afford any of that.'

'A reputable company will take pictures for your insurance company. In fact, you might want to give your insurance a call.'

'Are there any companies you recommend?'

The detective rattled off a couple of names. 'You can find them on any search engine. Both of those companies should be able to have cleaners there within twenty-four hours.'

She sighed. If only she'd done her laundry ahead of all this. 'Thank you. I appreciate your help.'

'We'll be in touch.' He disconnected, leaving her holding the empty line.

Right now, she couldn't even do a search, because she didn't have a phone.

'Kit,' she called from the back room.

Her co-worker turned around from the espresso machine.

'Can I borrow your phone?'

Kit shook her head and turned back to the nozzle.

Mandy muttered a rude word under her breath. She'd have to go home before she called anyone. It's not like there was a phone book anywhere these days, and the hospital help desks weren't usually manned, due to the lack of volunteers. She could get in trouble if she bothered front desk staff in any of the medical departments.

Five minutes later, she was in the parking garage, debating whether she should drive around and see if she could spot Ryan's car, but for all she knew, it had already been found and towed. She made a mental note of things she needed to do. Bring Vellum back home, but maybe not until the basement was cleaned. Call the crime scene cleanup company. Call her cousin Jasmine, even if her mother had already made contact.

When she reached her street, she turned left, ready to pull into her driveway, on autopilot as usual, but something caught the corner of her eye. She slowed down and squinted. Surely her eyes were deceiving her.

If they weren't, a child was sitting in her front yard, wearing only shorts and a T-shirt. Was that really a crying child on her icy lawn?

FOUR

Mandy forgot her to-do list and stopped her car beside the alley. She picked her way along the stone retaining wall that held up her lawn and ran up the steps to her front yard.

'What is it, honey? Are you hurt?' She skidded across the damp grass, hoping nothing on her property had injured the child. When she recognized the freckled face of Aiden Roswell, a ten-year-old neighbor, she really hoped that nothing was seriously wrong. His mother, Crystal, was nuts.

He offered her a blank stare and nothing more. Mandy's gaze flew past the skateboard on her mushy winter lawn – why? – checked his video game T-shirt for signs of rips, his elbows for signs of trauma, and finally found what she was looking for on his knees.

'You skinned your knee,' she exclaimed, picking up his skateboard and handing it to him. 'Let's just wash that out and put a bandage on it.'

He stared down at his bloody skin with mild interest. 'Is it bleeding?'

Mandy glanced at the blood dripping down his leg. Couldn't he tell? Was he freezing to death? She hooked her hands under his armpits and helped him up. 'We'd better get you inside. Is your mother home?'

'No, just Emilee.'

Mandy shook her head in disgust. Emilee was Aiden's twin sister. They were too young and foolish to be left home alone. Yet another parenting fail for Crystal. She felt bad that Crystal's husband had left her in order to pursue any other woman that might have him, preferably several at a time, but she had to do better with her kids.

'Come inside and we'll get you cleaned up.' She put her hand on his shoulder to guide him in. 'What were you doing up here anyway?'

He didn't answer, just dropped his skateboard right on the remains of her blue ivory Hosta. Mandy wanted to move it to the lawn, but then Aiden put one foot on the stair and immediately moaned and clutched at his knee. She took her concrete steps two at a time and pulled his hands away, afraid the bleeding had gotten worse.

'Let me see,' she encouraged.

He pulled his hands away. 'It hurts!'

He'd made things worse, having scraped off the drying blood. Fresh droplets welled up. 'Come on.' She hauled him up, half-supporting his sturdy eighty-pound weight. Glossy tears dribbled down his cheeks.

Her front door squeaked when she unlocked it and pushed it open. The hinges needed oil. 'Let's get you into the kitchen. The best light is in there.'

'Can I watch TV?' he asked.

'No, the kitchen doesn't have a television.' She had to encourage him past the forty-inch TV screen in her living room, a reminder of her marriage, and walked him through the dining room into the kitchen. 'Sit here.'

She pointed to a stool tucked under a counter along the back wall. Only then did she remember the crime scene in the hallway behind the wall. She'd brought this child into a home that needed a crime scene cleanup. Reacting like a mom wasn't always the right approach.

'Stay,' she commanded, pointing at him after he climbed onto the stool. She hurried into the bathroom and grabbed her first aid kit off the top shelf and brought it back into the kitchen.

She needn't have worried about Aiden exploring. He'd helped himself to a tin of shortbread on the counter. Crumbs dusted his lips.

'Yum,' he said, taking another huge bite.

She let it go. It wasn't her job to discipline Crystal's badly behaved children. She merely needed to minimize their presence on her property. When she lifted the lid of her kit, she saw the anti-bacterial ointment was missing, so she wet some paper towels and wiped grass off the wound. At this time of year, no dirt had gotten into it.

'Why were you skateboarding on my lawn?' she asked, as she dabbed a fresh spot of blood away.

'Mom yells at me if she sees tracks on our lawn.'

The little creep thought he'd use her lawn instead. *Nice.* 'It works much better on the pavement.'

'Mom doesn't want me out of the yard.'

'Then you should stay on your property,' she pointed out. 'My yard isn't your yard.'

He didn't say anything, just grabbed another piece of shortbread.

Oh well. She didn't need the sweets in the house anyway. They'd been a Christmas present from an elderly neighbor, but Vellum didn't like the coconut flavor.

'Please stay out of my yard.' She opened a big square bandage and carefully applied it over the wound. 'It should stop bleeding soon.'

'Huh.' He tried to peel away the edge.

'Don't touch it, Aiden,' she scolded. 'You want it to heal. Don't check it until bedtime, OK?'

He looked at her quizzically. She thought he was going to ask something about his wound.

'Is the body still here?' he asked.

Her hand shook. She turned away and dropped the bandage packaging into the trash can, hiding her upset. Had he been over here trying to get a look at the corpse? The Roswells all needed therapy. 'No, Aiden. I'm sure you're curious, but he is long gone.'

'Where is he?'

'I'm not sure. That's for his sister to decide.'

'What does that mean?'

'It means he has a sister who will be in charge now.' She closed the lid of her kit, ready to put it back in its spot in her bathroom.

'Is she a jerk too?'

'What, honey?'

Aiden screwed up his greasy lips. 'He had it coming.'

'You shouldn't speak ill of the dead,' she chided.

Aiden crawled off the stool. 'Ryan was a jerk. I hated him.'

'Did something happen?' Mandy followed him as he walked through the dining room toward the front door.

He shrugged. She touched his arm before he could open the front door. 'Is there something I should tell the police?' she asked gently.

He smiled sweetly at her, exposing the tip of an adult-sized canine tooth that hadn't quite come in yet. 'No.'

He went out the front door. 'You're welcome for the bandage,' she called as he went down the steps, hoping that would remind the child to say thank you – but no.

She watched until he'd disappeared through the bushes supposedly separating her property from the Roswells'. At this time of year, they didn't have enough leaf cover to make them impenetrable. Maybe she needed to plant something spiky like Japanese bayberry. If he really hurt himself here, like broke a bone, Crystal would probably sue her.

Had Ryan yelled at Aiden for crossing over to her lawn? Probably. Still, she was horrified that a ten-year-old would call an adult a jerk. Had she known Ryan at all?

A breeze washed over her, making her shiver. She shut her door and went down the steps, feeling for her car keys. Time to move her car into the driveway. She jumped down to the sidewalk and walked around the house, her arms wrapped around herself for warmth. A fast-moving, navy-blue truck came around the corner behind Linda's house as she went to her car. She stood by her bumper, waiting for it to pass. The light hit the side of her car oddly.

Oh no. Had her day just gotten even worse? She didn't have her phone with its flashlight app, so all she could do was run her fingers along the door. Nothing felt wrong, but when she reached the space in between the door and the metal above the bumper, she felt more air than should have been there. Someone had clipped her car.

'This is why I should never park here,' she muttered to herself. Another irritation to lay at the feet of her Roswell neighbors. They were a relatively minor headache, but still, one she didn't need. She opened her door, hearing a creak from the metal as it bent against the damaged part, got in and drove into her driveway.

The floodlights in the back came on, and when she hopped out she saw the damage. Nothing that made the car undrivable, though the area around the left headlight wasn't entirely intact. Pushing this latest issue to the back of her mind, she went in so she could look up crime scene cleanup companies and order their services. But first, she'd better email her insurance company.

This sort of thing was exactly what made journaling useful. A handy, simple place for to-do lists, checklists and the like, along with an easy method of tracking task status, what needed to be moved to a different day, or month, or even year, was heaven-sent for days like this. If she hadn't needed to leave her journal in a crime scene, of course.

Mandy lived by her lists, and her brain felt like scrambled eggs without that journal. Inside her back door she went past the freezer and her bill-paying table in what had originally been a tiny mudroom, then walked into the kitchen. The house didn't seem disturbed. The police must have focused their efforts on the basement.

She did a quick search through the main floor of the house. Her phone had been removed from the stand and taken as evidence. She snatched up her journal and cradled it. The police had left it alone, but this experience told her she needed to stop using her own personal journal for shooting her videos. From now on, or at least starting next month, she'd keep two separate ones. Maybe she'd even give the one from the video away in a contest. Some of her fellow vloggers awarded prize packs with every video. She'd been too cheap to do it, but she also hadn't tried to get free merch from the suppliers. Might be time to wave her follower numbers in front of Scribbles That Matter, Leuchtturm1917, Tombow, and other suppliers. Also her fellow online craft shop owners. Everyone traded product reviews and cross-promoted. No micro business-woman was an island.

She opened her journal and jotted these quick thoughts on her February brainstorming spread, then updated her to-do list. The house's silence bore down on her. She missed Vellum.

Ignoring loneliness and hunger pangs, she went into her bedroom and opened her laptop. In the next half hour, she made an appointment for a cleaner to come, then emailed back and forth with her insurance company, verifying the damage to her car wasn't enough to be worth a claim. The crime scene cleanup should be claim-worthy, though she'd have to pay her deductible. She debated starting dinner.

Instead, she decided to let her mother feed them. The last thing she did was creep into the hall and grab her laundry basket. It had been knocked over, but the clothes were still there. She tossed them all into a garbage bag and went out the back door.

Linda was just getting out of her car and waved from her driveway across the street. 'Time for a cup of tea?'

Mandy hefted her garbage bag and approached her friend. 'I feel like a weirdo, going into your house with my unwashed laundry.'

Linda laughed. 'Is your washer broken?'

Mandy shuddered. 'It's in the basement.'

'Oh, right,' Linda said sympathetically. 'Mine's in that little room off the back steps. Do you want to use it?'

Mandy shrugged. 'I was going to use my mother's, but sure. It's so strange not having my phone. No one can reach me and demand anything.'

'Where is Vellum?'

'My mom gave her the key to her house. Hopefully she's over there. I should go supervise.'

'I'll make the tea while you get your laundry going. You'll be out of here in ten minutes.'

Mandy followed Linda through the back gate onto her property. 'Did you hear anyone hit my car in the last hour? I had to park it alongside my yard and someone clipped it.'

'Bad idea,' Linda said. 'Sorry. The teenagers around here are terrible drivers. Must be all the weed.'

Mandy shrugged and told her about the Roswell drama as they walked up the back steps. She glanced at Linda's hot tub and felt a pang of desire. What she wouldn't give to climb into that hot warmth with a glass of chilled wine about now, even in February.

Linda unlocked her back door, then reset her security panel. 'Do you want me to have George look at your car?'

'That would be super neighborly of him.' Mandy wondered if she should get some security on her house, but it probably wouldn't have saved Ryan from whatever had happened. She had to keep reminding herself he was gone.

Linda pointed to the washer then went into the kitchen. 'I'll give him a call.' Her home layout was similar to Mandy's, without the sunroom addition. Mandy and Cory had decorated their home in a Neo-Victorian style, back when they were a two-income household. Linda had gone for country French décor. Lots of blues and yellows, with Provençal linens on the dining room table.

When she'd been married, there had been a lot of Hindu religious and cultural artifacts in cases, but Sanjay had taken them all when he left. Linda didn't seem to mind. She hadn't replaced any of the glass cases that used to line the walls, saying she liked the empty space.

Mandy emptied her bag into the washer. When she entered the kitchen, Linda handed her a ten- and a five-dollar bill.

'For Vellum,' she told her.

'Thanks.' Mandy felt her face go red. 'This is so embarrassing. I'll get it back to you as soon as I leave work tomorrow.'

'No rush,' Linda said. 'The tea should be ready by now.'

They sat down at the little iron table in the kitchen where Mandy's extra counter was located. Linda poured the tea and Mandy doctored hers with sugar to give her stomach something to feed on.

'Did you call your insurance company?' Linda asked.

'Yes, but it's not worth a claim. It will just raise my deductible.'

'It's drivable?'

'Yep, just one more thing I have to deal with. I'll have—' she paused. No, she couldn't have Ryan look at it. The one semi-reliable man in her life was dead. Tears burned her eyes. 'Thanks for asking George to help me.'

'But Mom, I have to go to school,' Vellum moaned as she handed her phone to Mandy on Friday morning in her grandmother's kitchen.

'I'm just going to post a quick note on our video channel, and a live video on our social media,' Mandy said. 'I'll be done before you finish breakfast.'

'I hate breakfast. Unless it's dinner.'

'Put something in your belly,' Mandy said. 'Hear my mom voice?'

Vellum stuck her tongue out at Mandy, then picked up an orange from her grandmother's fruit basket and peeled it.

Mandy signed out of Vellum's accounts and into the Mandy's Plan accounts. After she posted her notice about a death in the family, she fluffed her hair and stood in front of her mother's spotless refrigerator.

'I'm sorry, sweetie, can you record me?'

Vellum rolled her eyes. 'I'm on the clock, right?'

'Sure. For two minutes.'

Vellum fiddled with her phone.

'Make sure when you're done you set the video to post on all of the social media accounts,' Mandy advised.

'I'm not new at this,' Vellum groused.

'Of course not,' Mandy said. 'Ready?'

'Lights, camera, action!'

'Hello, friends!' Mandy said brightly. 'I'm sorry we haven't been posting on Mandy's Plan this week. We had a death in the family and I lost my phone. Crazy, right? Then last night my parked car was hit. Is something in retrograde?' she laughed lightly. 'We'll be up and running again as soon as I have my phone situation sorted. Lots of great content coming. Swipe up to visit our video page!'

Vellum turned off the recorder. 'I'll add the swipe.'

'Thanks, hun.' Mandy checked the pocket of her coat and pulled out Linda's money. 'Look at this. Cash!'

'Yes!' Vellum snatched it. 'Movie time. When do we get to go home?'

'Tonight, I think. I have to run over to the house and let in the professional cleaners. I assume they'll be done by the time I get home from work.'

'It's not like anything really gruesome happened.'

Mandy's stomach gurgled uneasily. She'd never be able to handle an orange right now. 'The police processed the scene, whatever that means. I couldn't bring myself to go down the steps so I went through the basement door and took a quick peek. It's a mess, lots of fingerprint collection material all over the place. They searched everything and pulled up some of the flooring on the stairs. Evidence, I suppose.'

'Was the door busted open?'

'No,' Mandy said.

'Are you going to change the locks?'

'I can't afford it.'

'Security system?'

Mandy sighed. 'I can't afford it.'

'Are we safe?' Vellum shivered.

'The door to the basement from the outside has a different lock to the upstairs door. Even if Ryan gave out keys to everyone, they can't get to us if we keep the door from the upstairs to the basement locked.'

'Can we add more locks?'

Mandy nodded. 'Sure. We can add a chain lock and one of those bolt locks on our side of the door. That way no one can get in.'

'Cool.' Vellum gave her a one-arm hug. She smelled like her orange.

The scent brightened Mandy's mood. 'I'll walk you to the bus stop.'

'You didn't eat breakfast,' Vellum pointed out.

Mandy grabbed an apple. 'The difference between us is that I can eat at work. Lots of choices.'

'All the coffee you can drink. So good for you, Mom.' Vellum snorted. 'And you should switch from dairy milk.'

Mandy laughed. 'I hear you.'

They went outside. Seattle offered up a typical misty morning. Light fog diminished the landscape and the drizzle bit at Mandy's cheeks. At the corner, they waited for a cluster of cars to pass.

'What am I doing?' Mandy groused. 'You pick up your bus on this side of the road.'

Vellum laughed. 'It's hard to sleep on a strange bed. You're in a daze.'

'That and no breakfast yet.' Mandy punctuated her words with a savage bite into her apple. They turned back and walked up to the bus stop. Vellum went to a private school, paid for by her Moffat grandparents, who'd insisted on it.

A couple of other teenagers were waiting there, so Mandy refrained from any embarrassing displays of affection and went back across the street to her house. She passed by her front steps, admiring the lattice work on her arched entryway. A white van was parked just in front of the steps. She read the name on the van. The crime scene cleanup people had arrived.

The mid-morning coffee bar slump had just begun when Detective Ahola showed up, alone this time, his hair covered in a slouchy blue cap. He still looked more handsome than anyone had a right to be. Mandy dropped her cleaning supplies into a bucket, wishing she'd been in a more elegant pose, and went to the cash register.

'Trouble on Pill Hill?' Mandy asked.

He lifted a brow. 'I came to see you.'

She felt a little flutter. Nerves? Attraction? She didn't know. 'No sidekick today?'

'My partner is taking a personal day.'

She frowned. 'With all due respect, you've got to be kidding me. My cousin only died thirty-six hours ago. Aren't you supposed to hit cases hard at the start because that's the best chance of solving them?'

Detective Ahola's cool stare shriveled her bravado. 'Detective Rideout's wife is dealing with cancer. He took the day to be with her during a chemo treatment.'

'Oh, well that's terrible. He seemed like a nice man.' She finished on a mumble. 'Black coffee?'

He pasted a false-looking smile on his face. 'Sure. A small one. Are you due for a break soon?'

'Not for another hour. I'm here alone because we don't get a lot of traffic at this time of day.' She rang him up and handed him an eight-ounce cup.

He glanced around. 'Look, Ms Meadows, I stopped by to let you know that Ryan Meadows' death is officially being treated as a murder.'

Her vision swam with dots, even though she'd half been expecting this. Clutching the edge of the counter, she asked, 'How can you tell?'

'The autopsy showed his nose was cracked and there were signs he'd been punched.'

She forced herself to let go. 'I didn't see any of that.'

'I would imagine you fixated on the journal. It isn't easy for a layperson to look at a body.'

Mandy used the heels of her hands to wipe at her eyes. She had to admit to herself that she hadn't looked at his face too closely. 'It wasn't a body. It was my cousin.'

'I'm very sorry.' He kept his cool gaze on her. 'I hope you aren't planning to leave town anytime soon.'

'No.' Mandy realized with sickening clarity that she or her daughter had to be the chief suspect since no one else was in the house. She needed to figure out what happened before she was arrested.

He handed her a couple of dollars. 'Keep the change for your charity box.'

They weren't allowed to take tips. Everything went into the hospital support fund. One of the downsides of working here, but Ryan had made it easy for her to get the job. It beat pounding the pavement and explaining why she hadn't worked a day job in years.

Alcoholic or not, she already missed Ryan. He'd been her oldest friend. She didn't think she'd gone a day without a text from him in years. And these days, between working in the same hospital and living in the same house, she was used to seeing him every day, too.

'Umm . . . do you need to interview me again?'

Fannah walked out of the back room and gave her a suspicious look. Mandy stuffed the change into the plastic collection box, praying her supervisor hadn't thought she was about to pocket the money. The detective did the lifted chin nod in Fannah's direction and put his hand into his inner coat pocket.

'I'll be in touch about that. For now, we took the video recording off your phone,' he said. 'You can have it back.' He handed her a plastic bag with her phone in it then walked off.

'Now him I could go for,' Fannah said into Mandy's ear in her husky voice. 'Single?'

She wiped her shaking hands on her apron front. 'He just told me officially that Ryan was murdered, Fannah. How would I know?'

'No ring. You have to pay attention to these things now, or you're going to be looking for a boyfriend on apps.'

Detective Ahola was the last person she'd go for under the circumstances. Mandy forced a laugh. 'Not looking for a boyfriend.'

'Why not?'

'My divorce just finalized.'

'Your husband cheated on you.' Fannah poked her shoulder. 'You need to move on. This is no life for you. Find another husband.'

Mandy enjoyed Fannah's Ethiopian-accented voice, the way she pronounced 'th' like 'z' and the musical cadence. She did not enjoy advice on how to live her life. 'I have a right to lick my wounds, which are considerable.'

'From a rich lady to here, working for an immigrant?' Fannah laughed. 'So it goes, hmmm?'

'I'm grateful for the job,' Mandy said earnestly, but Fannah walked off, not responding.

Would being a murder suspect get her fired?

FIVE

Mandy went to the cafeteria on her break and hid in the back-corner alcove along the windows. She could see the skeletal outlines of trees, a lot of pavement, and the I-5 freeway, never empty, even in the middle of a weekday. She'd snagged a handful of slightly burned ginger thins they couldn't sell, and a banana that had enough brown spots to be removed from sale, plus a café au lait.

After eating two cookies for courage, she turned on her phone, hoping it would have some battery life left. The newest model, it held a charge well, and she still had twenty percent. She sent Vellum a quick text to let her know she had her phone again, then plugged in her headphones and went into her pictures.

The video they had started that night was still on her phone. She didn't want to listen but she needed to. After squeezing her eyes shut for a moment, she hit the play button.

She watched their fingers, and the start of their inking process. Pride washed over her as she heard how grown-up Vellum sounded when she spoke. Then she heard those muffled bumps. She saw her torso move in front of the screen, then the video ended. She'd turned off the phone at that point. Unfortunate.

Noticing her battery had dropped a few percentage points, she closed the video and hit the button to call Vellum's father.

'Babe!' Cory crooned into the phone.

Mandy tried to ignore the muscle memory that had her melting at the sound of that old endearment. She'd met her ex-husband at eighteen at the University of Washington. He'd been in her Spanish 101 class and she'd literally met him on the first day of school. The pregnancy had been an accident but they'd married over their parents' objections and moved in together. He'd finished school; she hadn't. She'd thought they had a love story; he'd gone looking for greener pastures in the mid-life crisis zone. Two years older than her, he'd tired of his routine and annihilated it a year ago. 'I keep hoping you'll block my number.'

'Never,' he said. 'You're like a favorite pair of shoes. I'll never toss you out.'

'That's incredibly insulting, but I'm not rising to the bait. Did you hear the news about Ryan?'

'Haven't heard from Vellum lately,' he said. 'I took a cruise down to Mexico. Got some sun.'

'Lovely,' she muttered. On Mommy's dime, of course. 'Ryan was murdered in the basement on Wednesday. The police took my phone into evidence and just gave it back to me.'

His voice went low, intimate. 'Do they think you took him out?'

'It's not funny. You need to be prepared to take Vellum if I'm arrested.'

He went back to his normal tone, but he still didn't sound concerned. 'Don't you have an alibi?'

'I've thought hard about that. Vellum is my alibi, but she's my daughter. And there's my phone, too.'

'What's on it?'

'We had just started filming. You can hear the bumps, which must have been Ryan falling. My hands are visible so I obviously have an alibi for the fall, unless they think the noises were some kind of fake-out.'

'How long was the video?'

'Maybe four minutes?'

He made a noise in the back of his throat. 'It isn't much of an alibi.'

Mandy's hand shook, knocking the phone against her ear. 'No. I suppose he could have been dead before he fell. I'm sure I'm a suspect.'

'As is Vellum.'

Neither of them spoke for a moment, as they contemplated that. Finally, Cory said, 'He always had your back. I know you liked him and I accepted that, even if I didn't want him as a tenant.'

'It's not your house anymore.'

'That's still my daughter in that house,' Cory said.

'It's not like someone new is moving in tomorrow. I have to deal with everything Ryan left.'

'You'd better let me take a look at anyone you try to move in,' Cory said.

She wanted to make a biting comment about how rare it was

for him to take any responsibility, but if he was willing to do something, she had to be supportive of it. How had she turned into the grownup of this relationship? The alarm went off on her phone. It was set to go off on workdays, to remind her that lunch break was over in five minutes. Like Pavlov's dog, she got up instantly.

'What?' Cory asked.

'I need to get my charger out of my car. Battery's almost dead.'

'I just got you the phone for Christmas. The battery should last all day.'

'Thanks again for that,' she said. 'But the police aren't in the business of charging up suspects' phones.'

'Can't have my daughter without an adult to contact,' he said easily. 'You have her call me after school, OK? I can't keep her all weekend, but she can spend the night tonight.'

'Have fun with that conversation. You should be more appreciative that she actually wants to spend your two weekends a month with you.' She hung up, wounded by his total lack of concern over what she'd been through. But they were divorced. That was the point. He didn't have to care anymore, but every time he made it completely clear he didn't, it still hurt.

She raced to the parking garage and grabbed her emergency charger from the glove compartment. She made it back to the coffee bar just in time to clock in.

Fannah left work at two. She came out of the back room, flipping her keys around just before that. 'I apologize for the staff shortage today but you'll have to close at three.'

'We get a rush right about then. Do you really want me to stop everything and do the closing before that? We'll anger some of our best customers.'

Fannah sighed loudly. 'You want the overtime?'

'Sure. Lawyers don't come cheap, if I need one.'

'Mmm. Very good. Make sure you sign out by six-fifteen. You must finish the close by then.'

Mandy nodded. 'You got it.' She mentally pumped a fist into the air. Three hours of overtime at the end of a full week meant time and a half!

She contemplated their staffing shortage as she filled orders for the next forty-five minutes. Fannah had a hard time hiring good people with the wages she had to offer. Seattle had lots of openings in entry-level jobs right now.

Should she try to find a new position? Mandy laughed at herself while she made a sixteen-ounce white chocolate mocha with caramel sauce for a hospital chaplain. Most companies wouldn't be very tolerant of an employee who received visits from the police.

She set up cups for her usual orders this time of day, then took a second to text Vellum about Cory's plan. He would drop her off at home in the morning, which was fine from Mandy's perspective. They had plenty to do on Mandy's Plan and now she could afford to pay Vellum for the hours thanks to her overtime check.

She'd just finished with her two nurse regulars when Jeanie Christie trotted in from the ER. Not in the clique of nurses who were addicted to caffeine, Mandy only saw her a couple of times a week when she used a café table for her lunch break. She'd order a drink on those days and eat a salad she brought from home. Mandy admired the willpower demonstrated by her healthy lunch.

She made a quick note on her notepad app to play with the idea of a salad-themed journal month. How cute would that be?

'Hi, Jeanie,' she greeted. 'How fun to see you at a different time of day!'

Jeanie fumbled for her employee card. Her hand trembled as she extended it from her lanyard.

Why was she getting more coffee when she was so overloaded, visibly shaking already? 'Everything OK, hun? Just your usual short coffee?'

'Double shift,' Jeanie said.

'Ah,' Mandy said. 'I'm on OT, too. What can I get you?'

'Double Americano.'

Mandy blinked. Now this was a day for surprises. Once she had someone pegged as a regular, they rarely switched it up. 'You got it.'

'Are there sugar packets somewhere?'

'Behind you, next to the napkins.'

Jeanie swiped her card and Mandy hurried to make her order before a trio of techs she saw coming reached the counter. She handed the cup to the nurse and she sped off again, double-time.

Mandy considered the usual horrifying reason for overtime in the Emergency Department. *Flu season.* Had the ER been hit with a new batch of cases, cutting breaks short? Every year there were weeks where flu victims were all over the main floor of the hospital. Thank goodness the employee bathroom was nowhere near the germs on the ER end of the floor.

Mandy's feet were dragging by the time six came around. The insanity of the week had crept up on her and her phone had been dinging with messages because people expected her to be off work by now.

Scott popped out of his maintenance den just as she started washing up. 'Where's Kit?'

'She didn't work today. I think we might need to hire a fourth person for weekdays, though I love the overtime.'

'Aren't you busy with your calligraphy or whatever?'

'I can always fill my time.' She smiled at him, remembering he'd complimented her on the inspirational quote T-shirt she'd designed and worn over the summer, hoping it was a subtle way to promote her business. The quote was from Oscar Wilde: 'Be Yourself. Everyone else is already taken.'

'You're pretty good,' he said, taking out his employee card. 'I'll take a coffee with room for the road, but Kit always adds vanilla soy milk for me.'

'Sure thing. Does she charge you the extra fifty cents?'

'Now, Mandy, you can't ask me a question like that.' He winked at her.

'Hmmm,' Mandy said. She guessed not.

'Everything going as well as it can be with Ryan's death?'

She charged his card for the order, minus the alternative milk. 'The cleanup is done. Vellum comes home tomorrow, I think.'

'And you have to get a new tenant? What a pain.'

She grabbed a cup and went to the refrigerator to pour his milk. 'Yeah. Do you still have your rental house?'

'You bet. If you need any advice, let me know. You haven't tried to rent to a stranger yet.'

She grimaced instinctively, then turned back and handed him the cup so he could get his coffee. 'I need to talk to Ryan's sister and remove his possessions first. And then paint.'

'How long did he live with you?'

'A few months. He moved in to help me with expenses after Cory quit his job, but we don't need to talk about that again.'

'Cheer up, Mandy,' Scott said, walking over to the coffee urns. 'I bet you can get more hours here.'

Already, someone else was walking toward her to make an order and she had to clock out in fifteen minutes no matter what. Scott might be right about that overtime.

Mandy recognized her neighbor and friendly rival, Reese O'Leary-Sett, approaching. A nurse in a podiatry practice in the attached office building, she lived across the street from Mandy.

'I hear you're the bad news girl,' Reese said. She had her wealthy Bengali father's large dark eyes and her Irish mother's stunning bone structure. Mostly, Mandy envied Reese for her loose, dark curls, which never seemed to have the frizz of her own hair.

Reese, however, loudly envied Mandy for her social media career success, completely ironic given their relative positions here at the hospital.

'What can I get you?' Mandy asked. 'Less than five minutes until I close.'

Scott held up his cup toward Mandy in a salute as he walked out of the coffee bar area and toward the escalator that opened onto the skybridge to the parking garage.

'I never see you at this time of night,' Reese said.

'Overtime.'

Reese made a pout with her glossy lips. 'I'm glad your boss is helping you out.'

Mandy suspected Reese had injected fillers to augment her cheeks and lips. She had started her online presence as a makeup re-creator, using her face as a canvas for iconic movie looks, but had moved into journaling when that didn't take off.

In fact, they'd enjoyed their first journal class together, a workshop at North Seattle College, back last January, when Mandy was still a stay-at-home mom. Mandy had posted her first monthly 'Plan With Me' video the previous March, a couple of weeks after Cory had moved out. Reese's rival 'Plan With Me' video showed up in April.

'Would you like tea, Reese?' Whenever Mandy had been at Reese's house, she'd been offered tea.

'I have my own.' Reese lifted a logo-free metal cup. 'But I would like one of those ginger thins for the road.'

'Ginger thin coming up.' After Mandy took Reese's payment, she bagged up the cookie and handed it to her.

Reese put out her hand but didn't clasp the bag. 'I want to help you, Mandy, really I do.'

'You haven't even offered condolences yet,' Mandy said. 'Unlike half of the local population.'

'Oh.' The nurse smiled. 'I am so sorry you pushed your deadbeat cousin down your stairs.'

'Reese!' Mandy exclaimed. 'You don't really think that, do you?'

'I know you loved him.' Reese snapped her fingers around the white waxed pastry bag. 'But I wouldn't mind if you had. I'd be happy to buy your little sticker business so you can afford a lawyer.'

'My business?' The phrase burst out of Mandy's mouth, instead of more sensible words of self-defense. 'You can't buy a lifestyle business.'

'I can take over the social media accounts and your online shop, receive payments for the old stuff moving forward, and merge our presences together,' Reese said.

Mandy thought of a bad word, unworthy of someone who believed women had to support each other. Reese had obviously been thinking about this. 'Really,' she drawled.

'You make, what, about two hundred a month per video at your level? Then there's the shop. I don't know how much volume you do.' Reese warmed to her theme. 'I have a guy who can value the online presence, and there are formulas for the retail shop. I can even buy your cutting machines and such, though I probably have better ones than you do.'

'We all know you're rich,' Mandy said. 'But you're wrong about everything. I didn't push my cousin down the stairs. I was filming at the time, so I have an electronic alibi.' She hoped.

'Then why is everyone gossiping that you're going to be arrested?' Reese asked, all wide-eyed and innocent.

Mandy sighed. 'How can they not suspect me or Vellum? We were the only other people they know were in the house.'

'It's definitely murder, though?' Reese examined her French manicure.

'So the police say.' Mandy leaned in. 'I don't want to have to sell my business, but I'll keep you in mind if it comes to that.'

'You can't count on Moffat family money anymore,' Reese said sweetly. 'You let that ship sail.'

'For good reason.'

'Hmmm. I guess you'd better figure out what happened to your cousin.' Reese tucked her cookie into her Coach purse.

Mandy wanted to think Reese had picked it up from the discount mall down in Centralia, but probably not. She couldn't compete in fashion with her younger neighbor anymore. 'Feel free to help,' she invited.

Reese's lips curved. 'Me, solve a mystery?' She drummed her fingers on the countertop. 'I could do that.'

'So says the next victim in murder mysteries. Honestly, it's a police matter.' She noticed the time. 'I have to clock out or Fannah will have my head.'

'I'll wait for you,' Reese offered. 'It's creepy in the parking garage after dark.'

'OK.' Mandy shook her head, amused. Reese, being a no-filter sort, said the most off-putting things at times, though they really did get along. 'Have a seat at one of the tables. I have to clean up.'

'Off the clock?'

'Afraid so. I have to duck into the back room and then I'll finish up. Ten minutes, tops.'

Reese nodded. 'I'll just sit here, looking like a girl pretty enough to kill.'

Mandy felt queasy at the turn of the conversation. She wondered if Reese had even seen a dead body. Podiatry didn't have a lot of corpses coming through, just diabetes, bunions, and plantar fasciitis. Having just seen one herself, though, she felt horrified at her unpleasant joke. Why did Reese bring out the worst in her?

Mandy spent an uneasy night in her own bed, the first one since Ryan had died. She woke early, as if it were a work day, and started doing chores even before coffee. After putting away the laundry she'd done at Linda's, she stripped beds and dusted bedrooms, then ran a mop over the hardwood bedroom floors and wiped up the bathroom.

After that whirl of activity, she picked an espresso pod for her coffee maker. While it warmed up, she went into the art studio and reset the table for the April journal spread.

She couldn't imagine using the take they'd made, culminating in the horrible noises of Ryan falling, so she carefully cut out a page from an extra journal and pasted it over the page in Vellum's journal, then redid her daughter's cherry blossom and Space Needle sketch. After that, she drank her coffee and redid another sketch for herself, and taped it down to their desk. Poor Vellum. Her journal had been sitting here unused for four days. She hadn't been able to update her habit trackers, write in her Dear Diary spread, or anything. Mandy flipped through the pages, seeing that Vellum did faithfully keep up with her journal.

She was careful not to read the diary part but did have a pang when she saw one of Vellum's daily tasks was to message her dad. Did Cory know how much his daughter tried with him? Did he even care?

At eight, Mandy stood in front of the refrigerator, debating scrambling some eggs, when she heard the back door open. She whipped around, holding her spatula like a weapon, then recognized her daughter. Her heart began to beat again. 'Hi sweetheart, you're home early.'

Vellum closed the kitchen door and dropped her backpack inside. 'Dad had a golf lesson.'

Mandy refrained from commenting and gave her daughter a hug. 'I'm glad you're home.'

Vellum untangled her scarf and tucked it and her mittens into her knit cap. 'We have a lot of catching up to do.'

'You bet. I was awake early too, so I've set us up again.'

'Do I have to redo my pencil sketch?'

'I even did that.' Mandy shrugged. 'It was strange being here alone after the week we've had.'

'You went to your happy place. I get it, Mom.' Vellum peered into the open refrigerator. 'Anything for breakfast?'

'I haven't gotten that far.'

'Rats. I was hoping blueberry muffins had magically appeared.'

'Why don't you run over to the Shangri-La?' The bakery was across the street from Linda's house.

'You always say it's cheaper to make our own.'

'Didn't your father give you any pocket money?' Cory refused to do anything as reasonable as give his daughter an allowance, but he usually passed her a twenty-dollar bill when she came for one of their scheduled weekend visits.

Vellum brightened. 'Fifty bucks! I could totally go to the bakery. Do you want a latte, too?'

'Now *that* we can do at home,' Mandy said. 'But you don't have to buy me a muffin with your money. I'll just make eggs.'

'You deserve it, Mom.' Vellum kissed her cheek. 'After we eat, we'll shoot our video, OK?'

Mandy nodded. 'Can't wait! Our business is booming, so much so that Reese O'Leary-Sett offered to buy it.'

'She's not nearly as good as we are,' Vellum sniffed. 'It's no wonder.'

'She offered to buy it so I could pay my legal fees if I was arrested,' Mandy said sourly. 'It makes me wonder what she knows.'

'Or did,' Vellum said.

'Yeah, God forbid,' Mandy agreed, her thoughts flashing to Ryan's crumpled body. Her throat went tight and she turned away from her daughter to better control her emotions.

An hour later, they'd finished their muffins. Mandy ran across the street to give Linda her fifteen dollars back. She'd been able to verify her paycheck deposit on her phone the night before and had grabbed cash after leaving work.

'I'll start the laundry,' Vellum said.

'I set the basket with sheets at the top of the stairs. I suppose I should have done it.'

'It's fine,' Vellum said. 'I have my clothes from Grandma's and Dad's to do. I spilled root beer down my shirt at the movie last night and it's going to take some work to get the stain out.'

'I checked the basement. It's back to normal,' Mandy said. 'I'll set my phone to record.'

'I hope we can earn enough to get a better camera soon. Are we on track?'

'Sure,' Mandy said, remembering that conversation with Reese the night before. They were on track for something, at any rate. 'In fact, I'd better check sticker orders. We might have a backlog. It's been such a crazy week.'

'Not having your phone is awful,' Vellum agreed.

Mandy watched Vellum toss her backpack down the basement stairs, then handed her the laundry basket. She had just opened her phone screen to check her online store orders when the doorbell rang.

Odd. No one who knew her ever came to the front door.

SIX

Mandy opened her front door. Dylan Tran and Alexis Ivanova waited on the second step from the top. She didn't think they'd ever come to the front door before. The wind bit through her soft fleece pants. While she didn't want to entertain Ryan's ex-whatevers, she didn't want to stand out here and get rained on, either.

She stepped back and gestured them in. Dylan shook out his Mariners ball cap on the outside mat before he stepped in, and Alexis dropped her faux fur jacket hood to her shoulders.

'What brings you by?' Mandy asked. 'You probably know I work two jobs and I don't have more than a minute free.'

'We're sorry for your loss,' Alexis said. She had a heavy Russian accent and an emaciated body, with legs that looked like sticks under her jeans.

'Thank you,' Mandy said. 'I'm sorry you lost your friend as well.' But she didn't sense a condolence call here. People who made condolence calls brought food. Because of the crime scene factor, no one had thought to bring any to the house in the first couple of days, but Linda had brought brownies over to her mom's house on Thursday night, and Mandy's ex mother-in-law had sent a sausage-and-cheese gift basket that arrived yesterday. Kit and Fannah had signed a condolence card for her at work, along with some of their regulars.

Mandy was honestly surprised Reese hadn't stopped by with an offering. The fact that her neighbor, Crystal, had not was no surprise at all.

Dylan's thick black brows knitted together. 'Is there going to be a funeral?'

'I don't know,' Mandy admitted. 'His sister would be in charge of that, and since the police had my phone for a while I haven't caught up on calls.'

'Oh.'

Mandy waited for him to ask for Jasmine's contact information but nothing came. She didn't have time for this. 'Was there something else I could do for you?'

Alexis pulled up her hood, then let it drop again. 'Can we go downstairs?'

'No. I don't want anyone down there until Jasmine can look through Ryan's things.'

Alexis sniffed and lengthened from her slouched position. 'We helped Ryan build his coin collection and we'd like to have it.'

Dylan grabbed Alexis by the shoulder. 'To remember him by.'

'You want a keepsake?' Mandy asked, just to be clear.

They both nodded, a little too eagerly for her liking.

'I can't authorize that,' Mandy said. 'I'm sure Jasmine is the legal owner of Ryan's possessions. All I have in my part of the house are a couple of his coin-collecting magazines. You can have those.'

Alexis looked at her like she'd lost her mind. Mandy suspected they were looking for spendables.

'Why don't you let us come down to the basement?' Dylan asked. 'We can show you what we're talking about.'

Mandy moved quickly as Alexis tried to get around her. Her muscles tightened in flight or fight mode. Letting them in had been a bad idea. Were they going to try to take something valuable? The front door remained open and Mandy's only goal was to get the two of them out of it before Vellum came upstairs from the laundry room.

'Did he give you keys?' she asked bluntly.

'No,' Dylan said.

Alexis tried to edge around her again, but Mandy hopped in front.

'Stop that,' she ordered, as if Alexis was one of the Roswell twins. She wished she could afford a locksmith, just in case.

'Why were you two over Wednesday afternoon? I didn't hear you come in. Were you here before I came home?'

'What are you accusing us of?' Alexis asked.

'My neighbor said you left ten minutes before Ryan fell. Where did you go?'

Alexis's eyes narrowed. 'The police asked us all that.'

'It's none of your business,' Dylan said.

'I'm the homeowner. I have the right to know if unauthorized people have access to my home.'

Dylan scratched at a sore on his cheek. 'You're sad. I get it. You loved Ryan a lot.'

'So did we,' Alexis piped up.

'I'm going to ask you to leave now. I have to work.' Mandy took each of Ryan's young friends by the arm and moved them backward a couple of inches toward the door.

Thankfully, they took the hint and left. She watched them go through the archway and down the stairs to the street, waiting until they drove away.

Despite the cold, she stood there, thinking about how her mother had pointed her finger at the pair, how Ryan could have died because of them, until she heard a shriek from inside the house.

Mandy shut the door and ran into the hall. Oh God, had Vellum been attacked, too? 'Vellum?' she cried.

Mandy found her daughter at the top of the stairs. Vellum's skin had taken on a translucent hue. Her hands shook and her eyes were wide, staring.

Mandy grabbed her shoulders and pivoted her under the overhead light, her eyes scanning her daughter, looking for injuries. 'What happened?'

'G-g-ghost.' Vellum's teeth chattered.

Mandy frowned. 'Ghost?'

'D-downstairs.' Vellum coughed, then swallowed. 'He's down there, Mommy.'

'Who?'

'Ryan. I saw him in the washer.'

'I'm sorry?' Mandy wrapped one arm around her daughter and peered into her eyes.

'You know how things reflect into the outside of the washer? Like you can see the basket reflected when you put it behind you?'

'Umm, no,' Mandy said slowly.

'Maybe you're not looking,' Vellum said. 'But I always see reflections. I saw Ryan just now.'

'I'm sure you imagined it. Stress.' Mandy walked Vellum into her bedroom. 'Did you get any sleep last night?'

'I slept fine,' Vellum said impatiently. 'It was him.'

'Like his entire body? Or just the outline of a man?'

'No, it was his face, like something out of *A Christmas Carol*. You know, when Marley appears in the door?'

'Did he look like himself?'

'What do you mean?'

Mandy squeezed her shoulder. 'I don't know. Did he look tortured, like Marley?'

'His lips were moving. He wanted to tell me something.' Vellum shivered. 'I feel sick.'

'You're telling me you saw our dead cousin, and he was trying to tell you something,' Mandy summarized. 'Any idea what?'

Vellum shook her head. 'Sorry, Mom. You're going to have to go down there yourself and see if he appears to you.'

'But we have to do our video.'

Vellum put her hands on her hips. 'Seriously, Mom?'

Mandy waved hers in the air, trying not to laugh. 'He knows I'm busy. We don't have his rent money any more. It's more important than ever to get our videos out in time to sell our stickers.'

'Wow, Mom.' Vellum dropped onto her bed and curled up.

Mandy sat next to her. 'You are teasing me, right?'

Vellum shook her head. 'Sorry. I'll hold your hand when you go down there.'

Mandy grimaced. 'You'd better stay up here if you feel sick. We don't want to have to call the crime scene cleanup people again.'

'Mom!' Vellum shrieked. 'You can handle a little vomit.'

'You can,' Mandy shot back. 'I guess I'm going downstairs. Call your grandmother if I don't reappear and tell her to call an exorcist.' She went into the hall.

'I'm not joking,' Vellum called behind her.

'I know something spooked you,' Mandy called back. She investigated the dark stairwell. Having second thoughts, she went into the kitchen and grabbed her emergency flashlight.

Vellum came out of her bedroom and gave her a thumbs up. Mandy flicked up the light switch and went down four steps. Nothing happened when the light came on. The memory of finding Ryan flashed through her brain. She kept stepping down.

Something niggled at her. Something had changed. Not the cheap laminate flooring on the landing. The cleanup company had taken care of it. When she reached the landing, she turned slowly in a circle, and then she realized what was different.

The tiny built-in cabinet in the wall above the second step up from the landing hung open. Not good for much due to the size and place, it was original to the house. She had no idea what the original purpose would have been back in 1940. But it was never open. No one used it. Until now.

Mandy turned to face her daughter.

'What's wrong, Mom?' Vellum called from the top.

'Do you believe in ghosts?' Mandy asked, finding it hard to believe what she was seeing in the cabinet.

'Grandma does. She sees Grandpa all the time.'

'Huh.' Mandy had never been receptive to that sort of thing. But Vellum claimed Ryan had tried to tell her something, and now she was looking at what was probably the murder weapon. What hadn't the police been sharing with her?

'What's wrong, Mom?' Vellum bent into the doorway.

'The cabinet is open. Was it open when you came down here?'

'I don't think so.' Vellum started down the stairs. 'What's wrong?'

'I found a bloody hammer.' Mandy put up her hand. 'I need my cell phone, honey. Don't come down here.'

'I'll get it.' Vellum disappeared.

Mandy stared at the hammer and the dark substance smeared on it. Shuddering, she wondered if the killer had hit him with it. 'What did you do, Ryan? What did you get mixed up in?'

'I have your phone,' Vellum called.

Mandy stepped up and took it. 'Thanks, honey. Just wait a minute.' She went back down and took pictures, careful not to touch anything while she tried to get better angles, even using the flashlight as a spotlight.

Feeling five years older, Mandy walked back up the steps, closing the door behind her. 'The question is had it been there all along, or did someone sneak into the house and put it there?'

Vellum's lips trembled. 'Now what?'

'I need to find Detective Ahola's phone number and give him a call.'

'OK.' Vellum followed her like a puppy as she walked into her bedroom and pulled the card from her purse.

Mandy sent a text message with her address and the date, then loaded up the two best pictures. After her phone sent them, she dialed the detective's number.

He picked up on the fourth ring. 'Ahola.'

'This is Mandy Meadows. Did you see the messages I just sent?'

'I did not.'

She visualized his face, deepening the bags under his eyes to match his tone. 'You told me that Ryan looked like he'd been beaten up. I was assuming someone punched him. Was I wrong?'

'What do you want to know, Mrs Meadows?'

'Ms,' she corrected. 'Look, I found a bloody hammer in my house.'

His voice sharpened. 'Where?'

'In a cabinet on the basement stairs.'

'Did you touch it?'

'I didn't even touch the cabinet. It was hanging open.'

'Don't touch anything. I'll be there as soon as I can.'

'What does that mean?' she asked. 'I have to work.'

She heard the sigh. 'Twenty minutes.'

She put her phone in her pocket, a place where it was rarely found. 'How is your stomach, honey?'

Vellum let her tongue flop out of her mouth.

'That good, huh. Why don't you find my bottle of antacid tablets? Or I could make you a cup of tea.'

'Oh, please. I'm not forty.'

'Neither am I,' Mandy protested. 'I'd send you over to Grandma's, but I think they will want to talk to you.'

'OK.' Vellum's lips pinched.

Mandy saw her distress and took her daughter into the living room. They curled up together on the sofa and waited for the handsome detective to arrive.

'We should be filming,' Vellum said after a while.

'Do you really think you saw Ryan in the washer?' Mandy asked.

Vellum rubbed her face against Mandy's shoulder. 'Yep.' She sat up and walked into the art studio. A minute later she reappeared with her sketchbook. With quick moves of her pencil, she drew the outline of the washer, then began to shade it in.

Mandy was astonished by her daughter's command of light and shade. Then the creepy factor arrived as Ryan's face emerged to the left of the washer door.

'Wow,' Mandy said, with nothing else coming to mind.

'I know,' Vellum whispered.

'Don't show that to your grandmother or she'll want to hold a séance in the basement.'

'Maybe we should.' Vellum's voice cracked.

'I'm hoping that getting the murder weapon out of here will solve the problem,' Mandy said with a tone of certainty that she didn't feel.

The doorbell rang. Another front door arrival. Mandy had come to see that as bad news. The friendly news came in through the kitchen. She tucked a pillow under Vellum's cheek and opened the door.

Detective Ahola wore jeans, a Husky football T-shirt, and a studded leather jacket of the kind that mostly appeared on aging rock stars. She checked his feet for the requisite motorcycle boots but he simply wore some kind of black athletic shoe. Maybe she'd missed the trend.

Either way, his attire suited his athletic frame perfectly. She had to ask, 'How old are you?'

He raised his eyebrows. 'Thirty-five. Why?'

She shrugged. 'You're a year younger than me. Just wondering.' Not that she was wondering if he was single. She wasn't dating right now.

His gaze pierced into her for a minute, then his body language relaxed. 'You found a hammer?'

She nodded and let him in. 'I didn't touch it.'

He followed her into the hall. She opened the basement door again, flipped on the light switch and led him halfway down the stairs.

He glanced at the cabinet. 'You found it open like this?'

'I know it sounds nuts, but Vellum came down with laundry. She didn't notice it but came up in a panic, so I went down the stairs, made it to the landing, and then realized it was open.'

'She didn't notice this?'

'No.'

'Anyone else been in the house?'

'Ryan's friends, Dylan and Alexis, made it just inside the front door but I got them out of here. They had just left when Vellum shrieked.'

'Why was she upset?'

'I saw Ryan's ghost,' Vellum said from behind him, at the top of the stairs. Her face had taken on a mulish expression, like she expected him to make fun of her.

Detective Ahola turned to face her. 'What did you see? A shadowy figure?'

'No. His face, in the front of the washing machine.'

'Do you think someone might have sneaked into the basement to retrieve the hammer and you saw a real person?' he asked.

Mandy wondered that too, but Vellum had a note of certainty when she spoke. 'No, it was Ryan.'

'She did a sketch of what she saw,' Mandy offered.

'The brain can do all kinds of funny things,' the detective said. 'You see a man and you only expect your cousin to be there so that's what you perceive.'

'I didn't hear anything,' Mandy said, then rolled her eyes. 'Of course, I didn't hear anyone come in on Wednesday night, either. I thought I knew every creak this house makes.'

'You're probably starting to block out the noises you are used to,' the detective said. 'Why did Ryan's friends show up this morning?'

'They wanted some of his possessions. They claimed they'd helped him build his coin collection.'

'It's very common for people to try to grab expensive items in the aftermath of a death,' the detective said. 'A depressing reality.'

'I asked them if they had keys. They said no.'

'Could they have distracted you while someone else went in through the basement?'

'Maybe, but they seemed to be a trio. Ryan, Dylan, and Alexis. I never saw them with anyone else. If they were trying to pull something, I'd have thought one of them would come to the door while the other sneaked in.' She paused. 'I'm not sure there was really time for them to leave my front steps and get downstairs before Vellum shrieked.'

'You should check on those coins,' the detective suggested.

'That's a smart idea, Mom,' Vellum said.

Detective Ahola stepped down one more riser and looked at the cabinet from every angle. 'It's hard to see. The stairs aren't very well lit.'

'Low watt bulb,' Mandy admitted. 'It's a good one. I think it's been there for years.'

'I doubt we fingerprinted the area,' the detective said. 'I'd better call a technician to process this area properly.'

'That is blood on the hammer, isn't it?'

He pulled a flashlight from his jacket pocket and shone it over the interior of the cabinet. 'Looks like it.'

'You said Ryan had a cracked nose,' Mandy pointed out. 'I didn't notice that, but I'm sure I'd have noticed if someone had taken a hammer to his face.'

Detective Ahola glanced up the stairs at Vellum. She wrapped her arms around herself and disappeared. 'She doesn't need to hear this.'

'What?' Mandy asked.

He put his hand to the back of his head. 'Bashed in, I'm afraid. You couldn't have seen it from the way he was lying.'

'Oh God.' Mandy put her fingers to her mouth. 'I had no idea.'

He dropped his hand to his belt. 'I'll be interested to see if it appears that the hammer has been there all along.'

She understood his intent immediately. 'I know that finding it today makes me look bad, but it's my house. I couldn't lie about it.'

'I know.' He gave her an almost sympathetic look. 'I'm going to make a call. People will be coming. Stay out of the way for now.'

Mandy nodded. 'OK. Want a coffee while we wait?'

He bent down to examine something on the wall. 'Sure. I'll come up after I make my call.'

Even the sight of an attractive man bending over didn't dispel Mandy's sense of unease. 'Did you ever find Ryan's car, by the way?'

'It was in the USea parking garage. Someone must have driven him home that night.'

She felt the back of her own head as she went up the stairs. 'OK, thanks.'

Vellum stayed in her bedroom while Mandy made a pot of coffee and let the evidence technician in, along with Detective Ahola's partner, Detective Rideout.

'I'm sorry to hear about your wife,' Mandy said awkwardly, remembering what Detective Ahola had told her. 'It must be a very difficult time for your family.'

The detective grimaced. 'It's just us, most of the time. Our daughter works in Tacoma.'

'What does she do?'

'She's a program assistant with the Puyallup Tribe,' the detective told her.

'I'm glad Tacoma isn't far, though with our traffic congestion it might as well be,' Mandy said. 'Could I make your family some muffins while you're checking things out downstairs?'

'That's kind of you, but I couldn't accept a gift.'

He meant it could be a bribe. 'I didn't mean it that way.'

Detective Rideout touched her arm. 'I don't imagine you did, and I appreciate the kindness. Truth is, she simply isn't very hungry right now.'

The technician said, 'Excuse me, sir,' and pushed past them.

Mandy thought she recognized the man from Wednesday night. The detective nodded at her and followed the tech. Mandy decided to make muffins anyway. She and Vellum could eat them instead of going to the bakery. They could make a meal out of the muffins with the sausage and cheese that Vellum's grandmother had sent.

Mandy kept her ears on the noise of men's voices through the open basement door while she mixed up a batch of cinnamon streusel muffins. She thought she heard her daughter's voice once, but Vellum didn't come out.

A knock came on the back door while Mandy was sliding the muffin tin into the oven. Finally, someone she would probably want to see. Her mother, perhaps, or Linda, curious about the latest round of police vehicles outside.

Instead, her ex-husband stood outside the mudroom on the steps. Mandy's heart sank. No hint of the excitement she used to feel when she saw him had survived his infidelity. Nothing good came of his visits anymore. What did he want now?

SEVEN

Mandy opened the back door. 'What do you want, Cory?' He wore a navy pea coat, with a cashmere scarf tucked into the collar. She could see a hint of a Rolex peeking out from his sleeve. His still-thick blond hair was neatly trimmed into an executive cut, despite him not holding a job.

He didn't have anything so fancy as a trust fund, just two grandmothers who gave him fifteen-thousand-dollar checks each year for his incidentals, a suite in his mother's home, and a credit card that his father paid. His parents had been divorced for thirty years, following their own parents' divorces in the seventies, and Mandy should have known he wouldn't take marriage as seriously as she did. He came from a long line of philandering men. Unlike Cory, though, they had at least been hard-working. His father was a named law partner in a firm downtown, and Vellum said he showed no signs of retiring, though he was at retirement age now.

'Vellum texted me.' His forehead creased. 'Sounded panicked. What kind of trouble are you in now?'

'Same old,' she snapped. 'Just more about Ryan. If you want to help, pay to put in a security system to protect your daughter.'

He lifted his hands. 'Sorry, babe, no job, no money.'

'You piece of—' Mandy stopped, keeping the rest of her epithet to herself, especially with their daughter in the house. 'What do your parents have against me? I'm the wronged party here. How dare you refuse to pay child support?'

'My father is going to take this sad situation to court,' Cory said mockingly. 'Get my burden reduced since I'm unemployed now.'

'Whatever happens in the future, you need to make your payments,' Mandy snarled. 'I have yet to see a check from you this year.'

Cory glanced at the ceiling as if the answer to her demand lurked in the aging white paint.

'Ms Meadows?'

Mandy ignored the slight wince from her ex as she turned to the detective. As if Cory had any right to be upset that she'd changed her name. 'Yes, Detective?'

'We've secured the weapon and processed the area,' Detective Rideout said.

'Can I clean up the stairwell now?' she asked meekly, hoping he hadn't heard too much of her outburst.

'Is that what you were doing when you discovered—' he paused, glancing at Cory. 'The item?'

She shook her head. 'No, I found that cabinet open when I went down the stairs earlier. But I assume the tech left a mess.'

'Ah. Yes, you can tidy that up. Our apologies.'

She saw Detective Ahola come up behind his partner. He gave her a nod, then both men walked out of sight.

'I need to lock the front door behind them,' she told Cory, and sped into the living room. Once the men were gone and she'd bolted the door, she went and banged on Vellum's door. Cory no longer had the privilege of walking through the house like he owned the place. 'Your father is here.'

Vellum opened the door. Her eyes were red.

'Were you crying?'

'I'm tired of seeing the police in our house,' Vellum cried. 'And I don't want to be haunted.'

Mandy pulled her daughter into her arms. 'Ryan would never hurt you, sweetie. We'll do whatever your grandmother suggests to move him to the next phase of his existence.' Or at least whatever her mother suggested would make Vellum feel better.

Vellum sniffed. 'OK.'

'Now, go deal with your father. Maybe I should shoot the video alone today.'

Vellum rubbed her eyes. 'No, I can manage him better than you can. We'll do it.'

Mandy went back into the kitchen. She ignored Cory and turned on the oven light to check on the muffins, since he'd interrupted her before she could set the kitchen timer. They would probably be ready in another ten or fifteen minutes. She set the timer for twelve to split the difference.

Her cleaning supplies lived under the kitchen sink. After pulling on household gloves, she dragged out a bottle of all-purpose cleaning spray and a roll of paper towels. The last things she grabbed were a plastic bag and her emergency lantern.

On the steps, she turned on the lantern, which brightened the staircase considerably, and surveyed the damage. She couldn't detect any blood. Had it dried before the hammer had been placed in the cabinet? Had the killer sneaked back into her house, possibly while Vellum was doing laundry?

Maybe they'd have to do laundry in her mom's house for a while. She didn't want to take any risks with her precious child.

'I'll lock and bar the door at the top of the stairs,' she said.

'Do you have any bolt hardware?' Cory called.

'No. Sorry, just talking to myself.'

'I'll take Vellum to the store. We'll pick up a bolt lock for you and grab lunch.'

Vellum appeared in the doorway next to her father. 'I told you I need to work, Daddy. Mom pays me, remember?'

Mandy wanted to say something rude about Cory being the last person to understand commitment, but she kept her thought to herself.

'That's fine,' he said mildly. 'I'll run over to the hardware store and pick up some takeout from that Indian restaurant you like down the way.'

'You have to get some for Mom, too,' Vellum said.

Mandy turned back to the cabinet with a smile and tried to ignore the beautiful sounds of her daughter having her back. She sprayed disinfectant all over the wood shelves, then thought better of it and pulled them out, ancient wood crumbling at the edges, and tackled every inch of the framed-in cabinet.

Her small garbage bag filled with paper towels as she wiped out the cabinet, put the cleaned shelves back in, then scrubbed the wall. Finally, she tackled the basement steps, coughing from all the spray in the air. The enclosed space was hard to ventilate but she decided she didn't care. Her collection of fans was stored in the laundry room and she didn't want to go near it.

Had the police gone down there? 'Rats,' she muttered. What if they'd left a mess down there, too? She coughed hard, and decided she needed to get out of the disinfectant haze. She'd check the laundry room after Cory returned. He might be good for rescuing her from a ghost . . . or an intruder.

Upstairs, she dropped her garbage bag into the pail and took off the gloves, careful to remove them so that her skin didn't touch the outsides.

Vellum popped in from the dining room as she washed her hands. 'We're all ready, Mom.'

'We are?' Mandy noticed the muffins were cooling on the counter. 'Thanks for taking them out. I didn't hear the alarm go off.'

'I turned it off at ten seconds.'

'Were they good?' Mandy pointed at the empty hole in the muffin tin.

'Dad took it.'

'That will pay for my baba ghannouj.' Mandy dried her hands and turned to her daughter with a smile. 'Ready.'

Vellum pointed at her. 'How old is your manicure now?'

'It's at the outer limits, for sure. But we'd better not take the time to redo it.'

'Mom,' Vellum scolded.

'I'm sure you've noticed how bad some of the journalers' nails are. They joke about it.'

'But we don't want to be that kind of lifestyle maven,' Vellum whined.

Mandy grinned at her and wiggled her pastel pink nails. 'Joking, kiddo. I redid them last night.'

Back in their studio, Mandy replayed what they had done before Ryan's death. 'Let's get any shudders out of our system now. I liked what we had. Do you remember your lines?'

Vellum nodded. 'Got it, Mom.'

Mandy took a deep breath and circled her shoulders. Her right one popped, a disturbing reminder of heading into her late thirties. 'We got this.'

'We got this,' Vellum echoed.

Mandy set up her phone's camera app and started the filming. They did well, remembering what they had said on Wednesday night, and continued on through inking their drawings. They needed to let them dry before applying color, so Mandy stopped the recording after they had finished the ink.

Vellum stretched out her fingers, then did a couple of exercises Linda had taught them to keep their wrists and tendons supple. 'That went well.'

Mandy glanced at their artwork. 'Absolutely. What do you want to use to color?'

'I like the Koi brand pinks,' Vellum said. 'Why don't I use them and you use the Crayola Supertips?'

'You're supposed to be the student journaler,' Mandy pointed out. 'I hate to say it, but shouldn't you use the less expensive option?'

Vellum glanced at their array of pens, temptingly displayed in a set of glass boxes, the openings pointed outward so that the pens were easy to access. 'I'll use the Koi for the cherry blossoms and the Supertips for everything else. You use the Tombows.'

'I can do that.'

Vellum hesitated. 'Do you want to say what we're using, or just list it all below?'

'Both,' Mandy said. 'I know it's not exciting to us, but we aren't the regular consumer of our content. Most of them don't have our experience.'

'Right,' Vellum agreed. 'That's why we keep our palettes simple.' She selected a pink for the flowers, a soft gray for the mountains and buildings, then a yellow gold for highlights.

'I'm going to use a blue,' Mandy said. 'To add some definition to the mountain backdrop.'

Vellum grabbed another pen while Mandy flipped through the Tombows. 'So many blue choices,' she moaned.

Vellum chuckled. They both heard a bang at the mudroom door. 'Dad,' she said.

'Lunchtime,' Mandy agreed. 'We'll finish later. I can't believe your father gave up part of his afternoon.'

'He's not a terrible father.' Vellum stood and turned to Mandy. 'Just a terrible husband.' She smiled sadly and went to open the door.

After lunch, Cory promised to return that evening to pick up Vellum for the rest of the weekend she was supposed to have with him. She and Mandy finished shooting their video.

'One thing off the checklist,' Mandy said.

Vellum packed their pens back into the glass boxes. 'Are you going to script the voiceover this month?'

'I probably should. I'm so scatterbrained right now, though, with all the stress and grieving,' Mandy told her.

'I feel like we caught a lot of good stuff just while we were filming.'

'I agree. The problem is making it seamless. I'll see what we've got, edit it down, then figure out what to do.' Mandy yawned.

'What are you going to do tonight? You don't have to make dinner for us now.'

'Can of soup and a muffin. I'd have served that to you, too.'

'You don't have to add all those fresh veggies to make it healthier,' Vellum pointed out. 'You can be a slob.'

'In that case, I'm just going to eat a muffin. Maybe some sausage and cheese.' Mandy paused. 'Seriously, though, as you get older you'll actually appreciate taking care of yourself. It starts to make a difference, what you put in your body.'

'Dad will just order us pizza.'

'On top of chicken vindaloo?' Mandy shuddered. 'Better you than me. I'm going to take a bath and then look at the pages we did and decide about stickers.'

She had a different workflow than her competitors. Most of her competitors designed stickers that they then used in their journaling videos. She and Vellum created their pages and then she made stickers for the month. They always used some of their standard stickers like printed days of the week in spreads, and also sold number strips and blank calendars and such.

'Do a sticker page of cherry blossoms,' Vellum said. 'And use my designs. I like them better. Also, do a page of schoolbooks, like science and social studies and geometry. I think they'll sell.'

Mandy saluted. 'Yes, ma'am.'

Vellum rolled her eyes. 'I need to pack. I don't have any clean clothes. You can finish my laundry, right?'

'That's one of your chores, honey.'

Vellum blinked, all innocence. 'Special circumstances. They just need to be moved into the dryer and dumped on my bed. I'll fold everything.'

'You don't want to go back into the basement?'

Vellum screwed up her face. Knowing she was partly being played, Mandy gave her daughter a hug. 'I'll do it, but if I get eaten by a ghost you'll have to live with your father full-time.'

'Better eaten than possessed,' Vellum giggled, and went to her bedroom to pack.

Mandy contemplated braving the basement. What would settle her nerves? Wine? Some kind of ghetto alarm system on the basement door? A stacked set of cans, maybe? She had a case of garbanzo beans on a basement shelf.

While Vellum was still in the house, she ventured down and dragged the dusty case of beans over to the back door and stacked them. She didn't see any signs of forced entry, so if anyone had come inside they must have had a key. After that, she forced herself to go into the laundry room. Keeping her eyes averted from any reflective metallic surface, she dumped Vellum's clothes into the dryer and started a load of towels. She'd have to come downstairs one more time to retrieve her daughter's clothes. Experience had taught her that Vellum had a low tolerance for wrinkles, no matter what she said about just dumping her clothes on the bed.

On the way up, her phone rang. She averted her eyes from the cabinet in the wall and took the steps two at a time. As soon as she had the door slammed closed, she answered.

'Hi Mandy,' said a low, very tired voice.

'Jasmine,' Mandy exclaimed. 'I'm glad to hear from you.' She'd left a message with her cousin as soon as she had her phone back, but Jasmine hadn't answered or returned the call until now.

Their four-year age difference had prevented Jasmine from ever bonding with Mandy. They were never interested in the same things. While Ryan had become protective and basically a sibling, Jasmine had been distant and superior. Her parents hadn't had much money so Mandy hadn't inherited hand-me-downs that might have given her some insight into her older cousin's life, and Jasmine had gone to cosmetology school instead of college. They'd continued to have even less in common as adults than they had as children.

'It's too bad about Ryan,' Jasmine said slowly. 'Not that I expected him to make old bones.'

'I don't imagine his liver would have held out forever,' Mandy agreed. 'But I wanted him with us for longer than this.'

'Do the police have anything new to offer?'

'I learned something new today,' Mandy said. 'Something the police hadn't told me before, but it's horrible.'

'What?'

Mandy's eyes pricked. 'He was hit in the back of the head,' she whispered.

'How did you find that out?'

She swallowed. Her voice came out shaky. 'I found the hammer. In the house. I don't know if the police missed it, or if someone came in later on and hid it.'

'I hope it leads the police to the killer,' Jasmine said after a pause.

'Me too. Vellum is having some rough moments.'

Childless Jasmine didn't care about Vellum. Instead of making some comforting remark, she said, 'I can't afford to pay this week's rent because Ryan didn't have a bank account.'

'How is that possible? He had a job.'

'He signed the checks over to Mom and she gave him the cash. Stupid, right? But why save for retirement if you're just going to drink yourself to death?'

'Unbelievable,' Mandy muttered, then immediately felt bad for her tone of voice. She needed the rent payment to keep on top of the mortgage, but Ryan had lost his life.

'Not really.' Jasmine blew into the phone. 'Get his stuff together, will you? I doubt he has anything worth actual money, but I need something to cover his cell phone bill. I have his car now, since the police told me to pick it up from the hospital parking garage, but it's just junk.'

'He used a prepaid phone,' Mandy said.

'Well, I'm sure there are some bills.'

Mandy doubted it. If he lived entirely on cash, he couldn't have had credit card debt. He owned his car. But no doubt Jasmine would be happy to get some money from her brother's estate, if she inherited it. 'You don't want to box everything up?'

'I don't have time.'

Mandy wanted to point out that she had two jobs, but Jasmine couldn't care less. 'Should I toss out things like toiletries and underwear?'

'Gross,' Jasmine said. 'But you'd better box up every single thing.'

Mandy gritted her teeth. What she heard was Jasmine thinking she'd hide away some good stuff if she didn't pack up every single little item. What a suspicious nature her cousin had. She responded in a way that made her flaring temper calm. 'Very well. I'm happy to do this last thing for Ryan.'

'He's dead,' Jasmine said flatly. 'You can stop sucking up to him.'

She disconnected before Mandy could react. Had Jasmine been jealous of Ryan's relationship with her?

Mandy went up the stairs and locked the basement door behind her. That afternoon, Cory had installed a new bolt lock at shoulder height on the upstairs side of the door, so she shot the bolt home with a feeling of satisfaction. It would be difficult to break the door down from the steps. They should be safe in the house now.

She texted Linda to see if she could bring over boxes in exchange for wine. Linda kept every packing box she ever received in her basement. Then she went to check on Vellum.

A couple of hours later, Mandy had finished her intro and outro script for their April 'Plan With Me' video. She layered on a full face of makeup and recorded the script.

The knock came as she was turning off her studio lights. She went to the back door and let Linda in.

'I parked in your driveway so we only had to haul boxes from there to the basement,' Linda explained.

'Genius,' Mandy praised. 'Cory installed an extra deadbolt on the basement door to the backyard. I'll have to go down and open it from inside.'

'Is it really creepy down there right now?'

'He died on the stairs, not in the basement proper,' Mandy explained. 'Do you want to come in?'

'I'll get started with the boxes,' Linda said. 'Is your wheelbarrow still outside?'

'No, it's locked up in the old garage.' She used it for storage instead of parking since the roof was iffy since last spring's windstorm.

'Oh, well, boxes aren't heavy.'

A couple of minutes later, Mandy had the doors unbolted and Linda carried in an armful of large shipping boxes.

'What do you buy that comes in boxes that large?' Mandy asked.

'They dump a bunch of small stuff into a large box.' Linda looked at her pile of cardboard in satisfaction. 'You're wiping me out of probably three years of large boxes. I'm thrilled.'

'Soon to be Jasmine's problem,' Mandy said.

They brought in the rest of the boxes. The basement consisted of a hallway that opened into a laundry area, and then a warren of rooms, including a small bedroom and a larger family room, but also the furnace room, extra closets and a bathroom. Mandy uncorked a bottle of pinot and brought it into the family room.

Cory had stripped the basement of furnishings when he moved out. The room here had been a playroom when Vellum was little, but when she'd reached double digits, he'd taken it over and turned it into a man cave.

Linda came out of the bathroom, her hands still damp. 'I swear I can still smell Big Beastie Kitty in there.'

'Her litterbox was in there for almost ten years,' Mandy said, 'but I don't think I'm that bad of a housekeeper.'

'It's just memories, I'm sure.' Linda took one of the wine glasses. 'Are you going to get another cat?'

'Vellum cried for days when BBK died.' Mandy sighed. 'She was more emotional about that cat than about her grandfather's death.'

'Kids,' Linda said, and tossed back half of her glass. 'Think about it this way. She'll be off to college in two and a half years. A new cat can't go with her. She'll be long gone before your next pet passes onto kitty heaven.'

'You're trying to turn me into a cat lady?'

Linda smiled. 'Not really. I'm mildly allergic to them. A dog would be better. A protector.'

'Which animal is more psychic?' Mandy asked, as the thought struck her.

'Good question. Walk me through the haunting situation.'

Mandy picked up the other wine glass and sat in Ryan's creaking recliner. She told Linda what Vellum had claimed. 'Can you imagine? But I think it might have been an actual intruder, rather than a ghost.'

'That's even worse!' Linda exclaimed.

'I wish I knew what she really saw.' She rubbed her hand over the corduroy nub of the armrest. Her fingers came away with dangling white cat hairs. Odd. At least she hadn't discovered Ryan had secretly had a cat down here. Maybe the chair was a hand-me-down from a friend. She knew his brass headboard had been. 'It couldn't have been Dylan or Alexis. They were upstairs.'

'It wasn't me,' Linda said. 'I was at the shelter.'

Mandy frowned at her friend. Why did Linda feel the need to mention that? She'd barely known Ryan.

Linda took out her phone. 'Let's do a search on psychic pets.' She typed for a minute while Mandy refilled her wine glass.

'Any answers?'

'Not really. Cats seem to have an edge.'

'Do I want to have a cat who can see ghosts? I'd rather the ghosts left us alone.'

'I'd rather the ghosts did the packing,' Linda said. 'What's going to happen to the furniture?'

'Jasmine is paranoid. She wants everything boxed up, even Ryan's personal items. But she's going to have to pay someone and rent a truck to get his furniture out of here.'

'It's all his?'

Mandy nodded. 'Everything in here and in the bedroom and bath is absolutely his. The hallway, laundry and furnace areas are mine, but Cory took everything in here, even that breakfront that belonged to my grandmother. I didn't argue because it was so ugly.'

'You aren't supposed to care if family heirlooms are ugly.'

'This one was really bad. Her uncle had hand-carved it, and he wasn't an expert wood artist, to say the least. Every time I opened the cabinet doors I got a splinter, even sixty years after it had been made.'

Linda laughed. 'Poor old uncle.'

Mandy forced herself to stand and place a small box next to the stack of magazines on the battered coffee table. 'Thanks for helping me. It's much less spooky when I'm not alone.'

'Of course. I'll take the posters down from the wall. I think I have one box big enough for them.'

'I cannot imagine what she'll do with all this stuff,' Mandy muttered, dropping old copies of *Sports Illustrated* and other reading material into the smaller box. 'I'd better grab some bubble wrap for his iPad. That's probably the most valuable thing in here.'

Linda dropped a football poster into her box and rolled the putty that had held it to the wall into her hands. 'What about his coin collection?'

Mandy came over to the bookshelf. She pointed to a trio of

see-through plastic boxes. 'He's been collecting old and foreign pennies since we were kids. But I doubt they're worth anything.'

'What about these?' Linda picked up a couple of rolls of quarters. 'Were you running a coin laundry?'

'Ha, no.' Mandy stared at the rolls in Linda's hand. 'If only he'd been holding a couple of those. He could have fought back.' Tears pricked her eyes.

Linda set down the coins and gathered Mandy into a hug. 'I know it's hard, sweetie. It's going to take a while.'

'Who killed Ryan?' Mandy asked. 'What could possibly have happened down here?'

EIGHT

After a Sunday spent hunched over her iPad, designing sticker sets, then seated at her computer, loading up said sticker sets for sale and finishing up her 'Plan With Me' video with a fanned-out photo of the new stickers, Monday at the hospital felt like a vacation. Only an eight-hour day! With lunch and ten-minute breaks! Sometimes the side hustle felt more like slave labor than an actual paying job, even with a supervisor.

Having said that, both gigs needed to bring in income, or she would lose her house. Packing up Ryan's things had reminded Mandy that she wasn't receiving any income from a tenant, and having Cory around made it clear he had no intention of paying child support. If he ever went back to work, she'd have his wages garnished, but she couldn't count on anyone but herself for the bills.

'Doctor O'Hottie's coming,' Kit whispered to her mid-morning. 'I'll get out of your way so you can flirt.'

The room spun a little bit as Mandy was hit by a wave of anxiety. 'I don't remember how. You can have him.'

Kit batted her eyelashes and gave Mandy a gentle push toward the counter. 'He only wants you, princess.'

Too late. Dr O'Halloran stood front and center at the counter. His gaze danced down Mandy's front and looked quizzical. *Uh oh.* Had the girls gone crooked thanks to her aversion to underwire that morning? Mandy glanced down and saw a long black streak on her apron.

'Oh,' she winced. 'The chocolate syrup got away from me on that last mocha.'

The doctor pushed dark blond wisps off his forehead, displaying his manly brow. 'Better than blood. You wouldn't want to know what I had all over my surgical scrubs this morning.'

'Early start?'

'Afraid so. One of my patients needed emergency surgery at four this morning. Quad shot, please.'

'You got it.' She grinned at him and flashed four fingers at Kit, who put her hand to the espresso machine. 'Sorry, there's no hero discount.'

He chuckled. 'The employee discount will do, Mandy. How was your weekend?'

'Sixteen-hour day on my social media business, but I had a full night of sleep, so I can't complain.'

'How is that working out for you?'

'I'm a two-income household in the form of just me,' she said, running a hand down her body like a game-show model displaying a new washer and dryer.

'Art is good for the soul.' The doctor ran his card over the scanner. 'I painted models in high school. It trained me for detail work.'

'What kind?'

'Whatever came my way. Monsters, mostly. From fantasy role-playing games.'

'Do you still have them somewhere?'

'I think they went into the trash along with my first marriage. Not much survived from that bitter ending.'

'I didn't know you were divorced, too.'

'Long hours, career focus. It's hard on relationships.' He flashed her a grin. 'Better to date people with the same kind of lifestyle. I married my college sweetheart. She put up with med school but by the time I became a resident she was tired of it.'

'I'm sorry. Any kids?' Kit passed Mandy the espresso drink and she handed it to the doctor.

'No. We had some losses – well, you know. Never made it to the delivery room.'

Mandy touched his hand. 'I'm sorry, Doctor O'Halloran.'

He pressed his lips into a brave smile. 'One of these days. Children are a blessing.' Giving Kit a nod, since she'd come to stand behind Mandy, he walked away.

'If you don't date him I'll go through your phone, find your most embarrassing selfie, and post it on the cafeteria bulletin board,' Kit hissed in her ear.

'I can't imagine having a baby at my age,' Mandy said. 'Not even for Doctor O'Hottie.'

'Oh, come on. My ovaries just melted and he's not even my type.'

'What is your type, anyway?'

'I have terrible taste.' Kit stuck out her tongue.

'Why do you say that?'

'I don't date much. I just get these flashes of lust, and then I end up in bed with someone a few times.'

'Oh, to be twenty-four again. Not that I was twenty-four like you are. I was pregnant at twenty and had a pre-schooler at your age.' Mandy turned to face Kit. 'Anyone here ever possessed you with a lustful urge besides Doctor O'Hottie?'

Kit tugged at her left ear. Three round balls dangled from chains in her piercings. 'I'm almost afraid to admit it, but Ryan.'

Mandy's mouth fell open. 'My cousin? My old-enough-to-be-your-dad cousin?'

Kit sighed. 'I know, right?'

'When was that?'

'Last year.'

Mandy wiped up a spill at the espresso machine. 'Last year was like five weeks ago.'

'Summer,' Kit clarified. 'You invited me to your Fourth of July barbeque, remember?'

'Yeah.' She shoved her towel in the open space under the counter. 'He worked out.'

'I remember a phase,' she said cautiously.

'We were done before the weather changed, but he was looking good in July. I'm a biceps girl.' Kit shrugged. 'Flash of lust. We were hot and heavy for about two months.'

'He did like sleeveless shirts.' Mandy made a face, figuring Kit had kept the affair hidden due to embarrassment at dating such an older guy. In her opinion, tank tops on men were unseemly. No one needed to see all those tufts of armpit hair. And they had one less layer of defense between her nose and BO. But to each their own attraction.

Kit laughed, then sobered. 'Yeah. We had fun. He was probably drinking less than usual. I was drinking more than usual. You know. There was a drunken fight and that was the end of it.'

'It sounds like you helped him for a little bit. I remember him being in an unusually good mood in the summer. I'm glad he had a girlfriend for a while, at least.' Mandy hesitated. 'I knew he had herpes. I saw the medicine. Did you?'

Kit shrugged. 'We were careful.'

Mandy blew out a breath. 'Glad to hear it.'

Kit sighed. 'It was a bad breakup.'

'I would have preferred you to the friends who came next,' Mandy said, suspecting Ryan hadn't actually been drinking less than usual. He couldn't have seen Kit as often as she claimed or she'd have noticed her co-worker around eventually. But the story did remind Mandy that Ryan had a secretive side.

'Hello, ladies.' Scott sauntered up to them, followed by a jumpsuit-wearing underling carrying a ladder. 'I'm going to get in there behind you for a moment and install the new security camera.'

'No way,' Kit said, her face contorting. 'I don't want to be spied on.'

'It's going to look at the snacks, out over the counter,' Mandy said. 'Right? Not at us working.'

'That's the plan.' Scott gestured to his underling, who walked around the counter and set up the ladder behind the cash register.

'I want to see exactly what you pick up on camera,' Kit demanded.

Scott frowned. 'That's for Fannah, not you, kiddo.'

'Don't call me that,' Kit snapped. 'I'm an adult.' She stalked off. From the back, her narrow hips and thin frame made her look a decade younger.

Mandy glanced at Scott, who had an unreadable expression on his face. Considering Kit's behavior, had she had a relationship of some kind with Scott as well? Maybe she had Daddy issues.

When she looked past Scott, she saw a trio of administrative assistants approaching. It must be break time for them. 'Can you finish this during the pre-lunch lull?' she asked. 'Kit and I need to bust out some drinks.'

'Anything for you,' Scott said, motioning to his colleague. The kid, maybe Ryan's replacement, left the ladder where it was and slouched off behind Scott.

Mandy called to Kit and forced a smile in her customers' direction.

In the parking garage after work, Mandy pulled out her phone and leaned her head against her seat. Exhaustion had hit a couple of hours before. Her arms ached. Before she could second-guess herself, she called Detective Ahola.

'Ahola,' he said, answering on the second ring.

'It's Mandy Meadows.'

'Don't tell me you found another murder weapon,' he said, sounding distracted.

'Is there one?' Mandy asked.

He didn't answer.

Lovely. 'I'm just calling because I realized something today.'

'What's that?'

'I found out about another relationship my cousin had over the summer. With my closest co-worker, no less. I didn't realize Ryan could hide so much from me, much less someone I work with all week.'

'How long ago was the breakup?'

'Probably September. I'm not saying that gave her a motive or anything. Just that I thought I knew what happened in my basement and I'm obviously wrong. For instance, Alexis and Dylan might have been around far more often than I realized. Or anyone else, really.'

'Who is this co-worker of yours?'

'Kit Savva. She's only twenty-four, so I was surprised she'd dated a forty-two-year-old. And she acted funny when our maintenance supervisor came to install a security camera today. She's paranoid.'

'Why is a camera being installed?'

'We requested it because of pilfering.'

'Thank you. We haven't spoken to her.'

'I'll help anyway I can,' Mandy said, after another pause. 'I need the income from a tenant or I will lose my house.'

'Why can't you get another tenant?'

'How can I advertise the space, not knowing if someone might break in? I'm still afraid my daughter saw a person in the basement, not a ghost. Besides, Ryan's sister hasn't picked up his possessions yet. The bedroom and family room are both full of his furniture.'

He made an inarticulate noise. 'What do you think about your cousin Jasmine?'

'She seems to have been jealous of my close friendship with Ryan,' Mandy said. 'Or what I thought was a close friendship. She's greedy and suspicious. But she had no reason to kill him.'

'If you follow the money, she inherits his estate.'

'Not his mother?' She hadn't thought Jasmine had any motive to kill Ryan.

'He had a will.'

'I didn't know that,' Mandy said, confused by that bit of planning on Ryan's part. 'But Jasmine said there wasn't even a bank account. I didn't go through his stuff, just packed it up. I would assume there has to be a lot of cash somewhere, but where?'

'Maybe that's why you are having break-ins,' the detective suggested. 'I'd consider some security.'

'We've added bolt locks on the basement doors. I stacked cans inside the door to the outside.'

'You hear them fall, you call nine-one-one,' he advised. 'No investigating.'

'Nope,' Mandy agreed. 'Not a chance. I was thinking about getting a dog.'

'Do you have time to care for a pet?'

'No.' Nor the money for vet bills.

'Then think carefully about that,' he said. 'I need to go. Be safe out there.'

'Yes, sir.' Mandy disconnected and closed her eyes. Had she just suggested to a homicide detective that her co-worker had killed her cousin?

At home, Mandy felt guilty about the dishes and set about doing them before Vellum got home. When she arrived, she said she had a couple of hours of homework. Mandy sent her to her bedroom with the last of Linda's latest batch of late-night brownies and then washed that pan, too.

She needed to check her sticker sales . . . well, she needed to see if she had any. The big push would come after the video went live, and it was too early in the month to load it. Instead of looking at her statistics, she dried Linda's pan and walked it across the street.

No one answered at Linda's back door, so she opened the screen door and set the metal pan inside it. Since she'd already bundled up, she went for a short walk while the clouds were behaving. Across the street, the bakery beckoned her with far superior pastries than her workplace had to offer, and warmth, but she walked past it and crossed the street to the apartment building. Across the next side street, her mother's house was dark. Reese hadn't made it home yet either. She drifted down another couple of residential blocks, the air textured by cold. The entire landscape slumbered in gray, leafless winter. It should look very different a month from now. At this time of year, she found it difficult to gather artistic inspiration here. She went over her mental to-do list. She was due to film a weekly spread, something she didn't manage every week. It happened about once a month, to give her an excuse to use her new sticker sheets or highlight a product that wasn't moving. Her unfilmed weeks were much more basic bullet point list than artistic, though she used her journal daily.

When she reached her own small stretch of houses, she saw Crystal Roswell bent over in her doorway. Her neighbor straightened, a package in her hands.

Mandy called out a 'hello' but didn't receive a response, so she waved her arms and went up the stairs to Crystal's yard.

Over the railing, Crystal, clad in a thin T-shirt and jeans, her lank sandy brown hair in need of a wash, glanced at her impassively.

'Is Aiden around?' Mandy asked.

Crystal's brow creased. 'Why?'

'I wanted to ask you a private question, mom-to-mom,' Mandy said. 'Can I come in for a sec?'

'Yeah, sure,' Crystal said, in a tone that indicated her utter lack of interest.

Mandy followed Crystal inside. Her house was very similar to Mandy's. When Mandy and Cory had first moved in, Crystal's grandmother had lived in the house. A year or so later, she'd gone into assisted living and Crystal had taken over, first with her husband, and then alone. Mandy had no idea if the old woman was still alive, or who owned the property. Given that Crystal managed a small store in the mall, she couldn't possibly afford the house on her own.

Inside, Mandy saw the same furniture that had been there a dozen years ago. An overstuffed three-piece suite, now stained in places, a small television, and two bookcases filled with bestsellers from the era of James Clavell. Laundry lay in a heap on the loveseat and Crystal's oversized, drooling mastiff panted on a rug in the corner. The living room smelled like boy sweat and dog. Given the smell,

Mandy had to question Aiden's hygiene level. Or maybe the laundry mountain wasn't washed yet.

'Sorry, I don't mean to bother you,' Mandy said, then paused. A normal person would offer her a beverage and small talk, but this was Crystal, who offered nothing and said little more. 'Last week, Aiden was playing on my lawn and hurt himself.'

'Sorry,' Crystal mumbled. 'I told him to stop being so stupid.' She walked through the house and into her kitchen.

Mandy followed her. Crystal hadn't been doing her dishes. The kitchen looked far worse than Mandy's, even before she'd cleaned up, with bacon grease coating the stove, and fast-food wrappers from the mall food court on every surface.

'I don't know why he thought skateboarding on my lawn was a good idea, but as far as I know, he hasn't tried it again.' Crystal said nothing, so Mandy pressed on. 'He told me Ryan was a jerk, that he deserved to be murdered. Do you know why he said that?'

'I told him to stay away from your house,' Crystal said, staring at last year's giveaway calendar from an automotive place, still pinned to her wall. The month displayed was October.

'Because Ryan did something?'

'Because of last week,' Crystal said impatiently.

'Yes, thank you for that, but I'm asking about what happened in the past, between Aiden and Ryan.'

'Nothing.'

'Nothing happened? Then why did Aiden hate him?' Mandy's fingers itched to rip the calendar off the wall. Back when she'd first discovered journaling and had been sharing her excitement with the world, she'd offered to teach Crystal how, thinking it might help her to organize her life, but she'd declined. Apparently, she'd wanted to live her life four months out of sync.

Crystal's jaw worked. 'I guess it doesn't matter now.'

'What doesn't matter now?'

'Ryan.' Crystal's linebacker-sized shoulders went up and down, her unbound breasts jiggling with the movement. 'We hooked up a few times, until I told him to stop coming over.'

Mandy winced. 'What happened?'

'One time he fell asleep, spent the night. Not really appreciated, since he lived right next door, you know?'

Mandy nodded, too horrified to do more. Besides, she wanted to hear the rest.

'Anyway, the next morning he went into my kitchen like he paid for the groceries, even though he'd never bought me so much as a hamburger. And you know what he did?' Crystal's arms flailed.

Mandy averted her eyes from those pendulous breasts. 'What?'

'He ate the last of Aiden's Oreos for breakfast! Still had crumbs on his lips when the kids came into the kitchen. Jerk. Aiden lost it. I had to tell Ryan he wasn't welcome here anymore.'

'When did this happen?'

Crystal's gaze actually rolled over to her out-of-date calendar then back again. 'Summer. Late summer. He'd come through the side yard and call into my window, then climb in.' She almost smiled. 'Kind of sexy. Like a pirate boarding a ship.'

'OK,' Mandy said, holding up her hands. 'Would it surprise you to know he was with other women during that time?'

Crystal glared at her. 'I already said we weren't dating, OK? He never brought anything, even condoms or a joint.' Her eyes welled with tears and she brayed, a donkey-like cry of pain.

'A joint?' Mandy asked, confused. 'Ryan always told me he didn't use drugs. And I hope you used condoms. He had herpes.'

Crystal snorted, but the involuntary laugh mixed in with her tears and she choked. Mandy darted around her neighbor and pounded her on the back.

Emilee ran into the room and grabbed her mother's arm, her hands looking tiny against Crystal's flesh. 'What did you do?' she yelled at Mandy.

'I'll let myself out.' She walked rapidly to the front door, hoping Aiden wouldn't appear, too.

Once back on the sidewalk in front of her house, she breathed a sigh of relief. The frosty air felt good in her lungs, free of grime and dog and despair.

But she knew she hadn't just uncovered a motive for Kit killing Ryan, she'd found a new suspect for the murder. Not to mention the sticky issue of herpes. If her cousin had been having unprotected sex, someone could have been awfully upset with him when they'd picked up an STD.

NINE

On Tuesday, Fannah came in at six, Kit at seven, and Mandy at nine-thirty to cover the entire day. They were kept busy between the front counter and work in the back. Mandy baked cookies since they were in high demand and Kit preferred to run the cash register when she could. Since she tended to be a sloppy barista and often ended up covered in foam and espresso grounds, Mandy tried to accommodate her.

When they reached their pre-lunch lull, Fannah sent both Mandy and Kit on their ten-minute break.

'I need to get my blood moving,' Kit said, yawning. 'Want to walk up and down the stairs with me?'

Mandy's hands had been icy all day. Had the maintenance guy jostled a fan in the ceiling when he'd installed the security camera? Air moving in the wrong way could really make a job miserable. 'Let's do it.'

They grabbed their coats and dashed outside. The hospital and the attached office building created a 'U' shape around an attractively planted area, which gave patients something pleasant to look out on if they had a room on the right side of the building, and also gave stressed-out folks a place to pace.

'I'm glad we're getting a few minutes together,' Mandy said.

'Want to complain about Fannah?' Kit whispered loudly.

'No. Nothing to complain about.' Mandy scowled. 'It's about Ryan.'

'Oh,' Kit said, elongating the word until it trailed off.

'It sounded like you guys were legit in a relationship for a couple of months from what you said.'

'Pretty much.'

'I don't want to ruin your memories of him,' Mandy said, trying to be delicate.

Kit stuffed her hands into her REI trench coat. 'He wasn't that special to me.'

'That makes me sad, because he was very special to me,' Mandy said. 'But since he's gone, I'm learning things that would have upset me.'

Kit stepped up on the marble edge of a fountain and balanced on it, before hopping off again. 'Like what?'

'I hope your relationship was open, because I learned he was having late-night rendezvous with someone else.'

'That explains why he didn't always respond to my booty call texts,' Kit said, the ghost of a grin haunting the corners of her lips. 'I can accept he was a dog.'

'And another thing.'

'What?'

Mandy stopped at the end of the final fountain. They needed to return to work. She put her foot on the first step. 'Did he do drugs?'

'What does it matter now?'

Mandy worried at her lower lip and climbed another step. 'He told me he didn't, but I've heard otherwise.'

Kit ran up three steps and balanced on the side of the fountain again. She was being childish, or shady.

'Kit?' Mandy asked, climbing up a few more steps and turning back around. 'Please be honest. If he had a hidey hole somewhere in my basement, I need to find it.'

'Did you check his mini-fridge? He kept his weed in there. Rolling papers in a Christmas tin above it.'

'That's it? Nothing illegal?'

Kit shrugged and followed her up. 'If he did, I don't know where he hid it.'

An evasive answer, but at least Mandy knew the mini-fridge was empty. She'd pulled it away from the wall and unplugged it herself. No holiday tin had been on top of it either, or anywhere that she recalled. But maybe she wouldn't have noticed it. Did she need to unpack the boxes and look for it?

'Weed is no big deal. It's legal these days. But if he did anything else, do you know who sold it to him? Maybe they would know where his hiding place was. I have a kid, you know, and I need to get a new tenant ASAP.'

Kit laughed. 'Like I would tell you who was dealing around here.'

Mandy stared up at the façade of the hospital. 'Dealing around here? You mean an employee is selling drugs?'

'Welcome to the real world,' Kit said, running up the steps. She stopped at the top, huffing a little bit.

Mandy went up more slowly, heartsick at how her cousin had failed in his limited attempts at sobriety, then she and Kit crossed the multi-lane driveway together. The glass doors opened automatically and a blast of warm air hit them straight in the face. Their break had come to an end.

At least Kit wasn't acting like a murderer. Assuming Mandy could even tell what a murderer might act like. Angry, maybe? Kit seemed more tired than angry. And the relationship had been over for at least four months. Why would she have killed Ryan now?

Fannah took Kit's cash drawer toward the end of her shift at two-thirty. She replaced it with a fresh drawer that Mandy would be responsible for during the rest of her shift. Kit had to work the drinks station for her last hour.

Mandy bantered with Dr Burrell, who eagerly told her a silly coffee joke that one of his preemie parents had shared. She chuckled, since she'd never heard the joke before. After he wandered off, whistling, a sack of cookies in hand, Reese appeared with her shadow, a nurse-in-training.

Before Mandy could take their order, Fannah came out from the back.

'I need to see you right away,' she hissed.

Mandy turned her head. 'Now?'

'Not you. Kit.' Fannah adjusted her navy hair wrap and glided into the other room.

Kit went over to the doorway and leaned against the frame. 'What?'

Reese held up a finger when Mandy opened her mouth to take the order. She wanted to listen.

'Your till is short twelve dollars. You know our policy. It must be paid back immediately unless you want to be terminated right now,' Fannah said in her deadliest tone.

Mandy's eyes went wide. Kit should be deep in the back, where she couldn't be embarrassed in front of customers.

'I didn't take it,' Kit snapped. 'Mandy used the till today, and so did you.'

Mandy shook her head. In fact, she had not. She'd taken a couple of credit card orders, and that was it. She'd let Kit have the till.

Reese smiled at her sympathetically. Mandy lifted her chin, giving her neighbor the look of forbearance. But something caught her eye. She saw the new security camera in the corner. Could the till be seen in the footage, or only the counter snacks?

'It's your till. Pay it back now or suffer the consequences,' Fannah said majestically.

'No,' Kit snapped back.

'Mandy paid it back and she still has her job. If you choose not to do so, Mandy will be working overtime this week and you'll be out of a job.'

Reese's trainee's eyes went wide. Her hands fluttered nervously around the hem of her pink scrub shirt. Mandy couldn't believe customers were witnessing this. She turned and caught Fannah's eye, then pointed to the ceiling.

Fannah frowned and folded her hair wrap higher up on her forehead so she could follow Mandy's finger.

'Yeah,' Kit crowed, catching Mandy's point. 'That camera might come in handy.'

'You gave out bad change,' Fannah said in a bored voice. 'It's sloppiness, not theft.'

'Not twelve dollars' worth,' Kit argued. 'I could be short four dollars, because I gave out a five instead of a one, or something like that, but not twelve. Someone stole it and it wasn't me.'

'Kit,' Fannah said in a warning voice.

'This just happened to Mandy last week,' Kit said. 'Someone is pilfering and us poor shift workers shouldn't be paying for that.'

Fannah's lips tightened, creating little lines around them that displayed her true age for once. 'I don't have time for this.'

'You have to or we'll both have to quit,' Kit threatened. 'We can't afford to keep losing an hour's pay here and there.'

Now Mandy realized why Kit hadn't gone into the back. She wanted Mandy to hear her make her walk-out threat.

Fannah growled and disappeared. Mandy heard the safe open and close, then the former model swept past her and out from behind the coffee bar, heading for Scott's office.

It would have been more efficient to simply call him, but maybe

Fannah wanted to review the footage herself. Seven hours' worth, what a pain.

'Happy?' Mandy muttered when Kit went back to the drinks station.

Kit shrugged. 'I should have said something when it happened to you.'

'She gave me overtime. It did sort of make up the money.' Mandy paused. 'However, this happening twice in one week is unacceptable. Ten cents, sure. But over ten bucks? Less than a week apart? It feels like we're being targeted.'

'I'm glad you've got the camera now,' Reese said.

The trainee shuddered. 'Too Big Brother for me.'

'Mandy needs every penny she can earn,' Reese said, in pseudo-loyal fashion. 'She can't afford to lose anything. Isn't that right, dear?'

'What would you like, dear?' Mandy mimicked.

'Dark roast with a kiss of cream,' Reese said grandly.

Mandy gave her the stink eye and handed her a medium cup. 'You pour your own coffee here.'

Reese flashed her a toothy grin. 'You look tired. Why don't I take you to dinner tonight? Just us girls? You seem tense.'

The trainee spoke over her. 'A medium mocha please.'

'I'd love to have dinner with you,' Mandy said sweetly. 'And will that be one check or two for the drinks?'

Reese didn't offer to pay, so Mandy rang up the drinks separately. She wondered what that meant for their dinner. Would Reese woo her or conveniently forget her offer when it came time to pay? She'd better order the soup to be protected from a large bill.

Fannah sailed back in their direction twenty minutes later. She appeared cross and exhausted, about two minutes from the end of her shift.

'Did you see who took the money?' Mandy asked, every bit as interested in that topic as Kit was.

'There is no security footage,' Fannah snarled.

'They don't have the camera pointed over the register? Can they tilt it at all?' Mandy asked.

Kit came to stand next to her. She'd acquired a chocolate stain on her apron from her mocha making.

'The camera wasn't on.'

'He was just placating me?' Mandy asked, aghast.

'Of course not,' Scott said, walking up. Mandy hadn't seen him, since the free fruited water dispenser was in the way. 'Underling error.'

One of his crew walked past Scott with the ladder. He smiled and blushed as he pushed behind everyone at the counter. 'I'm sorry, I didn't install it correctly.'

Scott squinted and adjusted his tool belt. 'I had to write him up. I apologize, ladies.'

Fannah watched, impassive, as the kid fiddled with the controls.

'Umm, sir?' he said tentatively. 'I can't get it to turn on.'

Scott growled. 'Come on down.'

The kid climbed down the ladder, employing all safety techniques for ladder use. Scott rolled his eyes and went up after him. He fiddled with it, even batted at it, but nothing happened. 'It's broken,' he announced. 'I'll have to order a new one. Should I take this one down?'

'Leave it,' Fannah instructed. 'It might discourage thieves.'

Scott climbed down from the ladder.

'Sure didn't work today,' Kit muttered.

Fannah ignored the comment, probably preferring to believe Kit had either stolen the money or lost it in a change-counting error, given her own position in enforcing policy. 'You owe me twelve dollars,' she stated as she edged around the ladder and went into the back room. As a salaried person, she wasn't being paid for her overtime. Mandy was certain she wanted to get out of there.

Kit gritted her teeth.

'Do you have it?' Mandy asked softly.

Kit nodded. 'But it's not right.'

'I think they could relax the rule after we pass probation,' Mandy agreed. 'Once they know a new employee is honest.'

'People change,' Scott said, as he closed up the ladder. 'You can't trust anyone, any of the time.'

'Spoken like management,' Kit snapped.

Scott frowned at her, then gave Mandy a wink. 'See you around.'

Mandy closed down the coffee bar. Reese had already texted her, confirming dinner, so Mandy texted Vellum and her mother to make sure Vellum would get a hot dinner that night, then drove to a popular Italian restaurant in the neighborhood to meet her favorite frenemy.

As Mandy walked to the barstools in the tiny bar slash waiting area, the nurse was fingering her wine glass suggestively. She was glancing up at a well-dressed man in his thirties. Reese had managed to find the time to change into a cocktail dress, not the usual sort of thing for casual Seattle dining, and had put on a full face of makeup. Given the results, Mandy could see why she had made the effort. Reese looked stunning.

Just before Mandy reached the counter, the man took out his phone.

'What's your number?' he asked. 'I'll call you later.'

Reese glanced up and saw Mandy. Her slightly alarmed expression calmed. 'There's my friend now. Excuse me.' She descended from her stool much more gracefully than Mandy could have managed and edged around her would-be suitor.

'Do you think our table is ready?' Mandy asked. She'd been eager to get a wine glass of her own from the bartender.

Reese put her arm through Mandy's. Her heels clicked on the dark polished wood as they went toward the front desk.

'Didn't like him?' Mandy asked.

'He dated a friend of mine last year. Probably doesn't know she told me about it. He started off friendly, reminding me we'd met at a party, then slid into my personal space.'

'You are dressed to stand out. Some men, the disgusting ones, would say you dressed to be hit on,' Mandy said.

'Women dress for other women,' Reese announced primly. 'And this is nothing for a lot of cities.'

'You've lived in Seattle your entire life.' Mandy nudged Reese's shoulder with her own. 'Behave like it.'

Reese smiled at the maître d'. 'Is our table available yet?'

The seventy-something man checked. 'You are next. If you'd like to wait in the bar?'

Reese glared at the man. Mandy took her elbow and led her to the wall before they could be trampled by a large, exuberant group of young professionals coming in to celebrate a birthday.

'What ended up happening at USea?' Reese asked.

Mandy explained how the baristas had to make up till shortages.

'Sounds like a scam to me,' Reese said. 'Your supervisor could be pocketing the money herself and then you underlings have to eat the cost.'

Mandy sighed. 'If I was as paranoid as you, I wouldn't have been caught so off-guard by my divorce. I hope Fannah isn't crooked.'

'That security camera is more important than ever,' Reese said. 'Make sure it's pointing over the cash register, and make sure Scott isn't colluding with Fannah. You might need to review the footage yourself if money goes missing again.'

'Have there been rumors about any other petty theft in the hospital? Cafeteria, gift shop, any of those little trade shows that come through?'

Reese gave her a snooty smile. 'You'd be more likely to know about it than me. Don't you network with other cashiers?'

She frowned at Reese. 'Yeah, yeah, you have a college degree and I don't. The gift shop is run by volunteers and the trade shows by outsiders. I guess the cafeteria people fall into the same category as me, but I don't know them. I rarely go up there.'

'Ladies? Your table is ready.' The maître d' waved in their direction.

Mandy smiled at the server who approached them with menus, then followed her back to the dining room. The elegant space held less than twenty tables, causing the pile up in the main area and bar. Low instrumental music, white tablecloths, and elegant architectural swaths of braided vegetation on the walls made the diner aware that the bill would be high.

'What is your soup of the day?' Mandy asked as soon as they were seated. She'd just depress herself if she looked over the menu.

'Cream of mushroom,' the server said. 'What can I get you to drink?'

After she left with their drinks order, Reese leaned forward. 'That's not going to keep you on your diet, dear. Maybe a salad?'

Mandy fluttered her eyelashes. 'Is that what you're having? Dressing on the side?'

'No, I can never resist the stuffed salmon ravioli here. It's so quintessentially Seattle. I know Italian isn't the hippest cuisine these days, but I just love it.'

Reluctantly, Mandy opened the menu. She couldn't tolerate anything with red sauce right now. It looked too much like blood. Her gaze moved hopefully over a risotto dish but choked on the price. She settled on a watercress salad. Hopefully it was more than the size of a tea plate. If not, she had lots of leftover muffins, sausage, and cheese at home.

They made their orders. Mandy's glass of wine came. She saw two men in their mid-thirties at a table diagonal from them take turns checking Reese out, then obviously discussing her. Maybe there was something to this dressing for dinner idea. If she ever decided to date again, going out in a hot little dress to attract attention was much better than swiping through some dating app on her phone.

'You like attention,' Mandy announced, startling Reese.

She ran her fingers down one of her dress straps. 'I don't.'

'I think you do. Not that I don't admire your style.' She lifted her glass in a mock salute. 'I'd be quite proud of myself if I'd landed you for a date.'

Reese snorted. 'As if.'

'I may not be good enough for you, but I obviously have something you want.' She pulled on her most casual tone like armor. 'Did you kill my cousin in order to buy my business?'

Reese choked on her wine. Mandy stood and patted her on the back as the interested men watched, then discussed them again.

'As if,' Reese said again, after she could breathe.

Mandy grinned. 'I gained one hundred thousand followers in only one year, though my videos don't make a lot of money yet.'

'How much?' Reese said blandly.

'You were about right with your estimate. A couple of hundred dollars a month, especially on release month. You can't count on it, though. These massive companies are always finding a way to carve a chunk out of the take and put it back into their pockets.'

'I know. It seems like every month there is some new form of bad news in additional fees. I wanted to pay someone to help me with sponsorships on that photo site, and they wanted half of the sponsorship income. Can you imagine?' She took a large sip of wine.

'Not surprised. The fees for my online shop went up.'

'Are you selling many stickers? It's so brave of you to not use your own product in your spreads.'

'I do,' Mandy said defensively. 'In my dailies and weeklies. But we want all kinds of traffic to our vlogs and some of those people are never going to do more than reproduce our artwork or journal pages.'

'Hmmm,' Reese said. 'I just have trouble believing your numbers. How can you be so broke if your videos are doing well? If each one is making that much money?'

'Hello, Seattle mortgage,' Mandy said. 'And an ex who isn't paying his child support.'

'You should have at least made him pay off your house,' Reese said breezily. 'Any smart lawyer would have managed that.'

Mandy gritted his teeth. 'He paid off my car. I was lucky to get that.'

'I guess you have to be really careful.' Reese toyed with her glass. 'You must have thought you'd be set for life, marrying Cory, and now he's ruined your financial security.'

'I was too young to be anything but in love. Too dumb to fight the prenup his parents insisted on in case he inherited family money during our marriage. Case in point, me dropping out of college instead of figuring out how to make everything work.'

Reese tsked. 'You're right. You should have at least made sure your in-laws adored you. If you'd put in the time with them, you'd be eating off gold plates no matter what.'

Mandy stared into her wine as if it could be used as a divination tool. 'I thought they were on my side until the divorce. Then I learned his parents are just like him. Somehow Cory thinks it's all good as long as he is nice in person and responds to Vellum's calls. I mean, he literally hung out with us over the weekend, fixed stuff, bought takeout. Yet he doesn't give me the checks.'

Reese smiled at the server as she set a dinner salad in front of each of them. Reese's first course, Mandy's entire meal. 'I think you have to ask yourself why he's being so attentive all of a sudden.'

Ravenous, Mandy picked up her fork. Focused on her salad, she blithely walked right into Reese's trap. 'What are you implying?'

Reese tapped the table until Mandy looked up. She shot her

bolt right into Mandy's heart without even blinking. 'That he killed Ryan, of course. To punish you for divorcing him.'

Mandy's fingers went numb. The fork clattered to her plate. House dressing splattered. She squeezed her eyes shut tightly against a splash of lemon juice. Blinking rapidly, she stood and moved toward the back of the dining room, hoping to find a washroom to rinse out her eyes.

'I'll watch your purse,' Reese called helpfully as she darted away.

Ugh. And here she'd thought Reese was actually trying to be nice for once, rather than implying she'd married and given birth to the child of a murderer.

Had she?

TEN

Neither she nor Reese ended up paying for their dinners. While she was in the bathroom diluting the lemon juice in her eye, and frantically considering what Reese had said, Reese flirted with those two men in the dining room and they picked up dinner. Mandy said no to the offer of a date from the man who showed interest in her, but Reese gave the other one, a local architect, her number.

'I can't believe you let them pay,' Mandy groused in the parking lot. She was still trying to process Reese's words. Ryan and Cory had never, ever been close. Ryan had actually sent her a congratulations card through the mail when she'd filed for divorce. She remembered him standing guard over the house as Cory packed up his things, insisting he'd keep her husband from taking her few family heirlooms. There had been harsh words over crystal bar glasses that had belonged to their Meadows grandmother. But that had been almost a year ago.

'Why didn't you want to date that man?' Reese asked, unlocking her car door.

Mandy forced herself back into the moment. 'Seriously? He left his wife just before Christmas. They haven't even filed for a formal separation yet.'

'The perfect time to catch a man. He's lonely.'

'He didn't need to tell me all those personal details.'

'He was looking for a date. What is wrong with you, anyway? I'm sure you could get a date with Doctor O'Halloran if you played your cards right.' She stuck her finger in front of Mandy's nose. 'Don't give me that "just divorced" line. You chose poorly for your first husband, but even I might have not realized what a bad bargain Cory Moffat was. He hid it well. You can do better the next time. If you stay out of prison.'

'Thanks for taking me to dinner,' Mandy said, since she couldn't possibly respond to the rest of Reese's speech.

Reese nodded graciously and tucked her coat around her legs.

'You're welcome. If you really want just a girl's night, I'll take you to a little Indian place my father likes. No one will bother us there and you can eat heartily. I offered to buy you dinner, after all.'

'Sure. If I stay out of prison,' Mandy echoed.

When Mandy's phone rang, seconds after she'd arrived home from dinner, her first thought was that Reese had somehow slipped Recently Separated Guy her phone number. But she recognized the number. It belonged to Detective Ahola. What did he want at eight p.m. on a Tuesday?

The mere thought of what it might be made her hands shake as she dropped her mail and picked up her phone. 'Detective?'

'Hello, Ms Meadows.'

'Have you had some kind of breakthrough on my cousin's death?' she asked, thoughts of what Reese had implied about Cory running through her head. How bad of a judge of men was she?

'No, this is a personal call,' he said cheerfully. 'Got a minute?'

She perched on a kitchen stool, thinking she'd stop trembling if she sat. God help her if the homicide detective was about to ask her on a date as well. 'Sure. What is it? Need my muffin recipe? My coffee blend?'

He chuckled. 'I was thinking about your house.'

'What about it?'

'You were fretting about the basement apartment, about needing a new tenant.'

'Yes, after I clear it out. Ryan's estate isn't paying rent. His sister claims he didn't have any money.'

'I wonder if you'd let me rent it once you're officially cleared as a suspect.'

Mandy's first response was a hot wave of thrill. He thought she'd be cleared. What a relief. Her second thought was that she wasn't sure she wanted a strange man in her house. But having a police detective as a tenant was surely better than most possible choices. 'Gosh. I'm not going to say no. That must mean you're optimistic about figuring out what happened.' Even though it had been almost a week already.

'We're working on it.'

She wanted the police to work faster. 'I found out something new.'

His voice sharpened. 'What?'

'I learned the hospital has a drug-dealing employee.'

'It's not that unusual. Why do you think Ryan was involved? Do you think he was the dealer?'

'No. It's not like he seems to have had extra income. But maybe, the fact he didn't was a sign he was using.' She sighed. 'He wasn't the man I thought he was. Not that I had him on a pedestal. How could I? But I had no idea he was so promiscuous or that he did drugs. He slept with my co-worker and my neighbor.'

'The dead can't protect their secrets,' the detective said.

'That's for sure. I don't think he'd like that I've learned he lied to me about a lot of stuff.'

'Maybe he was lying to himself, too,' he said. 'Give me the details of these conversations you've had and I'll follow up. And please don't do any investigating on your own. I understand that you can't avoid gossip from neighbors and co-workers, but that needs to be the extent of your involvement.'

'No problem.' Though privately, she thought he'd done nothing but incentivize her to figure the situation out for herself. Not only might the killer be someone who was still close to her, but losing her suspect status would land her a new tenant.

'I'll talk to you soon. Don't go promising away that basement apartment of yours before you talk to me.'

'OK, but . . .' She hesitated, remembering a running gag about cops always finding the best apartments from the television show *Hawaii Five-0*. 'I can't give you a discount, even if a murder did take place there. I really do need the rent money.'

She heard him exhale. 'I wouldn't ask for one. Nor would I behave in anything but the most ethical manner. I believe in our ethics.'

'Amen,' Mandy said. 'That's what makes you one of the good guys, Detective. Thank you for the call.'

She hung up and stared blankly at the cork board attached to the wall backing the short counter. Did she really still have Christmas cards up? Where had her head been this past month?

She started unpinning them, counting a total of seven, then neatly stuck the push pins into the top corner in a diamond shape. Now that the board was empty, she could use it for planning ideas or art or something. She took a quick look through the cards, hoping she had sent a card back to each of them. Reese's smiling face twinkled at her from the bottom card, underneath a corporate one from USea. Cradled in Reese's angora-sweater-covered arms was a white fluffy cat looking cross-eyed in an elf hat, complete with pointy ears.

The cat flashed significantly in her memory. A white fluffy cat? She remembered the cat hairs on Ryan's chair.

In the hallway, she unbolted the basement door and went down, careful to take her phone with her in case of emergency. She went into the already musty-smelling, unused sitting room, and compared the cat hairs clinging to the corduroy to the cat in Reese's Christmas photo. They certainly could belong to Reese's cat. Had she given Ryan the chair, or had he picked it up from the side of the road? Mandy knew he'd selected abandoned furniture for his use. Or had Reese sat in this very chair, not too long before Ryan died?

Mandy rubbed her eyes. She was seeing potential killers everywhere, in a life that had been calm and normal just a week before. All those years of ignoring helpful aunties and cousins who had warned her that Ryan was bad news and to stay away from him, and he'd been the one who'd been victimized in the ultimate way. Who should people have been warning her about? Her own husband? One of her neighbors? Her co-worker? Or someone Ryan himself had brought into his life?

A dark shape fluttered in the corner of her eye. She turned quickly, her heart pounding in her chest. Had Vellum's ghost come back, or an intruder? Her gaze darted around the room, looking for a weapon, but every box had been filled and taped down. She'd been such a good cousin and landlord, clearing the space.

Uneasy, she crept forward. The fluttering happened again. Her body shook as if buffeted by a strong wind, existential terror filling her veins. But then she saw it. A hot-pink sticky note, hanging off the side of an old wooden bookshelf. The air vent had been catching it.

'Take a breath,' Mandy muttered to herself. 'In through your nose, out through your mouth. Calm down.' She reached up and pulled off the note, careful to touch only one little corner. Once she had it firmly in her grasp, she took it into the laundry room, where the light was better.

On the sticky note was a printed logo that said 'Planning With

Reese'. Then, handwritten, was a series of tally marks, like someone had been counting denominations of bills at a bank or something like that. It could have been anything.

She affixed it to the top of the dryer. Probably just garbage; she was unqualified to determine its importance, though it was another clue that Reese had been down here. At least she'd solved one ghostly apparition. She circled the laundry room, looking for similar fluttering items as her pulse slowed.

'Nothing.' Satisfied, she moved laundry from the washer to the dryer, then checked the back door to make sure the new bolt was securely fastened before she went back upstairs.

She wolfed down a muffin while she dressed again for the outdoors, then hunched against the nighttime cold and went out to bring Vellum home. Even though her daughter was fifteen, she didn't like the idea of her walking outside after dark. After the week they'd had she allowed herself a little mom indulgence.

She walked past her car, debated driving the half block, then told herself she needed the exercise.

Linda's security lights flared to life as she walked by her friend's house. Linda opened her kitchen window and leaned out. 'What are you doing outside?'

'Just walking over to my mom's.'

'Come in for a second so I don't have to yell.'

Mandy zipped through Linda's yard to the back door. Her friend let her into her inviting kitchen. The scent of chocolate laced with peppermint filled the air. The corner of one of Linda's ladybug curtains had caught in the window when she'd shut it.

Mandy pointed to it.

'Oops.' Linda pulled out the fabric and latched the window. 'I saw some traffic at your house today, but the nosy neighbor has to do a better job of keeping her own house locked up.'

'It's best to be careful until we know what happened,' Mandy agreed. 'I almost had a heart attack in the basement until I discovered a piece of paper fluttering by the heat register.'

'What did you think it was?' Linda absently licked at a knife she'd been using to frost brownies.

'Vellum's ghost.' Mandy's laughter sounded forced in her ears. 'Can you imagine? I've never believed in ghosts.'

'You've never been around violent death before,' Linda pointed out. 'Brownie? I added some peppermint extract to the frosting to change it up.'

'I could smell it from the back door,' Mandy said. 'But I need to get over to my mom's. Vellum needs to come home. It's a school night.'

'You've heard of a telephone?' Linda said innocently, cutting a big slice of her treat and dropping it into a square glass container.

'Would you send your daughter out into the night alone right now?'

Linda shook her head. 'I wouldn't even send out a pet without a guardian.' She snapped a lid on the container. 'So listen. I saw Vellum come home from school.'

'She went into our house? I thought she'd go straight to my mother's.'

'She was only there for a few minutes before I saw Dylan and Alexis pull up. She might have just been changing clothes or something.'

'I'm surprised she's willing to be home alone right now,' Mandy admitted. 'Mom always makes her comfortable.'

Linda brushed a few crumbs into the sink. 'Anyway, they parked on Roosevelt and went to the front door. I can't see that, of course, but they went back to their car only a minute later. Vellum refused to let them inside.'

'Good for her, but she probably shouldn't have opened the door.' Mandy took the container from Linda. 'Thanks. I'll share the brownies with Mom.'

'I did overhear Dylan and Alexis talking about their romantic relationship with Ryan,' Linda said.

'At my front door?' Mandy hadn't realized voices could carry that far across the side street.

'No. I was outside by then. I thought Vellum might need help. They were by their car.'

'Thanks,' Mandy said. 'I appreciate you looking out for her.'

Linda nodded. 'But you get my point, right?'

'I guess not,' Mandy admitted. 'It's been a long day.'

'Romantic relationship.' Linda emphasized the first word. 'They called Ryan their boyfriend.'

'Oh.' Mandy grabbed a fork out of Linda's drainer and scooped excess frosting out of the bowl, then stuffed it into her mouth.

Cream cheese and peppermint exploded on her tongue, instantly soothing her. She hadn't realized how complicated her cousin's lifestyle was. He'd been in a ménage. And now his ex-partners were harassing her daughter.

'Feel better?' Linda asked, after Mandy swallowed the bite of frosting.

'Pitiful, huh?' Mandy said. 'But I needed that.'

'Better than wine,' Linda said, then patted her hips. 'Even if it's worse on the waistline. I don't think Vellum should be home alone right now.'

'I agree,' Mandy said. 'I'm on it. I need to coordinate with her better until the killer is uncovered.'

Linda cut into her brownies and deftly scooped out a square, then deposited it on a plate. 'It must be hard for you, not knowing who you can trust.'

Mandy put her free arm around Linda's shoulders and squeezed. 'There are plenty of better suspects than you, my dear. After all, you never slept with Ryan. Right?'

Linda chuckled. 'No. I have George to keep me warm. And these fat old bones couldn't have made it across the street, into your basement, so I could murder someone, then back to my house and into my car in just five minutes.'

'Don't sell yourself short,' Mandy said. 'But it is unfortunate that your very welcome alibi also gives one to Dylan and Alexis.'

She went outside, holding her brownie container, then crossed Roosevelt to her mother's house. Traffic was sluggish. Roosevelt was an active street, almost all residential right here, with occasional businesses, parks and schools giving into a commercial core as it closed in on the University District around the University of Washington. Locals used the street to move between there and Northgate Mall to the east. But at this time of night, everyone was settled into their homes. Even Dylan and Alexis had given up for now.

She rang her mother's doorbell and waited. It took an unusually long time for her mother to answer. By the time she did, Mandy's toes were aching with cold.

'Everything OK?' she asked.

Her mother shook her head. 'Vellum isn't doing well.'

Mandy followed her inside, too chilly to take off her gloves or hat in the vestibule. 'Is she upset about Dylan and Alexis showing up again?'

'I'm sure that's part of it. She had a full-blown panic attack after she arrived, complete with hyperventilation. I had to have her breathe into a paper bag. I was afraid she was going to pass out.' Though her mother didn't have a hair out of place, her sweater buttons were askew and she had circles under her eyes.

Mandy's eyes pricked with hot moisture. 'My poor baby. Where is she?'

'In the den, watching one of the *Parent Trap* movies.'

'I hope she doesn't think her father and I will ever get back together.' Mandy handed her mother Linda's offering. 'Do you want to dish that up? The frosting is really good. Maybe chocolate will help.'

Her mother unsnapped the lid and looked blankly at the brownies. 'Good news would help more.'

Mandy pulled off her gloves. She tightened her icy fingers around them. 'All I've got is a story of the ghost that wasn't. That's about the only good news.'

'Are you sure you can't point the camera over the till when the new one comes in?' Mandy asked Scott during her break the next morning.

'The angle is wrong,' he told her, slouching back in his office chair.

'I only got a C in geometry,' Mandy said. 'Could you attach a camera from another angle?'

'There aren't many places where we can attach it. You can't seriously think Fannah is taking the money from the till?'

Mandy shrugged. 'Someone is.'

He leaned forward and cracked his neck from side to side. 'Even so, no one has time to go through hours of footage in order to figure it out. Especially when you don't even know what you are looking for.'

'It might be obvious,' she argued.

Scott drummed his fingers on his desk. 'I'll see what I can do, but you need to relax. Want to get a drink tonight after work? Maybe several?' He grinned.

Was he asking her out? 'I can't be out again tonight. I had dinner out last night and had to leave Vellum with my mom.'

'That's protective. She's old enough to be alone.'

Mandy didn't like his snide tone. 'Really? My cousin was murdered in my house a week ago. Anyway, my break is over in thirty seconds. Gotta run.'

'Some other time,' Scott called behind her as she walked out.

Or not. She stepped out from the employee corridor and into the main floor of the hospital. From a distance, she saw Dr O'Halloran moving toward the coffee bar, matching her step for step. He was with a female colleague, a prominent colon and rectal surgeon in her early sixties.

If Mandy was being honest with herself, she might have accepted a date with this guy, if he'd asked instead of Scott, but obviously that wasn't going to happen today. She darted through the door and made it to the cash register just before the surgeons arrived.

'What can I get you today, Doctor O'Halloran and Doctor Garcia?'

They cut off a conversation about fissures just before Mandy would have heard a great deal more than she would have wanted.

'Sixteen-ounce coffee,' Dr Garcia said, rearranging her surgical cap on her short, graying curls.

Mandy nodded. 'And for you?'

'Quad shot. Make it quick today, Mandy, we've got a schedule to keep.'

Mandy tapped the card reader so Dr Garcia could make her payment, then quickly put in Dr O'Hottie's order. The surgeon's intense mood made her wonder if he was doing some kind of complex procedure for the first time. She handed Dr Garcia a large cup, then started pulling shots for the espresso drink.

As Dr Garcia poured three French vanilla creamers into her coffee, she passed Dr O'Hottie's cup to him. The other surgeon turned back to him and said something about fissures again, and they strolled off together. Mandy's gaze followed them as she instinctively compared Dr O'Hottie's shape to Detective Ahola's.

Then she saw it. *Oh, no.* Dangling from Dr O'Hottie's hand was a biscotti, sealed into the plastic packaging of the brand they carried. He must have grabbed it from their counter. 'Doctor?' she called, but they didn't turn. 'Doctor?' No answer.

She darted around the counter and ran past the elevators, catching up with the surgeons in front of the volunteer station. 'Doctor O'Halloran?'

He turned around. Dr Garcia stopped and stared at Mandy, puzzlement on her face.

Mandy, out of breath, pointed to the biscotti package. 'I'm very sorry, but I didn't ring that up.'

The attractive surgeon stared at her. 'Excuse me?'

'The biscotti? It's from the coffee bar. I must have missed you telling me to ring it up. It's a dollar ninety-five. Ummm . . . two dollars thirteen cents with tax.'

'I need to get to surgery, Mandy,' the surgeon said, staring past her ear.

She worried her lip. 'I'll pay for it for now. Can you bring me the money when you're out of surgery?'

Dr Garcia reached into her scrubs and pulled out a five-dollar bill. 'Keep the change for the charity fund.'

'Oh, thank you,' Mandy said. Her cheeks were on fire. She turned away, careful not to look at Dr O'Hottie again, but her gaze caught on the volunteer desk and she realized that four of the senior citizen volunteers were perched there, staring at the scene with avid amusement. She wanted to crawl into the farthest corner of Scott's sepulcher of an office and hide.

She'd broken an unspoken rule of the hospital: never second-guess a doctor. Whether she could afford it or not, she should have paid for it, or at least told Fannah. This would have been a great time for a working camera. Not that it would have helped, to prove she was right. No one cared about two bucks in comparison to insulting a surgeon, possibly in front of his own patients.

The hospital administration would not want anyone losing confidence. Mandy chomped down on her lip until it hurt. She knew she'd have to confess all to Fannah.

But Fannah had taken away her opportunity to get ahead of the problem. She met Mandy's gaze from behind the pick-up block. 'What are you doing in the middle of the entrance hall?'

Mandy held up the five-dollar bill. 'Retrieving payment for a biscotti. I'm sorry, I didn't think.'

'From who?' Fannah demanded.

Mandy pulled her shoulders back and forced herself to meet Fannah's gaze. 'I'm sorry. A surgeon. I'm very on edge and I just reacted from instinct.'

'You aren't to exit from behind the counter during your shift,'

Fannah said, snatching the money from her hand. 'Do you hear me? I'm going to write this up as a formal warning.'

Mandy squeezed her eyes shut for a second. If an employee received three formal warnings, they were terminated. She'd threatened her job over a freaking cookie. 'Please, Fannah, don't do that. I'll remember.'

Fannah glared at Mandy as she set two lemonade iced teas on the pick-up block. 'You can't embarrass a surgeon. His department head would be fully in his rights to come to me. I have to document what happened.'

Mandy sighed. 'I know.' Why hadn't she paid for it herself? She could have spoken to Dr O'Hottie the next time he stopped by.

Fannah marched away. Her customers didn't meet Mandy's eyes as they reached for their drinks.

She forced herself to go back to her post behind the counter, just in time for two of the help-desk volunteers to show up, excitement obvious, to order small coffees and gossip about what she'd done.

Feeling sick, she took their orders robotically, and didn't respond to their questions about the biscotti. One of them picked up a wrapped cookie, managing to break it in half in the process, then slammed it roughly back into the plastic holder. Mandy didn't say anything, just took their crumpled dollar bills and handed them their cups. She bored the volunteers into leaving her alone, while in the back, Fannah wrote up a formal warning for her embarrassing a thief of a surgeon. Ugh. What had she done?

ELEVEN

Mandy woke at four a.m. the next morning. Her toes felt like little icicles. She hopped on the cold floorboards to the thermometer. Somehow, she'd turned the heat off, or not turned it on. Shaking with cold, she pulled on a robe and thick socks and went into the kitchen. She wouldn't be able to sleep again, but if she rattled around, she'd wake up Vellum.

After making a cup of coffee as quietly as she could, she went into her art studio. The feeling of desperation she'd had yesterday as she ran after Dr O'Hottie returned. She needed to take control of her financial life without letting the strain show at the hospital.

'You need to find a job where you aren't in danger of having to cover errors and theft with your own money,' she said aloud. Sitting down at her computer, she hunted around in her files until she found the footage for a journaling tools video. She'd done the shoot and edited it the last time Vellum had spent a full Saturday with her father, and had meant to record some footage with Vellum discussing her own tools.

Instead, she'd put up her own video now and do a part two with Vellum later. That would hopefully bring her some social media income. It might even sell some stickers.

Mandy opened her software and fine-tuned the video, cutting any sections that seemed awkward, and speeding up the action, ensuring the viewers wouldn't get bored. Watching herself demonstrating how she used various pens, papers, templates, paint and more, she took notes.

Finally, she set up the video in front of her and recorded a voiceover. At six, she ran into the bathroom and slapped on her makeup, then recorded an intro and an outro. After that, she started the process of loading the video to the social media site while she got Vellum up for school and finished readying herself for work.

While Vellum ate breakfast and she nibbled on toast, she took a picture of the loading screen and posted it to the social media photo site, so her fans would know a new video was coming.

When she returned from work, she'd update her website and do a better job with notifying social media, but for now, she'd done what she could. Her hundred thousand subscribers on the video channel would receive notice when the video had loaded. Hopefully they would watch and she'd add another couple of hundred dollars a month income-producing video to her portfolio.

'Are you OK, Mom?' Vellum peered into the art studio.

'Why?'

'I heard you moan.' Vellum frowned at her.

Mandy leaned back in her chair and heard her back pop. 'I've been up since four. I didn't realize how sore I was.'

'You're working too hard.'

'I need to.'

'You need to advertise for a new tenant. Can't you make Jasmine take Ryan's stuff?'

Mandy picked up the phone. 'I'll send her another harassing text.'

'Would it be easier for us to load everything up and deliver it to her?'

Mandy laughed darkly. 'We'd have to rent a truck to do that. I don't want to spend the money.'

Vellum nodded. 'I hear you. I've got to run to the bus stop.'

Mandy stood creakily and gave Vellum a kiss on the forehead. 'Be alert to your surroundings. Want me to walk with you?'

'No, I'll be safe.' Vellum blew her a kiss and walked away.

Mandy knew she'd regret getting up so early in a few hours, but at least she worked somewhere with tasty caffeine readily available.

Mandy saw Reese heading toward her just before the end-of-shift rush. As usual, she looked more stylish than other nurses, despite wearing scrubs. Did she have them tailored? Her dark hair hung around her shoulders in perfect waves, and she wore more makeup than Mandy had put on for her video shoot, though Mandy had to admit that Reese's eyelashes might actually be that lush without the use of false lashes.

'I saw your new video,' Reese cooed.

'Oh, good. I haven't had a break yet so I didn't know if it finished loading.' She'd been afraid to ask for one after yesterday. Fannah would probably tell her to use the time to read and sign her formal warning anyway, but she'd barely seen her supervisor.

Reese shook her head. 'Tsk, tsk, dear. You shouldn't broadcast that you use such cheap pens.'

'Why not?' Mandy put her hand on her hip. 'I'm happy to pass along a tip that you don't have to pay for expensive pens to have a vibrant journal.'

Reese shook her head slightly. 'That brand doesn't give vloggers freebies, Mandy. And without freebies, you have to pay for your own giveaways. Don't you want sponsorships? They can make all the difference.'

'I haven't thought about it. I'd rather be known as an honest content producer.'

'Also, it's a fact that those pens don't last as long as one of the more expensive brands,' Reese continued.

'But the ink is gorgeous. I've never seen a prettier purple, or a yellow that is so visible on the page,' Mandy argued.

Reese sighed. 'I don't care what you use, dear, but I suggest you promote the other brands. You didn't even add a giveaway. That's going to hurt your chance of going viral.'

Mandy nodded. 'You're right about that. I made the decision to finish the video in a panic this morning. It isn't in the form I meant it to have.'

Reese fluttered her eyelashes. 'I could tell.'

Now Mandy felt anxious. 'Do I have a bunch of thumbs down on it?' Should she take the video down?

Reese glanced up at the security camera. 'Only two when I looked.'

Mandy waited. 'Any other stats?'

'A couple of hundred thumbs up. Something under five thousand views.'

Mandy's eyebrows went up. 'Already? But that's fantastic.'

'All those girls who don't have a sweetheart to prep for on Valentine's Day,' Reese said carelessly. 'Who else would have the time to watch?'

'I get a lot of school-aged viewers,' Mandy explained. 'Because of Vellum. And school is out for half the country by now.'

'Then why wasn't Vellum in the video?' Reese asked.

'Because I put it up in a panic to earn money?'

Reese feigned sympathy. 'About to be fired after yesterday's drama?'

'Heard about that, did you?' Mandy asked, knowing perfectly well the gossip was all over the complex. In fact, she estimated that coffee bar sales were up twenty percent just so people could check out the nobody who'd dared to insult a surgeon. No sign of Dr O'Hottie today, either. At least he hadn't come to gloat. On the other hand, she hadn't been able to apologize.

'Everybody has.' Reese smiled brightly at her. 'You have to follow the pecking order around here, dear.'

Mandy took a deep breath. She had to change the subject or she was going to strangle Reese and really land herself in trouble. 'Did you want to buy something? I hear our biscotti is delicious.'

Reese smirked. 'Such a comedian. I don't think my delicate system can tolerate any of your lard bombs, much less caffeine. Do you have any herbal tea?'

Mandy pointed down the counter. 'Hot water and tea bags are down there. I just charge you and hand you a paper cup.'

Reese's lips turned down. 'You could offer teapots. Much more elegant.'

'Where do you think you are?' Mandy asked.

Fannah walked up behind her. 'Did you ever get your lunch break?'

'No.'

Fannah tsked. 'It's after two. What were you thinking?'

I was thinking that this was how you were punishing me for yesterday.

Fannah shooed her. 'Go, go. Be back in half an hour.'

'Should I ring up a tea?' Mandy asked Reese.

'No, just walk with me.'

'Hang on a sec.' Mandy went into the back room and clocked out. Unsurprisingly, she found a sealed envelope with her name on it in her cubby hole. This must be the formal warning. She stuck it in her purse and went back to Reese. 'I did want to ask you a couple of things.'

'What?'

Mandy took Reese's arm and pulled her toward the elevator up to the sky bridge that led to the parking garage. When she was out of earshot of anyone, she asked, 'Do you know anything about a drug dealer at the hospital?'

Reese shook her head and pointed to a couple of chairs perched along a wall. 'Since I work in the office building, I probably wouldn't know what goes on over here. I almost never use the cafeteria.'

'Or the coffee bar,' Mandy said. 'Well, I think there is one.'

'Why do you care?' Reese smoothed a long curl, then wrapped it around her index finger.

'Might have something to do with Ryan's death.'

'I ran into your mother the other day and she was convinced his boyfriend or his girlfriend had done it.'

'They have Linda Bhatt as an alibi. She saw them leave ten minutes before she heard the sirens.'

'Is it solid?'

'Not from that alone.' Mandy thought. 'Linda left five minutes after they did. Which gives them five minutes to have doubled back and killed Ryan. Maybe that's why the police don't seriously suspect me.'

'I don't understand why you aren't trying harder to solve the crime yourself. After all, it's costing you a lot of money to live without a tenant.'

'I'm well aware of that. Besides, I want justice for Ryan.' Mandy pulled the envelope from her bag. 'I think this is my formal warning writeup from yesterday. Think I'm about to lose my job and my health insurance?'

Reese plucked the envelope from Mandy's fingers and sliced it open with a sharp acrylic fingernail. She bent her head over the two sheets of paper. 'It's your lucky day.'

Mandy's heart fluttered. 'It's not a formal warning?'

Reese shook her head. 'Doctor O'Hottie wrote an apology note for accidentally taking the cookie. The second sheet is a note for your file, but it's just documentation, not a warning.'

Mandy's eyes widened. 'I wonder if having Doctor Garcia there saved my bacon. She's such a lady.'

'Yeah. I wouldn't put it past the average surgeon to have a tantrum, but she's a legend. All class.'

Their eyes met. Reese folded the papers back into the envelope and handed them to her. 'What?'

Mandy stuffed them into her purse. 'Strange. I don't want to ruin our friendship, but I have to ask you something.'

'What?'

'Were you in my basement recently? I found a sticky note with your logo on it.'

Reese frowned. 'Seriously?'

'So that's a no?' Mandy asked.

'Of course. I gave out those sticky notes all over the hospital and our neighborhood to advertise my business.' She spread her hands wide.

'OK then. You're sure you never hung out with Ryan?'

Reese snorted. 'I only date successful Hindu men. Mostly men that my mother's matchmaker sets me up with. I'd never have spent time with your cousin.'

Mandy nodded. 'Sorry I had to ask.'

'Why did you?'

'It's not just the sticky note. I found cat hair on Ryan's recliner and I know you have a cat with long white hair.'

'That's not unusual.'

'No, but it's not like a stranger killed him. It has to be someone I know.'

'Even so, you're grasping at straws. The cat hair probably wasn't left by the killer.'

Mandy rubbed her hands together and put her palms over her eyes. They still felt gritty from her early morning hours in front of the computer this morning.

Reese patted her shoulder. 'Don't fall apart on me now, Mandili. You can't seriously suspect me.'

Mandy lifted her head from her hands. 'Why not?'

'I'm like a younger, savvier version of you, and you're no killer.' Reese wiggled her shoulders. 'You even had a rich husband for a while there.'

'Don't be jealous over him,' Mandy advised. 'You're only twenty-five, right? Be pickier than I was.'

'It's hard.' Reese sighed. 'I feel like, with Indian men, they either want to move too fast or too slow. When a matchmaker is involved, they are ready to propose in a month, which is too fast for me, or they drag their heels.'

'I appreciate that you want to marry within your own culture,

but maybe you can meet someone in a social group instead?'
Mandy suggested.

'Who has the time?' Reese asked. 'But I do wish there was a
better way to meet medical professionals who share my heritage.'

'Lots of Indian doctors in these parts,' Mandy agreed. They
gossiped for a few minutes about a handsome oncologist who was
new in the office building, then Mandy excused herself to grab
some food before her lunch was over. She had to believe Reese
hadn't been friendly with Ryan. That didn't seem to match Reese's
worldview at all. Besides, it sounded like anyone might have had
one of those sticky notes, though Reese had clearly been careful
not to give her any.

Back at the coffee bar, Mandy had an hour to go on her shift.
Fannah had left for the day. She and Kit huddled behind the
espresso machine and whispered about what had happened with
Dr O'Hottie.

'I don't think you're going to ever get a date with him after
that, though,' Kit said.

'That's OK.' Mandy giggled. 'I'll just take one of Reese's rejects
when she finally selects a husband.'

'Who is she?'

Mandy described her. Out of the corner of her eye, she saw a
couple of their regular end-of-day people approaching. One of
them stumbled and put a hand to her hip.

'I'm aching today,' she said, rubbing the bony side of her torso.

'Me too,' the other nurse complained. 'I can't wait for spring.'

'Coffee, stat,' the first nurse barked at Mandy.

Kit raised her eyebrows and turned toward the espresso machine.

'What size?' Mandy asked pleasantly. No one was going to
bring down her unexpectedly good mood.

'Extra-large,' she snapped, rubbing her hip again.

The other nurse called over the first's shoulder. 'Dry cappuccino,
twenty ounces.'

Where had the courtesy gone? Sometimes folks were abrupt,
but when customers saw them every day, they usually added a
please or a thank you. Mandy quickly rang up the first nurse and
handed her a cup.

'Lid,' she snapped.

'Next to the coffee urns,' Mandy said politely. How could the nurse have forgotten that? She rang up the other nurse and Kit crafted her drink with double speed.

They exchanged glances after the pair had meandered off with their drinks, complaining about their joints.

'I hope we aren't about to see a new wave of flu,' Kit said out of the side of her mouth as the next wave of off-shift nurses approached. 'Remember last time? It was a ghost town in here and Fannah started talking about cutting our hours.'

'Yeah,' Mandy sighed, feeling her forehead. It was cool, no sign of fever. 'I sure hope not.'

Kit laughed at her. 'Hypochondriac.'

When Mandy arrived home, she found a long-bed pickup truck parked alongside her yard. She sighed and backed out of her driveway, then drove around the block to park in front of her house. She didn't want to park across from Linda's house and get her car hit again.

When she reached her back steps, she saw her cousin Jasmine coming out of the basement door, carrying a single box. Her elbow-length blond hair fluttered in the wind when she reached the yard. A wig or freshly dyed? Mandy couldn't be sure. Behind her, a couple of beefy guys who looked like they could have played for the Huskies a decade ago wrestled out Ryan's armchair.

Jasmine, a decade older than these dudes, but who had spent her time in cosmetology well and was made up like an ageless Barbie version of a Kardashian, dropped her box into Mandy's arms.

Mandy staggered back, regaining her balance. This must be the box of magazines. 'Why?'

'You're home. You can help.'

'I boxed everything up,' Mandy said. 'I did plenty.'

'The memorial service is on Saturday at the same funeral home your dad's was,' Jasmine called over her shoulder as she went back to the basement. 'Ryan's body has been released.'

Mandy shook her head as she walked to the pickup. Ryan was being buried on Valentine's Day. That seemed appropriate somehow.

She handed the box to the guy who was standing in the pickup bed and went to demand Ryan's set of keys back from Jasmine, then escaped into her house before Jasmine could ask her for any more favors. Vellum walked in through the front door a few minutes later, complaining about her homework. Mandy set her up with a muffin and a glass of milk in her bedroom so she could focus on work.

Fifteen minutes after that, Mandy ventured down the basement stairs. She had left large sticky notes on the items that were hers and these had been respected. Her grandmother's sideboard was still in the hall. The bedroom and the sitting room had been stripped, though. She opened the closet. The hanging bag containing her old wedding dress still hung on the rail, and the Christmas ornament boxes were on the shelf.

Dust bunnies dotted the carpet in both rooms. She went into the laundry room and grabbed her vacuum, to clean what she could. A couple of dark stains colored the carpet around where the easy chair had been. Beer maybe. She'd need to get a steam cleaner in here.

Vellum crept down and looked around. She said 'hello', then frowned. 'It's so empty there's an echo in here.'

Mandy put her arm around her daughter. 'I know. Let's take a quick look at the walls and make sure we don't need to paint, then lock it all up.'

Vellum sighed. 'It sucks that Ryan died.'

Mandy changed the subject before her emotions took over. 'Do you have big plans for Valentine's Day?'

Vellum stuck out her tongue. 'As if.' She brightened. 'I filmed a video for us, though.'

'You did?'

'Yeah, I was bored at Grandma's so I filmed myself doing a sheet of fifty heart doodles. Do you think you could edit it tonight and put it up? I thought we could use the money.'

Mandy smiled at her daughter. 'Absolutely. What a great idea.'

Vellum patted her arm. 'I saw the tools video. You really should have waited for me, at least to do your makeup.'

'Yeah. Reese already made fun of me.' Mandy kicked one dust bunny into another, forming a larger gray lump.

'It's getting lots of views and likes though.' Vellum nodded wisely. 'I'll do a teen version, maybe on Sunday.'

'OK. Upload your video from your phone to my computer?'

'It's already on the Cloud.'

'Let's take a quick look at the walls then, so I can get to work on the video. The faster we load it the better.'

Vellum went to the short wall next to the closet. 'Yep. I talked while I did the doodles. An intro and outro should be enough.'

'Great!'

Vellum rang her fingers along the wall then moved onto the next one. 'We need to get the cobwebs off the ceiling, and this shelf is really dusty.'

'The paint is marked over here, where his sofa rubbed against the wall,' Mandy said. 'We've got a few hours of work to do in this room.'

'Of course we do,' Vellum said. 'Let's just lock it up for the night and update our "to do" lists.'

Upstairs, Vellum redid Mandy's makeup and helped her set up to film an intro and outro for the new mini-video. Mandy threw on a relatively new red mock turtleneck and put a heart necklace over it that Cory had bought her one year. She spoke cheerily and wished their viewers a Happy Valentine's Day, then watched through Vellum's video. She made a couple of cuts, but Vellum had done a good job of showing her minimal supplies and remembering to announce each doodle as she did it.

Mandy added one shot of the entire page at the end, moving the camera over it in loving fashion to highlight the doodles one last time, then spliced in all four of the video segments and set it to upload.

While her computer was digesting the video, she went into the kitchen, realizing they had skipped dinner. Vellum had gone to her bedroom to finish up an English Lit report.

She scrambled some eggs with cheddar and chopped tomato and delivered a plate to her daughter's room, then sat on a stool in her kitchen to eat and read the mail. Dreaming of a bubble bath and an early night, she was not happy when the doorbell rang.

TWELVE

Mandy set down her fork, then picked it up again to gobble her eggs. Why should she let them get cold? But she found she had lost her appetite. At this point, she couldn't think of a single person she wanted to see at her front door. Anyone she loved or liked would have come to the back, or at least texted her first.

She hoped Dylan and Alexis hadn't appeared again. With that unpleasant thought, she slid off her stool and went to the front door, still holding her fork.

When she checked through the door, she saw a single figure. Large, male, imposing. Relief that it wasn't Ryan's friends warred with concern for her and her daughter's safety. No, not opening her door without more information. She flicked on the outdoor light so she could see.

When she peered through the peephole again, Detective Ahola was staring right at her. She reared back, dropping her fork.

'Everything OK in there?' he called through the door.

She kicked the fork out of the way. 'Sorry.'

When she opened the door, he furrowed his brow. 'What's going on?'

'I was eating. Dropped my fork.' She unlocked her screen door.

He stepped into her living room, looking like a modern Viking with that strong chin, prominent cheekbones and fashionable beard. He wore a long-sleeved white T-shirt under a navy quilted vest, form-fitting jeans and hiking boots. He looked ready to scale her mountain.

Her face flushed. Any mountain, that was, of which there were plenty to choose from around here.

He frowned. 'You OK?'

She put her hands to her cheeks. 'Hot flash?'

'Aren't you a little too young for that?'

'A lot too young,' she said emphatically.

He grinned at her, making those model-worthy cheekbones pop. 'Maybe you're catching the flu.'

'I hope not. Some people at work were complaining of body aches. That's never good news.'

He held up his hands. 'Don't touch me.'

'You're armed,' she pointed out. 'I'd be crazy to come within three feet of you.'

His eyes slitted. 'Smart.'

She shifted from side to side, testing her joints for aches. Nothing, thankfully. 'Any Viking marauders in your family history?'

'No clue.' The frown reappeared. 'I have an update. Don't you want to hear it?'

'OK.' She guessed the family genealogy chat could wait for some indeterminate point in the future.

He sat down on her couch without being invited.

Her brain said 'Manners, manners', but she was hardly going to suggest a homicide detective might have asked before taking a liberty. She perched on the armchair by the fireplace, waiting.

His blue eyes pierced into her, as if he could read her history on her face. 'At this time, you are no longer a person of interest.'

She broke into a wide grin. 'No?'

'There are good prints on the hammer and on the journal. They match to each other, but not to you.'

She put her hands to her cheeks. 'What about Vellum?'

He shook his head. 'Not to her either.'

Vellum appeared in the doorway, her arms clamped across her chest. 'I heard my name. Is everything OK?'

Mandy gestured to her daughter. Vellum came over and perched on the arm of the chair. 'Detective Ahola just told me we're not under suspicion anymore.'

'Who is?' Vellum demanded.

'The fingerprints aren't in the system,' the detective explained. 'And material on the hammer is a match to Mr Meadows.'

Mandy winced. 'That's unfortunate.'

He nodded as Vellum squeezed Mandy's hand. 'Still, it means we aren't dealing with a sophisticated killer.'

Mandy squeezed back. 'Why weren't my fingerprints on that journal? Wasn't it mine?'

'You thought you'd marked it up some, right?' he asked.

'Pen tests,' she said. 'Probably just a page or two.'

He rubbed at one of his brows. 'I don't think it was yours, then. A few lists of numbers and such in pencil, no pen marks. We have research to do.'

'I did find a sticky note with tally marks after that,' she offered. 'It was caught on a bookshelf, as if by accident. The note had the logo of a local business on it, but the owner said she gave them out as promotional items and she'd never been downstairs.'

'I'd like to compare the handwriting. Do you have it?'

She thought back. 'Yes, it's in the laundry room. I'll get it for you. But it's just marks. I don't know if you can compare marks.'

'Maybe. If they're distinctive in some way.'

She stood. Vellum sidled out of the room with her, then went back to her bedroom. 'Hey,' Mandy whispered.

'What?'

'I'm ready to celebrate. Maybe I'll run out and get milkshakes. Does that sound good?'

Vellum rubbed her eyes. 'OK. Mocha, please.'

'At this time of night?'

'It won't affect me. I have a lot of boring reading to do.'

'What do you have to read?'

'*The Crucible.*'

'Oh, you should enjoy that.'

'You have to be joking,' Vellum exclaimed.

Remembering her ancestry question to Detective Ahola, Mandy said, 'We had an ancestor arrested for witchcraft during the Salem Witch Trials.'

Vellum's eyes went wide. 'Cool. Seriously?'

'Yes, on my mother's side. You should ask about her sometime.'

Vellum watched from her doorway as Mandy unbolted the basement door. She sighed and went downstairs, knowing she had to get over this sense of dread and loss every time she stepped into the stairwell.

The note was where she remembered it, on the dryer. She snatched it up and climbed upstairs, careful to bolt the door at the top. With an air of triumph, she flourished it at the detective.

He shook his head at her and pulled out a plastic bag. 'Your fingerprints must be all over it.'

She dropped it in and he sealed the bag and labeled it.

'It never would have occurred to me that it was valuable evidence. It was caught in the movement of the heating duct so I have no idea where it originated from. It couldn't have been floating from Ryan's body.' Her voice caught. 'It was in the sitting room.'

'You'd better show me for the documentation.'

She took him down and pointed to the spot on the bookcase. He took a photo and noted everything.

'I think I'm done here,' he said, glancing around.

'It looks bigger without the furniture.'

'Not really.' He pointed at the closet. 'Anything in there?'

'I use it for holiday decorations and that kind of thing.'

'Could you clear it out? I could fit my gun safe in there. I like to keep it out of view.'

'Umm, I guess.' She needed a tenant. 'When did you think you might want to move in?'

'We should discuss that.' His phone rang.

He answered, and by his lowered voice, she could tell it was a work call. She went back upstairs and pulled on her coat so she could leave as soon as he did. A couple of minutes later, he came back up. She heard the snick of the bolt.

'Where are you going?' he asked.

'Kidd Valley, to pick up some milkshakes.'

'Celebrating?'

She lifted her palms into the air. 'Vellum's got a lot of home-work. I have no mom guilt if I enable both of us.'

His lips quirked. 'I could use a burger. Which one are you going to?'

'University?' Even though she shouldn't. It definitely catered to college students.

'Sure. I'll meet you there. We'll talk about the basement.'

Mandy wanted to keep her prospective tenant interested so she went to her car, happy now that she hadn't finished her eggs. When her car stereo came to life, she found a pop station and hummed along to the latest Ariana Grande female empowerment earworm. For the first time since Ryan had died, she actually felt happy again. Her arrest wasn't imminent and she might have a tenant.

She walked into Kidd Valley and ordered her milkshakes. The detective was only a minute behind her and made his order without speaking to her. She glanced around. The restaurant was mostly empty at this time of night, but given that he was still running an active murder investigation, she didn't want to seem too chummy with him.

That instinct served her well. The door opened again and in walked Dylan and Alexis. They had always seemed inseparable, almost like twins, and here they were again. He had traded his ball cap for a bright blue Eddie Bauer beanie. Alexis wore her faux fur coat again and her blond hair hung as thin and lank as her skinny legs. Had they followed her to the restaurant?

They spotted her and came in her direction. No hint of a smile or any sort of welcome expression met Mandy, just a certain resolve. With the confidence of knowing Detective Ahola knew exactly who they were, she stood her ground.

'I've never seen you here,' Dylan said in an aggressive tone.

'I usually can't waste money on fast food,' Mandy said, then went on the offensive before they could badger her. 'But I'm sure glad I ran into you two.'

'Why?' Alexis ran her fingers through the split ends of her ragged hair.

'Jasmine has picked up all of Ryan's possessions,' Mandy announced. 'There is no point in you coming to my house anymore.'

Dylan glanced over her shoulder. Mandy saw him stiffen the moment he recognized the homicide detective. He smirked. 'One last milkshake before you're taken to jail?'

'I didn't kill Ryan,' she said sweetly. 'The police have cleared me. What about you two?' She heard her order called. Perfect timing. She sauntered away to collect her shakes, a little Ariana Grande bounce to her step. Behind her, the door opened and closed. She hoped the useless pair had been frightened away.

'Small world,' Detective Ahola commented.

'I'm afraid so. Ryan got around. He'll be hard to forget.'

His gaze raked her face. 'Who do you think killed him?'

'I don't know. Can't you figure out who hit him?' she countered. 'I thought you could tell the killer's size, and what hand they used, all that kind of stuff, from the injury?'

The detective scratched his cheek. 'We don't know where he was standing. There's no obvious mark on the stairs, no blood spatter.'

'And you don't know where the murderer stood either,' Mandy mused. 'I guess whoever it was got away while I was coming to the door to see what had happened.'

He nodded. 'And after your neighbor Mrs Bhatt had driven away.'

'What about my neighbor behind me? The lower level is blocked by bushes, but they have a partial second story.'

'They weren't home.'

Mandy set her drinks on a railing and pushed her straw into her shake. She took a slurp, hoping the sugar bomb would hit her bloodstream fast and boost her intellect. Alas, sugar failed her in the way caffeine never did. 'I should have gotten a latte,' she mused.

The detective lifted a brow and gestured her to a booth in an empty corner. 'But then I wouldn't have been able to pick up a burger.'

She perched on the edge of the seat. 'We shouldn't eat together.'

He leaned over her. 'Not the best idea, not right now. Unfortunately.'

Was he flirting with her? Suddenly unsure of the situation, she tucked Vellum's straw into her pocket so she wouldn't lose it. 'I wish I could help you. I want it to be Dylan or Alexis. I wouldn't mind if it was my next-door neighbor, except for wondering who would take her kids if she gets arrested.'

He ran his tongue over his upper lip. 'I don't want wishes, I want a killer.'

'I don't have an answer,' Mandy said, watching his mouth. 'But it's motive, means and opportunity, right?'

He squinted at her. 'The hammer belonged to your cousin. His fingerprints were on it, and his toolbox was open on the floor in the closet of his bedroom.'

'I didn't recognize it.' Mandy hoped she wasn't blushing.

'Who is this Reese person?'

'How do you know that name?'

'Sticky note?'

'Oh, right,' she said eagerly. 'She's a nurse at the USea office building. Kind of a friend. Also does vlogging like me. She lives down the street.'

'Do you have any concerns about her?'

'Ryan wasn't her type. She's serious about only dating within her religious faith.'

'We'll fingerprint her because of the sticky note,' the detective said. 'Who does have a motive, in your opinion?'

'That's the problem, right?' Mandy took another suck of her sweet chocolate shake. 'This is a guy who was dating my co-worker and cheating on her with my neighbor, but that was a few months back. Then he started a relationship with Dylan and Alexis. He was about to get fired at work. He was lying to me about drug use. No relationship with his family other than me. No bank account, but also no outstanding debt. He paid his rent.'

The detective nodded. 'He was written up for being drunk on the job. Not because he had personal conflicts.'

'Right. I missed all the sex stuff.' She shook her head. 'I've been too wrapped up in my own drama to notice other people's.'

His lips tilted in a sympathetic almost smile. 'What is your gut telling you? Oblivious or not, you were Ryan Meadows' best friend.'

She stared at the table for a moment before meeting his gaze. 'I can't believe Jasmine was involved. Is there anyone you've run across with a white cat? I found cat hairs on his chair and I can't imagine why. They must have rubbed off on it recently. Reese is the only person who has a cat like that.'

'There weren't any on the body or the hammer.'

She slurped on her shake again. At this rate there wouldn't be any left to enjoy with her bath. She tightened her jaw to suppress a yawn. 'Probably not relevant then. How did he hook up with Dylan and Alexis? Was he cheating on them?'

'Good questions. I also find very interesting those things he felt were important enough to lie to you about. Drug use. Where did his paycheck go?'

'Right,' Mandy said. 'Where? Meanwhile, I really need someone to take over his rent payments.'

'I really like the space and location,' he said. 'Count me in as soon as we close the case.'

'Good incentive.' Mandy clasped her hands together. It was a good thing she didn't want to date right now. A man with a steady job and a well-kept appearance was also perfection as a tenant. 'Will your significant other be on the tenant agreement?'

He lifted his brows. 'Just me. My ex-girlfriend moved to Austin over the holidays. Now I've sold our house and I need to move.'

Mandy nodded soberly. 'Let me tell you the details about the property, like what the deposit would be.'

In preparation for a family dinner across the street the next evening, Mandy was in the bathroom testing a new lipstick her mother had given her for Christmas. She heard the mudroom doorbell ring and quickly pressed her lips together to smooth out the brown-red color.

'Friend or foe?' she asked, opening the inner door.

Reese, her hair tucked into the hood of a violet parka, held up a tote bag. 'Friend. Are you going to let me in? It's pouring out here.'

'Hold on.' Mandy unlocked the screen door and held it open so Reese could get past. 'What are you doing out in this horrible weather?'

'I was halfway down the block before the rain hit. You know how it goes at this time of year.' Reese pushed back her hood. Water streamed off the water-resistant fabric. She fisted her hands. 'My fingers are frozen.'

'I'll help you.' Mandy tugged at the resistant zipper of Reese's soaked coat. Finally, it engaged, and she pulled it down.

'I feel like a toddler,' Reese joked, dropping the tote to the floor. 'Can this go in the dryer?'

'On low, I think. Does this mean you're going to show me your basement?'

'You want the murder tour?'

'Yes! Especially since you sent the police after me.' Reese adjusted the cowl neck of her lemon-yellow sweater.

'It's not my fault that Ryan had your sticky note.' Mandy considered the nurse's innocent expression. Maybe if they went down to the basement together, Reese would give herself away with some sort of observation that only the killer could know. Or maybe Reese would try to kill Mandy, too. Or recover some kind of cache?

Her head spun. She leaned back against the counter in the mudroom and casually slid a pair of scissors into the back pocket of her jeans. Thus armed, she said, 'Lead the way.'

Reese frowned at her. 'Do our houses have the same layout? I don't know where your dryer is.'

'You knew it was in the basement.'

Reese blinked. 'Everybody's dryer is in the basement. And I remember you complaining about coming downstairs with the laundry, and Ryan would come out of his bedroom in his shorts and hand you his clothes to throw into your load.'

Mandy shuddered. 'He did do that, didn't he? And to think Kit heard me complain about it and still got involved with him.'

Reese's eyes sparkled. 'Do tell.'

With a sigh, Mandy gave up trying to lead Reese into a confession and took her down the stairs. She turned on the landing to see if Reese's eyes went anywhere interesting.

'It's creepy,' Reese said, walking right past the little cabinet where the hammer had been hidden. 'Did he fall down this flight or the bottom stairs?'

'He landed where I'm standing.'

'What did you think at first?'

'That he slipped on my journal.'

Reese experimentally slid the sole of one boot across the steps. 'You could slip down these and break your neck. I can see why you thought that. Have you thought about carpeting the stairs?'

'I should have done it before Cory left.'

'Back when you had the money.' Reese sighed. 'It can't be easy to keep up this place on minimum wage.'

'USea doesn't pay that badly,' Mandy said defensively. 'But yeah, that's why I need the journaling business.' Refusing to look at the landing, she walked down the last few steps and went into the laundry room, careful to keep the coat to the side so she didn't slick up the floor in front of her feet.

'You should mop up the water,' Reese said.

'You should.' Mandy grabbed a mop from the hook in the laundry room and thrust it in Reese's direction.

'You could have at least offered me a cup of tea first,' Reese complained.

'Feel free to put the kettle on after you've done the mopping,' Mandy said sweetly. Turning her back on Reese, she pulled a dry load of laundry from the dryer and put the coat inside. She set the dial to twenty minutes on low heat.

When she went back into the hall, she saw no sign of Reese, but she heard water running in the kitchen. Wincing, she realized she'd lost her shot at walking Reese through the basement and getting her to slip up. Had Reese outsmarted her or had she outsmarted herself?

THIRTEEN

Upstairs, Mandy found Reese sitting on a kitchen stool while Vellum poured boiling water into a tea pot.

'You remember that we're going to your grandmother's for dinner, right?' Mandy asked. 'We have to go in half an hour.'

'That's OK. It's Friday. I don't need to do homework tonight.'

'By the way, Reese,' Mandy said. 'I wanted to tell you that I'm no longer a person of interest. As a result, I don't need to hire a lawyer and I definitely won't need to sell my business.'

Reese's full lips went into a pout. Mandy didn't sense any anger in the woman, but she wasn't sure why Reese was hanging around, either. 'What was in that tote bag?'

'Oh, right.' Reese bounced off the stool and went to retrieve the bag, just as Mandy spotted the dripping mop in the corner.

She grabbed a kitchen towel and soaked up the puddle of water, then carried the mop into the bathroom and put it in the tub, half afraid that when she saw the water against the porcelain it would still show the rusty color of blood. But the crime scene cleanup people had been as thorough as advertised and the water ran clear when she squeezed out the mop.

In the kitchen, Vellum poured tea and took her cup into her bedroom.

Reese took her cup and blew into it, holding out her tote bag with her free hand.

Mandy opened it. She pulled out a few sheets of notebook paper with spread ideas, and a round canister of Scribbles That Matter brush pens. 'What's this?'

'I thought we could have a matching theme for March,' Reese said. 'You see people doing that from time to time. Three different vloggers use the same idea in their own style and then cross-promote each other. We'd only have to find one more person.'

Mandy glanced over the spreads. 'Why sunflowers? They don't bloom until the end of summer?'

'I thought they'd be cute.'

She put the sheets back into the tote. 'You have to think more seasonally.'

'That's why I'm asking you now.'

Mandy handed her the tote. 'I get it, but I'm close to two weeks ahead of you. I've already made my spreads for March and filmed them. It's not a bad idea, just not for March.'

'We could do the same thing for April,' Reese said eagerly.

Mandy chuckled. 'You just want a shot at my audience.'

'Can you blame me? But I've done my research. Look.' Reese held out her phone and showed Mandy an email she'd written back and forth with another video journalist. 'She liked the idea, but I didn't want to propose a theme until I talked to you.'

Mandy pulled out her own phone and checked the woman's followers on her video channel, then took a quick glance at her social media. 'You did your homework. This woman doesn't have the followers I do, but she has more than you.'

'Her work is cute,' Reese said. 'Did you see her flamingo month from last summer?'

Mandy flipped past. 'Yeah, you're right.'

'How about a teddy bear picnic theme for April?' Reese said eagerly. 'I've been wanting to do that.'

'Adorable but complicated,' Mandy said. 'I need something more universal for my stickers.'

'What was your plan?'

'Not was, is. I already filmed cherry blossoms for April. My backup plan was tulips. Obvious, and I haven't done it before.'

Reese licked her full lips. 'Yeah, let's do tulips.' Before Mandy could say another word, she typed into her phone and sent an email back to the other vlogger.

Mandy drank her tea with a sigh. She could do two sets of stickers and videos for April. It might earn her more money. 'Anything else?'

Reese pointed at the canister. 'I thought you could review those next, since you like cheap pens.'

'They came out last year. It's much too late to do a review or a swatch video.'

'I never even opened them.'

'Then use them for a giveaway,' Mandy suggested.

Reese nodded. 'I guess I have to do something to increase

engagement for March. I have no idea what I'm going to do now. I need to go.'

Mandy watched openmouthed as Reese disappeared into her mudroom. She heard the screen door hit the side of the house as she went outside. Mandy followed more slowly and locked up as Reese trudged across the yard, coatless, her head down against the elements.

Mandy shook her head, hoping Reese had her house key in the pocket of her sweater.

An hour later, Mandy sat shivering at her mother's dinner table next to Vellum. She wished she'd worn a fleece-lined hoodie like Vellum, instead of an aging cashmere sweater with holes here and there. 'Why is it so cold, Mom?'

'I had to open the windows upstairs to dilute the new carpet smell,' her mother said. 'How is your job now, sweetheart? Any more problems with the till?'

'Not for me, but more money was missing during someone else's shift.'

Her mother tsked. 'It's time to find a better job. The less you make, the less respect you receive. That's what my father always said.'

'I remember,' Mandy told her, 'but job-hopping is bad, too. I'll have been in this spot for a year in May. Maybe I'll look around then.'

Her mother lifted her chin. 'What does being a barista prepare you to do for your next step up?'

'I have no idea.'

'Our business is doing well,' Vellum announced defensively. 'Mom's really smart. She just started a year ago next month. And we're projected to make as much as her day job by summer.'

'You're still running short,' her grandmother said. 'I'm glad you are learning money management early, Vellum. School doesn't prepare girls for the real world like it should.'

'I still need a tenant to break even,' Mandy agreed. 'Unless Cory would pay his child support.'

'One of my regrets is that I was never able to foster a truly positive relationship with the Moffats,' her mother said. 'But that woman is cold. I never could find a way to ally with her.'

'Grandmother isn't that nice to me, either,' Vellum said.

Her grandma shuddered. 'Who asks their grandchild to call them "Grandmother"? So formal.'

'Better than Mrs Moffat,' Mandy interjected. 'Enough about them. We just have to keep Vellum front and center so she's in the will.'

'Mom!'

Mandy shrugged. 'It's the only way we're ever going to get your child support out of those people.'

'Did you find a tenant?' her mother asked. 'I saw a truck arriving at your house yesterday.'

'Jasmine took Ryan's stuff, and no sooner than that, my prospective tenant showed up. It's the homicide detective, Mom. He's asked about the apartment once the investigation has closed.'

Her mother's finely tweezed blond brows raised. 'I like that. I'll feel like my girls are safe with a man in the basement again.'

Vellum gave her a quizzical look. 'We don't need a man to feel safe.'

'Amen.' Mandy held up her wine glass.

Her mother looked at her with disfavor. 'It's not as if you are a black belt, sweetheart. Why is this man moving in? Is romance in the air?'

Mandy coughed as her wine went down the wrong pipe. 'Nah. I'm dead inside and below the waist.'

'Mom!' Vellum shrieked.

'It's for the best,' Mandy's mother said calmly. 'The police have a high divorce rate and, given the poor odds of success in a second marriage, he would not be a good option for the long term.'

Mandy had to laugh. She needed a tenant, not a boyfriend.

On Valentine's Day, Mandy dressed in a black cocktail dress. She called for Vellum, then ran back into her bedroom and grabbed a tartan scarf Ryan had given her for Christmas. Vellum appeared from her bedroom, wearing a dark jacket and khaki skirt.

'I don't have funeral clothes,' she fretted.

Mandy pulled on her coat and tucked the scarf under the lapels. 'It's close enough. You look nice.'

She let Vellum choose the music in the car for their half-hour drive north. Her mother had told them that Ryan would be cremated after the memorial service because his mother, who was Mandy's father's sister-in-law, wanted him buried with her when the time came. Mandy wondered where the ashes would be stored before then, but felt too queasy to ask.

'I want to be buried,' she told Vellum. 'I should buy a plot now and pay for it on installment.'

'But if you get married again you might want to be buried with your husband.'

'How about a family plot?' she suggested.

'I can think of better ways to spend our money.'

Mandy poked her daughter's leg. 'Don't want to spend eternity next to your boring old mom, huh.'

'I might marry a billionaire who has his own cemetery,' Vellum explained. 'On the moon.'

'Would I get to join you?'

'Only if you're cremated like Ryan,' Vellum said, hitting buttons on her phone to bring up a new song. 'I suppose they can tuck you in at my feet.'

'Nah. I'll take a nice raised stone. I don't care if it's wasteful.'

'Would you like a weeping angel statue too?'

'Absolutely.'

Vellum sang along to the song she was streaming. Mandy blinked back tears, though from laughter or sorrow she wasn't quite sure. She knew she needed to have these conversations, but thirty-six seemed much too early for them. Still, people did die this young. Princess Diana, for instance.

She shook her head, and wished she could sing along, but she didn't know the words. 'Do you still want to be a rock star when you grow up?'

'Ummm, no, Mom.'

'Why not?'

Vellum rolled her eyes. 'I'm going to be a business major in college.'

'What about art?'

'You don't have any training and you're a good artist. Business is something else. I want a degree and one of those high-end jobs that you can retire from at thirty-five. Then I can have kids and relax.'

'Wow. You have it all figured out, huh?'

'It's not like I'm deliberately choosing the opposite life to you,' Vellum said.

'Yeah,' Mandy said. 'I hear you. And if you are really sure that's what you want, don't let some man persuade you otherwise. Live your life, not his.'

'Is that what you did?'

'I lived inside your father's fantasy, rather than my reality. I should have paid more attention to the money, so I wouldn't be in this fix now.'

'Is it really that bad?'

'We're fine as long as nothing goes wrong. Most people can't do what we're doing with Mandy's Plan.'

'No. People would kill to be in our position after only ten months.'

Mandy nodded. Had someone done that? Could the journal have been left on the step for her to trip on, the hammer there to finish her off? Had the assailant, Reese perhaps, killed Ryan because he would have died eventually from his injuries?

She'd stayed on the arterials rather than entering the clogged, rainy freeway. They sped past endless fast-food restaurants, big box stores, and streets snaking off into residential areas. She remembered where they had gone to say goodbye to her father, and made the turn easily. Then they were pulling into a surprisingly small parking lot. She saw her mother stepping out of her car with her sister-in-law, Ryan's mother. Her aunt looked diminished, like she'd lost a lot of weight since Mandy had seen her during the holidays.

Mandy parked in the first spot she saw and hurried Vellum out of the car to join their family. She didn't want the older women to be alone in their grief. It didn't seem like there were any men left in this family, at least not in the Seattle area.

An hour and a half later, the brief family-only visitation and open memorial had ended. Despite Mandy's closeness to Ryan, she hadn't been asked to participate. An extremely elderly uncle of her father's, whom she hadn't seen since that funeral, read a poem in a shaking voice, and her aunt gave the eulogy. Jasmine sang the song 'Hallelujah' at the end. Few of the attendees teared up, but Mandy and Vellum both did.

The guests had been invited to a reception in another room in lieu of a graveside service. Mandy saw Dylan and Alexis corner Jasmine within ten minutes of the doors opening. She winced, wondering what the pair were still after, and what it might have to do with his murder.

Making sure her daughter was comfortable chatting with the teenagers who belonged to Ryan's mother's side of the family, Mandy crept toward Ryan's friends, hoping to overhear the conversation.

'No, you cannot have his coin collection,' Jasmine snapped. 'I don't care if you helped him build it.'

'But it has no value,' Dylan said.

'Just sentimental,' Alexis added in her low rumble of a voice.

'I'm taking every cent to the bank,' Jasmine said. 'Who do you think is paying for this funeral? I had to put it on an installment plan.'

'Just the pennies, then?' Dylan said hopefully.

'Not. One. Cent,' Jasmine hissed. 'Where did all his money go? He didn't have a car payment. He lived in a freaking basement.'

'He drank very expensive liquor,' Dylan said with a smile.

'The best vodka.' Alexis smacked her lips.

'I thought his drinking was under control,' Jasmine said. 'Mandy promised me he was doing better.'

The pair shrugged in unison, just as Jasmine glanced up and saw Mandy hovering.

Her cousin's eyes narrowed. 'You as good as killed him!' she shrieked.

Mandy stepped back, as if the words were a physical blow. 'That's absurd!'

'He probably owed someone money,' Jasmine yelled. 'He probably got killed over a loan. It's your fault! You should have been honest about what was going on!'

'Nothing was going on,' Mandy protested. 'He paid his rent on time. I talked to him every day.' She paused, unable to deny she'd missed so many things. The lovers. The drug use.

Vellum ran up and put her arm around her waist protectively. 'My mom was good to Ryan. You need to back off.'

Jasmine raised a finger and pointed it at Vellum's nose, then stepped closer. Just then, Jasmine's mother and aunt arrived. Her mother took Jasmine's arm, and Barbara put her hand on Vellum's shoulder.

'Let's get you home,' Barbara told her granddaughter. 'Valentine's Day traffic is terrible.'

Jasmine sneered at Mandy as her mother steered her away, saying, 'Let's get you a drink, dear.'

No wonder Ryan had developed a drinking problem. She made a mental note to tell her aunt to intervene before Jasmine took the coins to a bank. Was it possible that he had some valuable coins in his collection?

Mandy turned away from Dylan and Alexis, examining the guests. Most of the forty or so people there were from Ryan's maternal side, not related or known to her part of the Meadows family. She tried to talk to her great-uncle, but he was hard of hearing. No one had come from work, not even Kit. She would have thought Scott would feel obligated to come, but maybe since Ryan was about to be fired, he couldn't be bothered. At that moment, even Crystal Roswell would have been a welcome sight, but Jasmine wouldn't have known to invite her.

Mandy decided it was time to leave.

When she pulled into her driveway an hour later, a text appeared from her mother saying she and Vellum were going to order pizza and watch a movie.

She climbed out of her car, exposing far more of herself than she wished to a stiff breeze in her short skirt.

'Happy Valentine's Day,' Linda called from behind her.

Mandy turned and saw her neighbor with a Pyrex baking dish. More brownies, exactly what she needed after a funeral.

As if pulled in by the treats, Reese appeared behind Linda.

'I have come here to bury Caesar, not to praise him,' Mandy said, quoting Shakespeare.

A twinkle appeared in Linda's eye. 'The evil that men do is remembered after their deaths, but the good is often buried with them.'

'Umm,' Reese said. 'I haven't read that play since sophomore year.'

'Vellum had the audio playing a few days ago in the kitchen. She's doing it in school,' Mandy explained, grabbing her purse from the back seat.

'How was the funeral?' Linda asked.

'Like any funeral. Jasmine called me a murderer.'

'Oh my,' Reese said, eyes sparkling. 'Want to go get Chinese food? It's so early we can probably get in no problem.'

Mandy glanced at the brownie dish. 'Lock it in my trunk and we'll go.'

Linda handed it to her and thrust her arms into the coat she'd just thrown over her shoulders. Mandy unlocked the doors and dropped the brownie dish in the trunk. The trio got in and she drove them to Snappy Dragon, a local institution a few blocks away on Roosevelt.

Mandy glanced at her phone as they walked in. 'I can't believe it's just before five.'

'Funerals make for a long day,' Linda soothed, rubbing her back.

'Was there a bunch of sobbing exes there?' asked Reese, after she spoke to the woman at the desk.

'Just Dylan and Alexis, following Jasmine around, asking for Ryan's coin collection again.'

'What's that all about?' Reese asked.

'I'm convinced loose change isn't what they're after. Like, maybe, Ryan was buying antique coins instead of drugs,' Mandy suggested. 'They aren't wasting all this time to get pennies.'

'Even a roll of quarters has value,' Linda pointed out.

'Yeah, but in the end, Dylan wanted to get his hands on the pennies. Strange, huh?'

'Can you talk your cousin into giving you a look at the pennies?' Linda asked.

'I doubt it. She called me a murderer,' Mandy said. 'Maybe the police can get a warrant for them? Except, how would they do that?'

'They're the police,' Reese said.

'No, I mean how would they justify asking for it. They had full access to the coins at the start and didn't find anything.'

'Yeah,' Linda said. 'Manpower is limited.'

Their server appeared and took them to a table. Mandy ordered asparagus in black bean sauce and a tofu clay pot stew. Reese chose another stew with seafood, and Linda went more traditional with salt and pepper chicken.

'What do you guys think about funeral etiquette?' Mandy asked. 'Should his boss have been there? What about his last serious girlfriend?'

'Your neighbors?' Linda suggested warily.

Mandy sighed. 'I'm not calling you out for not coming, Linda. You had your shift at the animal shelter today.'

'His supervisor was Scott Nelson, right?' Reese asked. At Mandy's nod, she said, 'He's not Mister Friendly. I doubt he'd bother. I heard he was better before his wife left him, but now he'll chew people out if they're to blame for overloading outlets, banging up walls or anything, really.'

Mandy pushed her hair behind her ears. 'I know he didn't like Ryan, and it's not like there weren't people there, but once my mom and daughter left, it was like there was no one there for me. Mostly relatives of his on the other side of the family.'

'You could have asked me to go,' Reese said.

'Did you know Ryan?' Mandy asked bluntly. 'Did you remember spending time in my basement after all?'

'I . . . no,' Reese said. 'I mean, I knew he was your cousin from seeing him at your house. I said hi a few times.'

'Hmm.' Mandy said, and decided to change the subject. 'Did you decide on a March theme?'

Linda ignored her attempt to redirect the conversation. 'I wonder how Ryan had so many hookups and lovers and none of us have anyone.'

'What happened to George Lowry?' Mandy asked. 'I haven't seen him since he pulled out my car dent with a crowbar.'

The server delivered their pot of tea. Reese poured them each a steaming cup of oolong before Linda responded.

'He went to Hawaii for a couple of weeks.' Linda rolled her eyes. 'These couple of weeks, around Valentine's Day.'

'Did he send flowers?' Reese asked.

'Not even a text.' Linda pantomimed holding her phone. 'I could text. I could sext, even.'

Mandy chuckled, imagining the rotund, retired dentist. 'With George Lowry?'

'But then there was Ryan. His looks weren't entirely ruined,' Reese said reflectively, picking up her teacup.

'He smelled wrong,' Linda said. 'That hot, yeasty alcoholic smell.'

'What if he was a drug dealer?' Mandy asked suddenly. 'That would attract people to him.'

'He'd have more money,' Linda said.

'He wouldn't be living with a prude like you,' Reese added. 'You'd have noticed all the visitors he would have, probably late at night.'

Mandy shook her head. 'He could just deal at the hospital. I've heard someone is.'

'No money,' Linda said again. 'He'd have had a stash if he was dealing. It's a cash economy.'

'Someone did break in, maybe, after he died. I can't be sure the murder weapon had been there all along, given where I found it. Maybe someone did steal hidden cash.'

'It's gone now, if there ever was any,' Reese said.

Reese might have wanted Mandy's business, but she didn't need cash. Still, Mandy wanted to be clear, even if she wasn't certain, that no money remained in the house. After all, she had the gnawing sense that the murderer was someone close to her world. But how close? An actual friend? Or a frenemy?

FOURTEEN

Mandy went to her mother's house on Sunday morning. The trio ate a quick breakfast and tried hard not to revisit the memorial service drama.

'Are we going to livestream?' Vellum asked as they dashed across the street.

It had warmed up a little and Mandy found it bittersweet to consider the coming of a spring that Ryan would never enjoy.

'Sounds good to me. I'd rather do that than shoot a video that we have to edit.'

'Let's make sure to use stickers so we have a bump in shop sales.'

'Great idea. In fact, let's take a look at our orders. We have an hour before our usual livestream time.' On Sundays, lots of vloggers went on live camera with their fans on the social media sites. Fans could watch and work along with them as they set up their journals for the week. They could also comment live, which was great for suggestions but bad for concentration.

'Do you need a quick manicure first?' Vellum asked, as they hung their coats in the mudroom. 'I did my nails last night.'

'It always seems to come last on my list,' Mandy admitted.

'Let's check our orders, get them printing and cutting, and then we'll do your nails quickly after that,' Vellum suggested.

'Look at you. So organized,' Mandy said. 'I think you might be right about belonging in business school.'

Vellum grinned. 'I can't decide if I want to be the CEO of a massive business, or be an entrepreneur and build my own massive business.'

'The path will become clear in time, tadpole,' Mandy said with a mysterious air.

'Funny, Mom. Well, not really.' She took Mandy's arm and pulled her into the art studio.

Mandy opened her computer while Vellum went to choose manicure supplies. Mandy's Plan did have orders, but most of the requests were sticker sheets she had ready, like the snowflakes she'd designed for January and the cacti she'd done for February. After jotting down what she needed on an inventory sheet, she set the cacti sheets to print to one printer and the customer address labels to another. Finally, she went to the plastic racks in the dining room to start assembling.

As the pages came off the printer, she set up the cutting machines so they could follow the specifications she'd set up to make the stickers lift easily from the backing paper. Sticker creation was a bit more complex than people realized, both in the initial computer setup and then the cutting process. She needed her iPad, her laptop, her printer and her cutting machine to make it all happen, but in the end, order fulfillment took the most time of all. Today, she had twenty orders piled up.

By the time Vellum returned, she had the label sheets and twenty envelopes spread out on the table. Vellum stamped each of the envelopes with a cute 'thank you' rubber stamp and affixed the labels while Mandy switched out the sticker sheets and started assembling orders.

'Did you sign in?' Mandy asked, reminding Vellum to record her hours worked.

'Oops.' Vellum dug out her employment record and signed in, then readied the postage meter.

For the next half hour, they assembled orders. Mandy made an announcement on social media that they were going live at eleven. They finished their orders just in time for Mandy to set up the camera.

'We forgot your nails,' Vellum fretted.

'Oh, well. Better content than appearance.' They both sat down and opened their journals. 'Rats.' Mandy jumped up again and flipped through their racks, pulling sheets of her new cherry blossom stickers and the lettering sheets that matched the color scheme of those stickers.

She set one of each page next to them, then said, 'Ready?' At Vellum's nod, she switched on the phone camera.

Vellum set the computer in place, so they could see the scroll of comments from their viewers.

'Hi everyone!' She and Vellum waved into the camera. 'We're going to set up our spreads for the week. Can you believe it's Sunday already? I'm sorry we missed last week.'

'Did everyone have a good Valentine's Day?' Vellum asked. She made a face. 'I had pizza with Grandma.'

'I had Chinese with girlfriends,' Mandy said. 'We're going to be setting up our weekly spreads with our new April stickers. I just love these.'

'I feel like I'm cheating to work with them,' Vellum said.

'Actually, they are already in our shop, and we just filled our first set of orders,' Mandy said. 'So no, we aren't cheating, you can order these now!' She held up the sheets, feeling like an infomercial hostess. Still, she had to do these things to make money.

'I love the new garden stake stickers,' Vellum exclaimed. 'They came out perfectly.'

They responded to the comments on the screen as they used their rules to mark out days, lettered headers, and used their stickers judiciously to make everything look colorful and flowery. Just like on the cooking shows, they had to sell their work by squealing how delightful it was at the end, so they did that too. Mandy was certain more sales would pop up on the online shop by the end of their forty-minute livestream.

Mandy clicked off the camera, then slumped into her chair. 'I need to get the envelopes out the door. Then I can mark everything processed in the shop.'

'I can walk them to the mailbox,' Vellum said. 'Then I need to do homework.'

'OK. I'll clean everything up, and if we do get more orders, I'll get them done and drop them in the mailbox later today.'

'Sounds good.' Vellum kissed the top of her head and walked into the dining room.

Mandy stayed at her pretty desk, staring at the half-used sticker sheets and the matching pink and black pens they had used for their weekly spreads. She'd zigzagged a swatch of pink across the top and neatly calligraphed February, with that week's dates.

A bolt of inspiration hit her. Why couldn't she use her organizational strength to solve Ryan's murder? Almost mystical connections occurred in her brain when she wrote things down. Once they were in writing, it was as if the task had been released and her brain was free to focus on details, new information.

Resolutely, she pulled a red marker from the clear box and carefully wrote 'Murder Spread' on a blank page. As she always did, she went back over the outline of her red calligraphy with a thin black marker, to accentuate the words. She added suns around the words, meaning to indicate to herself that she was making insights, but when she set her pen down and looked at the page, she saw that the red pen suns looked like nothing more than blood splotches. Her stomach rumbled uneasily, but perhaps nothing was more appropriate.

She grabbed a template from a stack in another clear box and drew a circle in the center of her journal page. Inside, she wrote her cousin's name, Ryan Meadows, and underneath, she added basic details: age forty-two, single, no kids, janitor, alcoholic.

Those were the bare facts of her cousin. They ignored his handyman and gardening skills, the way he'd stood up to bullies for her, his strange charisma that sucked both women and men into sexual entanglements.

But in these bald facts, the reason behind his death must be hidden.

She'd never done anything like this before, so she used her template to create symbols that would add meaning. Drawing a diamond, she added the word 'family' beneath, then, in smaller circles vertical on the page, she wrote Jasmine, Mandy, Vellum and Barbara, noting the relationship of each.

Then she added a rectangle and wrote 'co-workers' underneath that. The names that went in those circles were Reese, Kit and Fannah. She didn't know the names of Ryan's fellow maintenance techs because they didn't frequent the coffee bar. Instead, she wrote 'Maintenance Dept' in another circle.

She moved to the right after glancing at her template and catching sight of a heart. She added the word 'lovers' and in the circle boxes wrote Dylan, Alexis, Crystal and also Kit. Kit did double duty here. Frowning at her spread, she erased Kit from the co-worker list to avoid confusion. She added another circle to the right and placed Aiden next to Crystal. Who knew what that kid was capable of?

Up at the top, she drew a shield emblem and wrote 'neighbors.' Here she put only Linda, since Crystal, Reese and Barbara were already listed.

Ryan's family, co-workers, lovers and neighbors were all intertwined.

What else might go on a murder spread? She added a banner close to the top, under one of the bloody suns, and wrote 'weapons' neatly across. Those were stairs, journal, hammer, and alcohol. Nothing helpful there. Anyone could have had access to any of those items. They didn't help.

Mandy turned the page and drew her diamond, shield, rectangle and heart emblems again, this time intertwined. She wanted to see who fit into multiple categories. Her mother and herself she ignored, but Reese was a neighbor and a co-worker, Crystal was a neighbor and a lover, and Kit was a co-worker and a lover.

It made all too much sense that Crystal or Reese had the most opportunity. Theoretically, whoever had killed Ryan had only a few minutes to get inside, those minutes after his friends had left and before Mandy heard the fall. Reese and Crystal were the obvious suspects.

But Crystal seemed too uninvolved, and she was actually starting to like Reese. Also, she hadn't caught her out on anything after spending more time with her in the past few days. Mandy stared down at her paper. That meant her murder spread was telling her that Kit, the co-worker who didn't want a security camera, and ex-girlfriend who'd been cheated on, was Mandy's person of interest.

Her phone rang, pulling her from her thoughts before she could consider further. She closed her notebook and took the call.

On Monday, all signs of Valentine's Day had vanished from the coffee bar. Fannah kept Mandy and Kit busy in between customers, hanging four-leaf clover cutouts and a ridiculously oversized cardboard decoration of a pot o' gold with a rainbow leading into it. At least they'd been spared the leprechaun images.

Finally, Fannah went on her break. The surgeons had finished their morning rounds of short surgeries. She'd had a friendly chat with Dr Burrell about an art exhibit he'd seen at the Seattle Art Museum. Dr O'Halloran had arrived, very business-like, with a resident and two interns, and bought a round of coffees for all four. Nurses had streamed by, volunteers, moms with babies having their wellness checks at the pediatrician's office, the elderly visiting specialists, most of them ordering coffee instead of fancier drinks. It was the kind of gray day that required basic caffeine to regroup after a sugary holiday.

Kit washed used milk jugs in the little sink while Mandy ran into the back and put a tray of fresh chocolate chip cookies into the oven. Afterwards, Mandy checked the front. They had a lull.

She took a deep breath, preparing herself to interrogate her person of interest. Walking up to Kit, she stood at her elbow.

'What?'

'Why weren't you at the funeral?'

'Whose funeral?' Kit asked without turning around.

'Your ex-boyfriend. Ryan?'

'That was over the weekend?' Her tone was careless.

'Yeah.'

'Sorry. I mean, I know he was your cousin, but I hate funerals.'

'Yeah, it wasn't a lot of fun for me, being called a murderer and all.'

Kit turned off the faucet. 'Who did that?'

'His sister. She claimed not to know his drinking was out of control.'

Kit glanced at her. 'Who spilled?'

'His creepy friends, Dylan and Alexis. Were they around when you were dating?' Mandy pressed.

'Never heard those names.'

Mandy tilted her head. 'Do you know anything about Ryan's coin collection?'

Kit started putting everything she'd washed away. 'What coin collection?'

'I'm not sure if it was actual collectibles or if he just rolled all his change before taking it into the bank, but Dylan seems very intent on gaining possession.'

Kit shrugged, her back turned to Mandy. 'Dunno. But want to duck into the back for a minute? I have something to tell you.'

'OK.'

Kit went into the back room. Mandy leaned against the wall so she could see Kit and the counter. 'What's up?'

Kit stared at her. She had dark shadows under her eyes, almost like bruises, but probably just exhaustion. 'I'm planning to quit this job soon.'

Mandy's brows lifted. 'Why? Because of the thefts?'

Kit shrugged again. 'I'm already working a second job at Starbucks. It's not such a dead end, working there.'

Mandy tried to force her brain to work like a detective's.

'Anyway, don't tell Fannah, OK?' Kit added.

'No, you need to choose your own time,' Mandy agreed. 'I guess you don't need a reference or anything.'

'No, I've already been working there for a month. I work Tuesday, Wednesday, Saturday and Sunday.'

A bell sounded in Mandy's brain. 'Wednesday evening?'

'From six until close, yeah. My shift here ends at five on Wednesdays because Fannah works the late shift for doing inventory. And since I work the earlier shift here on Tuesdays, I go to work at Starbucks at four that day.'

Mandy's thoughts rearranged themselves. 'I know what the schedule is around here.' That's why Fannah had never been a suspect, even if she'd had some kind of motive. But Kit could have killed Ryan, or so she'd thought. 'You were at Starbucks when Ryan died?'

'Yeah, that's my regular shift, after work here. It's an exhausting day, a shift and a half. I'm working seven days a week.'

'No wonder you've got circles under your eyes.' It hadn't been guilt keeping her up, but endless hours on her feet.

A couple of nurses appeared at the counter. Mandy nodded sympathetically at Kit and went to take orders.

Only twenty minutes later, when she'd finished with the customers and was putting the cooled cookies onto a tray, was she able to process the fact that Kit had an alibi for the murder. Now what? Who was left?

Fannah returned and gave Mandy her break. Mandy took her journal and a small cup of intellect-boosting dark roast coffee over to one of the pair of sofas in the corner, out of sight of her co-workers. She decided she needed a color code for her murder spread. Since she had a couple of highlighters in her purse, she decided yellow would be 'no alibi' and pink would be 'alibi'. That way she could color pink over the yellow if the status changed.

She made her key in a corner and then colored a strip of pink over Kit's name. After staring at the list, she colored a strip over her name and Vellum's. Finally, she added pink to Fannah, who had never been a suspect. While she didn't have proof Fannah had worked her normal Wednesday shift, she hadn't heard the coffee bar had closed early, and on the rare occasions something went wrong with their hours, people usually complained the next day.

If only she knew all the facts the police did. Based on her update, that made Reese her person of interest. And being honest with herself, she didn't like that one bit. Especially since Reese would have had a better reason to kill *her*. But if Reese felt like a bad suspect, who was the right one?

She spent the rest of her break monitoring Crystal's social media, but from last month to this, she didn't see much change. In fact, Crystal had done a phone check-in at Snappy Dragon at 5:03 p.m. the night Ryan died. That was practically an alibi since the notification picked up her location from GPS. She added pink above Crystal's name.

At 3:25 p.m., just before the end of her shift, Dr O'Halloran, looking like a model in blue scrubs that brought out the light in his eyes and showcased his muscular chest and legs, arrived and asked for a quad shot Americano. Mandy smiled brightly at him. Business had been down ever since she'd embarrassed him with her demand that he pay for the 'stolen' biscotti in front of people, and she was grateful that he hadn't stopped patronizing them.

'Where are all your co-workers?' he asked as he swiped his card. 'Could I get a little vanilla powder on top?'

She could have told him to do it himself, since the vanilla was available on the customer side of the counter, but mindful of his surgeon status and their incident, she went to get it and sprinkled until he held up his hand. 'Kit closes tonight, so she's on break, and Fannah only works late on Wednesdays.'

'What night do you work late?'

'Tuesdays. Which is nice, because I can be home with my daughter the other four nights. On Tuesdays she spends time with my mom.'

'But she's old enough to be home alone.'

'Of course, but most fifteen-year-olds don't think about making themselves a healthy meal.'

'She must be responsible.'

'In some ways I'm very lucky. I haven't had to remind her to do her homework for four years.'

'College bound?'

'Definitely.' She didn't want to run on about her daughter, given his lack of children. The doctor was certainly chatty this evening.

He ran his tongue over his teeth. 'Any super-fresh cookies hiding in the back?'

'Just some brown-on-the-edges ginger thins. I couldn't put them out for sale.'

He smiled disarmingly. 'I'll take them off your hands. They should get me through my workout.'

As he'd no doubt expected, she glanced at his arms. Under his scrub top he wore a long-sleeved performance athletic shirt that molded to his biceps in a way that would have made anyone single and not dead-below-the-waist very excitable. Even in her uninterested state, she became aware of how skimpy her USea shirt really was as he gave her the once-over.

'Better than the garbage can,' she said, taken aback. There were a few cookies still in the glass case. Why wouldn't he just pay for some of those? Smiling thinly, she said, 'But remember I didn't sell them to you.'

He winked. She went into the back and grabbed the best three of the slightly burned treats and dropped them into a bag, then handed them to him over the counter.

'Why don't you have dinner with me tonight?' he asked. 'I'll be done with the gym at six. I could meet you at six-thirty, give you time to run home and put on something pretty. Art of the Table?'

She blinked at his naming of the expensive, artisanal restaurant. Straightening her shirt so that her cleavage was better covered, she said, 'Thank you, but I need to go home and get on with my second shift.'

'It's a fantastic restaurant,' he wheedled. 'I have a cousin who works in the kitchen.'

'How nice, Doctor O'Halloran, but I'm afraid I have a policy of not dating anyone in the hospital.' She didn't really, though of course she never had, but she was afraid he'd expect free food and coffee if they dated. She needed her job more than a date with the hospital's Dr O'Hottie.

His expression changed. A noise came from her right and she glanced over her shoulder. Kit was back from break. She hoped her co-worker would come out to have her back.

'I'm not used to being turned down,' he said, brows furrowed in a rather adorably confused way, like the hero of a rom-com who'd just been rejected. His floppy hair reminded her of the same sort of film cad.

Four nurses appeared from the elevator bay, heading in her direction for their coffees. They were a bit late, and must have been having a unit meeting. She saw another pair descending from the elevator, including Reese. Some of the offices must be done for the day, too.

'I'm sorry, Doctor,' Mandy said as Kit hurried out. 'I'm afraid I have to get going. Fannah doesn't like me to clock out late.' She would hide in the back for a few minutes until she knew he was gone.

'I get what I want, Mandy,' he announced.

'I'm not a product we sell at the coffee bar,' she replied, forcing what she hoped was a disarming smile over the sound of her pounding heart.

But his expression hardened. He hadn't taken her comment in the way she'd hoped. He leaned in. 'Listen here,' he snapped.

The nurses converged behind him, forming a line, their mouths open and eyes wide. Kit stepped to the counter, shoulder-to-shoulder with Mandy, looking fierce.

Dr O'Hottie, no fool, could read Kit's protective body language if not the reactions of the women behind him. He narrowed his eyes at Mandy, then relaxed his face, picked up his cup and strode away. Mandy watched him head out the door toward the parking garage. None of the women spoke for a second.

'I'll get your orders,' Kit said quickly. The first two in line always ordered the same thing.

Mandy rang them up quickly, figuring she could defend a few minutes of overtime to Fannah given the run on the coffee bar.

Reese was next in line and stood in front of Mandy as the first nurses stepped to the side. 'What was that all about?'

'He asked me out,' Mandy said in a low voice.

'He's been very irritable lately,' said the nurse behind Reese, while her friend, a decade older than the others, put her hand over her heart, displaying her wedding ring.

'Maybe he just needs to get laid,' Reese said.

The nurses waiting for Kit to finish snickered.

Mandy rolled her eyes. 'You can have him. Although I doubt he's a Hindu.'

'I'll take him,' said the sentimental nurse.

Her friend bumped her shoulder. 'What would your husband say?'

The half-dozen nurses all laughed. Mandy quickly rang up the rest of the orders while Kit made them, then she went into the back and clocked out, only seven minutes late.

In the back, she grabbed her coat, purse and planner, but instead of leaving while the nurses were still out there, sat in Fannah's office chair and decompressed. What a strange end to the day.

She opened her planner and took a look at her murder spread. While she needed to think some more about Reese, she added Dr O'Halloran to her co-worker list, given his temper. Maybe Ryan had infuriated him at work somehow. She needed to find out if something had happened between them.

Scrolling through her phone, she looked for Scott's number, but it appeared that she'd never had it. She peeked out of the back room. The nurses had dispersed.

'Kit,' she called in a low voice. 'Do you have Scott Nelson's number?'

'Why?'

'I want to ask him a work question.'

Kit gave her a suspicious glance, then pulled out her phone and read out the number.

'Thanks,' Mandy said. Was she right? Had Kit had a fling with the maintenance supervisor? Before she thought too hard about it, she typed out a text. *Hi Scott, this is Mandy from the coffee bar. Do you remember if my cousin ever had a run-in with Dr O'Halloran?*

FIFTEEN

When Mandy arrived home, she found an unfamiliar car at the end of her driveway, effectively blocking the entire entrance. She snapped a photo of the Washington State plates with her phone and drove around the block so she could park in the front of her house. Her thoughts churned. Vellum could have a friend over, but she didn't have any friends who had their licenses and permission to drive with fellow teens in the car.

She parked and called Vellum.

'Mom, I have a yearbook meeting today,' Vellum said in an irritated voice when she picked up.

'I just wanted to make sure. There's a car blocking our driveway.'

'I'm still at school.'

'OK. Have fun. Call me if you need a ride home.'

'I'm fine,' Vellum said, still exasperated.

'Love you.' Mandy hung up. Should she call the police?

A knock on her passenger window sent her stomach plummeting into her intestines. Mandy shrieked and flung out her arm. Her phone dropped into her lap. She ducked her head to see who'd knocked and saw her cousin Jasmine.

Mandy closed her eyes. Now what? She grabbed her phone, her purse and her tote bag and climbed out of the car, making sure to be out of punching distance when she stepped onto the sidewalk.

'I honestly don't think a single thing that belonged to Ryan is still in the house,' she said defensively.

'I'm not here for that.' Jasmine shifted from side to side. Her hair was short and dark, making it obvious that the blond had been a wig. Her heavily made-up eyes hid her feelings, but her mouth held distress.

'What's wrong? I mean, other than just losing your brother.' Mandy's voice caught with emotion.

She fidgeted uneasily again, ignoring the intensifying shards of rain. 'I spoke to my therapist today. She said no one could be blamed for Ryan's drinking.'

Mandy nodded. 'It's a disease. I didn't enable it in any way.'

'You gave him a home,' Jasmine said in a dark tone.

Mandy didn't see that as a problem. 'He had a steady job. He could afford it, here or somewhere else. Honestly, I think he was enabling me to stay here.'

Jasmine folded her arms over her chest. 'I never understood your relationship.'

'I know. But he was good to me.'

Jasmine sniffed. 'And now neither of us have him.'

Mandy's lips trembled. She closed the distance between them and pulled Jasmine into a hug. Her cousin pressed her face into Mandy's knit cap and squeezed her hard. After a long moment, they pulled away simultaneously.

Mandy blinked away tears. 'You have my dad's ears. I never noticed that before.'

Jasmine touched her ears. 'My hair usually covers them.' They stuck out a little bit.

'Want to come inside for a cup of coffee? I might still have some cinnamon streusel muffins in the freezer.'

'Just coffee. I don't eat carbs.'

Mandy didn't want prickly Jasmine back, so she just smiled and went up the steps and under the archway. At her front door, she found a package from an art supply company, probably some swag to review, and a number of envelopes. 'If you want to go into the kitchen, I'll be there in a second.' She bent to pick up her mail and then took off her coat before following her cousin.

Mandy filled her coffeemaker and switched it on. 'I think I have some edamame in the freezer. Should I heat that up?'

'That's OK,' Jasmine said, leaning against the stove. 'You don't have to feed me. Where is Vellum?'

'At a meeting. We have at least an hour until she gets home.'

'Do you think Ryan had any hidey holes?' Jasmine asked.

Mandy hesitated. 'I honestly don't know of any in the basement, but I'm as stumped as you are about where Ryan's money went. He had that job for years. It's not like he'd have debts to pay off, you know, interest rates eating up his income or anything.'

'He had a girlfriend about five years ago who was a real opportunist.'

'Keep going,' Mandy said, pulling a pint carton from the kitchen. 'You still put coconut creamer in your coffee, right?'

'Yes. Anyway, she would demand expensive gifts and Ryan supplied them. I'm sure every penny back then went to her. It's possible some of the jewelry was on instalment plan.'

'I remember her, I think. Wore a lot of leopard print.' Mandy considered the idea. 'It might have taken a couple of years to pay off.'

'Right. But not five.'

Mandy hit the button to start the first cup of coffee brewing. The machine churned. Mandy's phone burbled from a distant room. She went into the living room and retrieved it.

Scott had texted back. His text said, *Dr O yelled at Ryan once for bringing the wrong lightbulbs for his assigned locker. It made the lights flicker.*

When was that? Mandy texted back.

Around Christmas. I can't remember anything else. Why? replied Scott.

Just wondering. Mandy thought quickly and typed again. *You know, how stable Ryan was toward the end.*

The answer came just as fast. *I told you his job was at risk.*

Yep. That tells me all I wanted to know. Thanks. Mandy texted back, then shoved her phone into her pocket and went back to the kitchen. The first coffee cup had filled. She handed it to Jasmine, then started another pod brewing for herself.

'You didn't keep any cans of coins, did you? Maybe they are in an out-of-the-way place? I'd understand if you did,' Jasmine said quickly. 'I remember Grandma complaining about all those heavy jars of Grandpa's pennies that were in the garage and what a pain they were to deal with.'

'I remember that too, but why do you think there were more coins around?'

'There was a box of empty coin rolls.' Jasmine took a drink of her coffee, then licked her lips. 'I thought maybe he rolled up his change, you know, to keep his hands busy? Something to do to keep from drinking.'

'I know he picked up coins all over the place. He always did, remember?'

'I remember when he saw a penny on the ground, he always pointed it out to you so you could pick it up for good luck.'

Mandy smiled. 'He did look out for me when we were kids. I wish alcoholism hadn't caught him. Who else drank in our family?'

'Grandma's father, from what I've heard,' Jasmine said.

Mandy retrieved her cup from the coffee machine. 'Ryan probably rolled his change and put it in the bank.'

'No bank account, remember?'

'Maybe Dylan and Alexis took them to their bank,' Mandy said. 'Let's go downstairs. We can comb the basement and see if I'm missing something.'

Jasmine unzipped her four-inch heeled boots. 'Let's do it, but not because I'm accusing you of hiding anything.' She smiled at Mandy.

Mandy took the boots from her and set them against the wall. Maybe she couldn't have Ryan back, but perhaps with the jealousy terminated because of his death, she could have a friendship with her other cousin.

She and Jasmine spent a delightful couple of hours together. That had not been a guaranteed result, once they discovered one pasta sauce jar full of American pennies and a Cool Whip tub full of Canadian coins in Mandy's Christmas decoration closet.

She had genuinely thought she and Linda had packed everything and hated to be caught in a lie. But Jasmine poked through the containers and determined the pennies weren't covering anything more valuable, so she remained calm. She'd even helped Mandy bring it all upstairs to clear out the closet.

After that, Mandy had been forced to play detective with Jasmine, checking the carpet edges for pulled up spots, wandering along the walls looking for hidden compartments or old cabinets like the one on the stairs. They had opened Great-Grandma's sideboard and gone through the cabinets, poked around the laundry room, and found nothing more that belonged to Ryan.

Jasmine had left in a good mood, and Mandy had been left with an empty stomach that had sent her over to Linda's for a brownie before picking up Vellum at the bus stop.

When she walked Vellum home, she saw Crystal drive by. She

sent Vellum inside and waited for her neighbor to get out of her car, then pounced.

'Did the police ever talk to you about the night Ryan died?' Mandy asked, crossing her arms over her chest for warmth.

Crystal frowned and scratched a scab on her chin. 'Yeah, but I wasn't home. I didn't hear anything.'

'You were out?'

'Yeah, getting take-out. Why?'

'Well, someone got into my house. I thought maybe they crossed through your yard or something.'

Crystal shrugged. 'Wasn't home. The kids had the TV going so they didn't hear anything.'

'Right.' Mandy forced a smile. 'Well, thanks.' Even the Roswell kids had each other for an alibi. Aiden might have pushed Ryan down a flight of steps, but the kid would have a tough time striking a grown man on the back of the head with a hammer. On to the next idea.

Mandy loved Tuesdays. For a couple of hours, she could pretend she worked from home full-time, before reality hit and she had to climb into her car for a drive to the USea Hospital for the start of her shift. At least she wasn't Kit, having to go straight from one job to the next.

Oh, right, that *was* exactly her life too. When she booted up her computer that morning, she found a dozen new sticker orders, all of them including the new cherry blossoms. Her latest designs appeared to be a hit.

Warbling 'Happy days are here again,' she filled out her inventory sheet, but since she had no idea what the rest of the song was, just hummed as she drank coffee and readied her orders. By the time she updated her finance spread and grabbed the envelopes, she had just enough time to drop them off and still make it past the University of Washington sprawl, the Montlake Bridge, and on to the hospital.

At the hospital's front entrance, she saw a couple of police cars driving away as she walked up the slope between the parking garage and the main doors at nine-twenty. Nothing unusual, as they often came to take reports from victims, but she noticed the police more often now and wondered if Detective Justin Ahola ever handled cases around here. She had only the foggiest notion of how the police were organized.

Still though, when she walked into the main hall, it seemed more chaotic than usual. A bad accident, or even a murder?

'There you are,' Fannah snapped as Mandy walked through the door. 'I've been texting you since seven-fifteen!'

'My shift starts at nine-thirty on Tuesdays,' Mandy said evenly, trying to hold onto her good mood. She clocked in then went to stand next to Fannah, who was shuffling through papers on her desk.

'Kit didn't show up for her shift, so I tried to reach you.'

Mandy reached into her slacks for her phone, then realized she was wearing a pair without pockets. What had she done with her phone after checking it this morning? She thought back. 'I must have left my phone on my bed. I never went back in my bedroom after I put my makeup on. Sorry.'

Fannah huffed. 'That's very irresponsible of you.'

'Sorry,' Mandy said. Had Kit decided to ghost the coffee bar? 'Did you find her?'

'Oh, yes,' Fannah said. 'A security guard came by to tell me, but not until eight-fifteen a.m., mind you, that Kit was assaulted in the hospital parking garage last night.'

Mandy's mouth dropped open. 'Is she OK?'

Fannah rolled her eyes. 'Just bruises, but she decided to take the day off without notifying me. Can you imagine? I could fire her for that. I had a rather harsh phone call with her.'

'I would start looking for a new hire,' Mandy said in her most delicate tone. She didn't want to betray Kit's trust, but she knew they'd need another person soon. 'At least you'd have a backup for emergencies. Which this certainly is.'

'Yes, poor Kit.' Fannah muttered something in another language and pointed at the door. 'You need to get out there and open up.'

'Open up?' Mandy gasped. 'You mean we've been closed all morning?'

Fannah's face shuttered. 'I couldn't track her down and run the counter, could I? We've been open intermittently.'

Mandy ignored Fannah's commentary and rushed through the door. She turned on the lights and took the 'Emergency Closure' sign off the counter. As if by magic, the ant-like trails of people in the front hall changed course and began to line up in front of the cash register.

While Mandy frantically took money and filled orders, her brain churned with questions about what had happened to Kit. First of all, had it actually happened at all or was it just an excuse?

She supposed if Security and the police were involved, something had occurred. Therefore, the next question was: was it random or related to Ryan's death somehow?

She had no answers, but was shocked to see Kit appear behind the coffee bar at noon, with dark pink and purple circles under her eyes and a visibly cut lip. One hand was bandaged around her palm. 'Are you OK? What are you doing here?'

Kit sighed. 'It was a rough night, but I can't afford to miss more hours.'

'Oh, Kit,' Mandy said, going to her for a hug, but Kit stood, wooden-doll like, instead of returning her gesture. She stepped away. 'What happened?'

'Someone punched me in the face just as the elevator door opened. I fell into a garbage can and cut my hand.'

'Security cameras?'

'Not at that angle. They probably knew what they were doing.'

'Did they take your backpack?' Kit carried one everywhere she went.

'No, they shoved their hands into my pockets, but then they ran.' Kit pointed to the counter. 'Incoming.'

Mandy whirled around and forced a fake smile at Dr Burrell. 'The regular?'

He pulled off his glasses for a moment. 'I thought I didn't have a regular order?'

For the first time, she realized he had the looks of a craggier Chris Pine. Dr Burrell could fit in on a *Wonder Woman* set. 'I'm trying to turn it into our little joke,' Mandy explained.

His face lit with a smile. He put his glasses back on. 'I'd like that. And I'll take this last egg salad sandwich and a coffee.'

His glasses didn't do anything for his face. They were the wrong shape. He went back to being invisible Dr Burrell. 'Anything for you, Doctor B.' Mandy rang him up. Silently, Kit pushed a cup over the counter toward the surgeon.

'How did you avoid having your nose broken?' the surgeon asked, staring at Kit's eyes.

She pointed to the cup until he picked it up. 'I don't know. It's all a blur.'

'I hope we don't lose you over this,' he exclaimed. 'What a thing to happen.'

'Don't worry,' Kit assured him. 'I'm not quitting. It could have happened anywhere.'

'Unfortunately true,' he agreed.

The customers behind him inched forward, eager for their caffeine fix. Mandy sent the surgeon on his way and waited on the next batch of customers, keeping very busy until Fannah sent her on her lunch break.

Mandy went into the back room. She needed to remain alert on hospital grounds from now on. No daydreaming or staring at her phone while waiting for elevators. When she remembered her phone, that was. Before she headed to the cafeteria, she called Vellum from the backroom's extension and left a message about not having her cell on her.

Then she went up the steps to get her lunch. She hadn't seen Dr O'Halloran at all today. The surgeon continued to make her nervous. Could he have somehow mistaken Kit for Mandy and attacked her as revenge for his public humiliation? It didn't seem as if whoever had done it had been very serious about robbing Kit. Maybe there had been another motivation. But it seemed odd that her cousin had been murdered and her co-worker attacked just two weeks apart.

Dr O'Hottie appeared at the coffee bar at two o'clock. Kit waited on him as Mandy was busy making specialty drinks for a half-dozen family members there to see a new mother. Listening to Kit flirt with the surgeon, Mandy didn't sense anything sinister in his actions or behavior. She added his order to her list and kept making drinks as customers swarmed the coffee bar.

Kit clocked out promptly at three-thirty, leaving Mandy's hands full as they had not had a lull since one-thirty. She worked steadily, her arms aching and her head spinning as she turned to the cash register, then made drinks, then spun again, rinse and repeat. A conference let out at five and she had a run on coffees for the participants' drives home, meaning she had to brew coffee and refill the urns.

Finally, at five-thirty, it slowed down and she could clean up the mess. Staring at the puddles of espresso, dots of milk froth, and all the containers around the sink, she sighed and wished she could turn on some peppy music to keep her going like she could when she cleaned at home. Some early 2000s' pop music would be perfect about now.

She had just finished with the sink when she heard footsteps. When she turned she saw Jeanie Christie, the ER nurse, along with a younger woman in scrubs who she saw rarely enough that she hadn't been introduced.

'Double shift, Jeanie?' she asked.

'Emergency surgery,' Jeanie said. 'Listen, I like you, so I'm giving you a heads up.' She nodded at the other woman.

'I'm Doctor Nguyen,' the other woman said.

'She's an intern,' Jeannie explained.

'Doctor O'Halloran's hands were shaking so badly he was dismissed from the surgery today,' Dr Nguyen whispered.

'Oh my goodness,' Mandy breathed. 'He was here at two.'

'Are you sure?'

'Yes. My co-worker Kit took the cash register just in time to wait on him because I was busy with other orders. I didn't talk to him.' She didn't explain why the encounter had been memorable.

'Did you make his drink?'

'Yes. His usual quad shot.'

Dr Nguyen's brows lifted. 'Well, he's blaming you for his hands. He said you gave him a quad shot instead of a double.'

Mandy frowned. 'He always orders a quad shot. I'm sure that's not it.'

'Maybe he only asked for a double?' Jeanie suggested.

Mandy opened her mouth to deny that, then realized she didn't know. 'I made it on autopilot in between multiple orders. I suppose it's possible but, oh . . .' She rubbed her eyes. 'The cup would have been equally full either way. We get so busy sometimes you just assume regulars want their regular order. It's kind of a badge of honor to have one.'

'Did he have a quad shot earlier in the day?'

'Not when I was working,' Mandy said. 'But if there is going to be an investigation, they'll have to talk to Kit and Fannah as well.'

'He's being forced to take a blood test,' Jeanie told her.

'What kind?'

'Certainly they'll order a Theophylline and Caffeine Blood Test,' the nurse said, 'but also a basic blood workup to see what else is wrong.'

'He's been a little erratic lately,' Dr Nguyen whispered. She pulled her surgical cap lower on her forehead as if to help herself hide. 'The chief's policy for an incident like this is a drug screen, then a medical exam, and maybe even a chat with a psychiatrist, depending on what happened.'

'Wow.' Mandy's hands shook. Could she be fired for making a surgeon the wrong order? Why did all the bad things in her work life suddenly seem to revolve around Dr O'Halloran?

SIXTEEN

The next morning, Mandy arrived just before seven. She opened on Wednesdays, and unless someone had contacted Fannah outside of work, the boss lady wouldn't hear the latest Dr O'Halloran story until she came in at nine-thirty.

Kit arrived at eight-thirty. As she tied on her apron, Mandy gave her a passing glance and saw Kit had applied makeup around her eyes to hide the damage.

'So glad you're here,' Mandy said out of the side of her mouth. She'd been run off her feet since she turned on the lights. Most of the customers had been visiting patients.

'Full moon,' Kit told her, and bumped Mandy's shoulder so she could take over the cash register. 'Makes everyone hungry.'

Mandy moved aside to the espresso machine to make the drinks she'd just rung up. 'Donuts are sold out and there are only two muffins left.'

'Cool,' Kit said. 'Make some cookies as soon as you're done with that order. I'll hold down the fort.' She moved her jaw as if it ached, then forced a smile as she took a five-dollar bill from a customer.

An hour later, Mandy had just pulled cookies out of their toaster oven when Fannah clocked in. 'Running late?' Usually she appeared a few minutes before clock-in time.

'Accident on Broadway has everything snarled up.' Fannah was at the sink washing her hands when Kit poked her head into the doorway.

'You need to get back out here. There's a line four deep.' Kit dashed back to the cash register.

When Mandy saw Fannah's glare, she said, 'We don't have any baked goods to sell.' She quickly moved the cooling cookies to a tray, careful not to bend or break them, and rushed out to put them in the display.

Fifteen minutes later, all the cookies were sold. They sold even faster than black coffee, though Kit had more brewing. Fannah came out with another batch of ginger thins, an uncharacteristic smile on her face.

Fannah gestured at Mandy then returned to the back room. Mandy leaned through the doorway as Fannah pulled off her disposable gloves. 'I'm glad business is up again. I was getting worried.'

'It's been crazy since yesterday.'

'Full moon?' Fannah said.

'Too cloudy for me to tell but Kit says so,' Mandy said, remembering she had created a journal-sized lunar calendar for her online shop. Even though science had basically disproved lunar involvement in things like births, people still believed the old wives' tales.

'Hmmm. I hope it keeps up.'

'I need to get back out there.'

'I just want you to mix up more cookies. All the batter is gone,' Fannah said. 'I'll take over the register.'

Mandy cleared her throat. 'I need to give you a head's up.'

'On what?' Fannah dropped her gloves into the garbage can.

Mandy told her about Dr O'Halloran's quad shot claim.

'I can run a report and see what he paid for,' Fannah said. 'But someone who is used to quad shots shouldn't react so severely as to be removed from a surgery.'

Mandy nodded her agreement. 'Probably he's just coming down with something. I've seen signs of another flu outbreak.'

'Those surgeons like to believe they are superheroes,' Fannah said disdainfully. 'Hopefully Doctor O's craziness won't get out and hurt him, or us. But I'll run a full report on his employee payments from yesterday, since we don't know if he ordered multiple times.'

'I had better tell you something else,' Mandy said, wishing she didn't have to. 'You know about the biscotti betrayal, but the thing is, he asked me out recently and I said no. I feel like I have a target on my back where's he's concerned.'

'These alpha males love to cause trouble when we say no,' Fannah said. 'Look at Scott.'

'What about him?'

'The security camera drama? He's jerking us around because I shot him down,' she said with an expressive roll of her eyes.

'Right.' Mandy hadn't even considered that possibility. 'I should have figured that out.'

'Men.' Fannah clicked her tongue against her teeth.

'Men,' Mandy echoed.

Fannah pointed toward the toaster oven and stepped around her.

Mandy realized their scant moment of bonding had ended, and headed into the prep room. 'Right. Cookies.'

When Mandy returned from her lunch break, she found Fannah in the back room, leaning against their cubbies while the ER's chief medical resident took her desk chair. Zvonimir Krygier wore a thick gold wedding ring and spoke of his wife often, which kept him from receiving too much attention from female staff, so he wasn't there to flirt with Fannah. Mandy thought he looked younger than Dr O'Halloran, who reported to him, and wondered why her surgeon frenemy was still a resident.

'Doctor Krygier came to give us an update on the O'Halloran matter,' Fannah announced.

Mandy nodded, all pleasure from her excellent salad lunch vanishing.

The doctor's gaze narrowed on her. Mandy shifted uncomfortably as he considered her for a long moment before speaking.

'Fannah tells me that you informed her of the gossip regarding our surgical incident yesterday.'

Mandy rubbed at her eye. 'This morning.'

'In the ER, we follow a three-step policy when surgeons have been involved in an incident of this magnitude, which includes blood tests.'

She nodded.

The doctor continued. 'Doctor O'Halloran's blood test showed a therapeutic dose of Adderall, but he does not have a prescription.'

'What is that?' Mandy asked.

'It is a central nervous system stimulant. It is used to treat ADHD, among other conditions. It is also commonly abused.'

Mandy didn't want to ask the question. 'It's like an amphetamine, then? He was taking it to stay awake?'

'It is an amphetamine,' Fannah clarified.

'It can increase alertness, attention and energy level,' Dr Krygier confirmed. 'Which is why people abuse it. But the side effects include shaking, dizziness and paranoia.'

'Paranoia?' Mandy queried.

Dr Krygier stared hard at her. 'I'm telling you this because Doctor O'Halloran blames you for the medication being in his system.'

Mandy clutched one hand in the other. 'Me! What on earth . . .?'

'He claims you somehow gave it to him in his drink.'

She stared at the chief resident. 'I'm flummoxed. I'm just one of the baristas.'

'I told Doctor Krygier about Doctor O'Halloran asking you out,' Fannah said.

Mandy's memory flashed through a few high-school dramas, but she'd been with Cory so long that a lot of dating problems had not been part of her life. She could not fathom why someone she'd rejected in such a casual manner could have betrayed her so completely that he could cause her to be fired.

'Did you give Doctor O'Halloran Adderall in any way?' the resident asked.

'Of course not. I don't have access to it,' Mandy said. 'I've never given anyone anything except what they ordered from the coffee bar.'

'Very well,' the doctor said, in that calm surgeon's voice. 'We're done here for now.'

'Go give Kit her break,' Fannah said.

Mandy felt like her face had been frozen in confused horror as she turned back around. How was she supposed to hear these accusations and then return to work, helping customers, like nothing had happened?

On the other hand, she was lucky to have the opportunity to serve them. Dr O'Halloran could still cost her this job.

Mandy felt absolutely wrung out by the time she arrived home. They had worked double time all afternoon, serving many more customers than usual, and nearly all beverages because she couldn't keep up with cookie production. Even the string cheese and hard-boiled eggs in the refrigerated case were gone. On her way home, an accident on Madison had cost her twenty minutes. After a stop at Safeway to pick up a few groceries, she finally trundled home.

'Where have you been?' Vellum demanded, grabbing one of the bags from her mother's hand when she struggled into the mudroom at almost six.

'Long day,' Mandy said. 'But I have soup fixings.'

'You don't have time to cook tonight,' Vellum said impatiently. 'It's the eighteenth. We need to get the March 'Plan With Me' up and then the sticker orders will start pouring in.'

Mandy yawned, only covering her mouth with her hand halfway through. 'We'll fulfill orders all weekend. I do need to cook tonight or we're going to be living on pizza. I'll start the upload and then get that veggie quinoa soup together. It's mostly cans.' She waited for her daughter to say pizza was fine, but she didn't. Either Vellum actually wanted to eat healthy, or she knew money was tight.

'Fine, Mom, but don't wait, OK? I have a paper due Monday. I'm going to be busy at least half the weekend.'

'I thought you had an early-release day tomorrow? Some teacher in-service?'

'Yeah, but I have a test on Friday, so I'll use that time to study.'

Mandy regarded her. 'Will you be OK here alone all afternoon? If the traffic gods are kind I'll be home by four, but that's at least a couple of hours here alone. Do you want to go to Grandma's? Or the library?'

'I'll lock myself in my room,' Vellum said. 'And put my headphones on while I study. No ghosts in my bedroom.'

'I haven't seen anything in the laundry room, either,' Mandy said.

Vellum fixed her with a stare, then flipped her thick hair over her shoulder. 'Would you rather believe I saw an intruder? The murderer returning?'

'Ghost it is.' Wearily, Mandy saluted her, waved her hands vaguely at the grocery bags, and went to her computer. Even if there really had been an intruder, they'd have been after Ryan's possessions, which were long gone now. And she had all those new locks, too.

Mandy woke at five a.m. to the sound of her phone alerting her to a text. She struggled to a sitting position and blinked until her eyes focused.

I'll pay OT if you come in early, said the text from Fannah. *We need to restock.*

Mandy groaned and texted back. *On my way.* At least she'd pay off all the excess groceries from yesterday. When had the price of everything gone up?

Mandy arrived in the parking garage just as Fannah exited her car. They entered the back room together and clocked in. A full hour of overtime.

'Cookies,' Fannah ordered. 'I'll restock the cases.'

'Coffee?' Mandy croaked. She hadn't been able to get anything into her system at home.

'I'll do that first,' Fannah agreed. 'Who knows what today is going to be like.'

They worked frantically until Fannah turned on the lights at six-thirty. A line had already formed of nurses still gossiping about Dr O'Halloran. The general consensus seemed to be that he needed to be nursed back to health, since he was simply too good-looking to forget.

Mandy hid her revulsion and continued to take orders on auto-pilot. Fannah went around with a smile on her high-cheekboned face, looking more like a catalog model than a high-fashion one because of her expression.

'What's got her so happy?' Kit muttered, as Mandy walked past for her lunch break hours later.

'Ka-ching,' Mandy said in her ear. 'I think she gets a monthly bonus if our sales reach a certain point.'

By the time she arrived back from lunch, the coffee bar had slowed down. Mandy took the time in the prep room to change her USea T-shirt, which had acquired a coffee stain. When she walked into the back room to clock in, she found Fannah standing with two suit-wearing middle-aged men.

Fannah glared at her, all geniality vanished. Mandy clocked in, pretending to ignore the meeting, then went to take over the cash register from Kit.

'What's going on?' she whispered.

'They're from administration,' Kit said. 'I saw their titles on the badges when they walked by.'

'More about O'Hottie?'

'Probably.' Kit smiled as a harried young couple appeared at the cash register, holding balloons and a pink teddy bear.

After the pair was gone, Fannah appeared in the doorway.

'Put up the closed sign,' she snapped, and then turned off the coffee bar lights.

Mandy's pulse jumped. This couldn't be good.

Fannah gestured impatiently. As Kit walked forward, Mandy saw Scott and one of his jump-suited minions walking their way. She shrugged in their direction and went into the backroom.

The space wasn't tiny, but with five people in there it felt it. The aftershave one of the administrators wore filled up the space, instead of the usual delicious cookie smells. Mandy hoped it didn't infuse her precious baked goods.

'I'm Jason Cho, assistant hospital administrator,' one of them said.

The other man didn't speak, but Mandy spotted the word 'director' on his badge, though she couldn't read of what. 'Hello,' Mandy said.

Jason cleared his throat. Maybe the other man's overpowering cologne was bothering him too. 'A few nurses are ill. All of them reported coming here to the coffee bar.'

'We've had hundreds of customers this week,' Fannah said.

Jason pinched the bridge of his nose. 'All of these nurses have been vomiting about half an hour after they visited the coffee bar.'

'Is it one group of people?' Mandy asked. 'Like they all drank from a single coffee urn?'

'They all ordered cookies,' the director said, wafting fresh cologne in her direction as he turned.

Mandy squeezed her eyes closed. 'I cleaned out the oven just this morning.'

'Cleaning supply residue?' Fannah said.

Mandy shook her head. 'I clean it the same way every time. The products are the same. I wore gloves. I'm not ill, nor is my daughter.'

'I'm glad to hear that,' Jason said. 'We're going to bring in a team to disinfect your prep room and the bakery case. All the ingredients will be thrown out. Your supervisor will do the reordering.'

'Are we being laid off?' Kit asked.

'I'll be in touch when you can return to work,' Fannah said. 'But there has to be an investigation.'

'How many nurses?' Mandy asked. 'Why just nurses?'

'Three. We might not know if non-hospital employees became ill,' Jason said. 'Nurses are a specific population.'

'Yes, but we serve cookies to doctors, technicians, administrative personnel. Only nurses becoming ill makes no sense.' Mandy squeezed her fingers around the hem of her T-shirt, as if she could anchor herself to the bar. Hearing she might have made people sick made her own lunch sit uneasily in her stomach.

'We're investigating,' Jason said.

Mandy locked her muscles together to keep from trembling. 'I apologize if I did anything to make people sick, sir. But I genuinely can't think of anything.'

'We'll be in touch if we need to interview you further,' Fannah said formally. 'But I've been here with you all day and saw no sign of anything amiss.'

Mandy nodded, glad at least that Fannah wasn't turning her back on her employees in order to save herself.

'Keep the lights off,' Jason said. He and the odiferous director stepped around them. 'We'll be in touch.'

'We should empty the urns and do the cleanup,' Mandy said.

'Clock out,' Fannah said. 'I'm not in charge right now.'

'Fine,' Kit said. 'This is crazy. But I need to get my ID out of the till. I left it there for safekeeping.'

'Why?' Fannah asked.

Kit shrugged. 'I always do that. Remember when that janitor was stealing from desks a couple of years ago?'

Fannah handed her the cash register override key. 'Clock out first, then get your ID. And don't leave it there again.'

'I guess I'll head out,' Mandy said. 'Kit, do you want me to wait for you?'

'Don't bother. I took the bus today,' Kit said, not looking at her.

Mandy wanted to ask if she'd still receive overtime pay for her first hour, but she knew the answer was no. She was only getting a seven-hour shift today, and who knew when she'd get more hours.

Or if she had a job at all after today. After she clocked out, she grabbed her bag from her cubby and went out the back way, heading for the parking garage. Her emotions felt muted, maybe by the onslaught of cologne, but still, tears welled up in her eyes as she headed into the sky bridge that led to the parking garage.

'What's wrong?'

Mandy glanced up to see Dr Burrell, his eyes kind behind his glasses. He wore a plaid-lined jacket that looked like it belonged in a lumber camp, but it fit tightly enough to display his wide shoulders. They looked perfect to cry on, and she wished she could lean her head against the rough-looking coat and hide from the world.

'I was just coming to get coffee. You're off early.'

'We're shut down. Some nurses reported getting sick after they ate our cookies.'

'That's terrible,' he said softly. 'I love your cookies.'

'I know,' she choked out, then started to sob as she tried to tell him the story. 'Sorry.' She wiped her eyes.

'Don't worry,' he said after she slowed down. 'Most foodborne illnesses don't cause a reaction after just thirty minutes. They'll probably find out that the nurses all ate something tainted yesterday evening.'

She lifted her gaze. 'Really?'

He smiled at her. 'Really. Now why don't you go enjoy your unexpected afternoon off? I'm sure you have some calligraphy orders to fill.'

'Sticker orders,' she said. 'I probably have those.'

An unexpected dimple appeared in his right cheek as his smile deepened. 'There you go. Always with a plan. I have to get to surgery.'

She liked that view of herself. Always with a plan. 'Of course, Doctor Burrell. Have a good surgery.'

'It's Tristan,' he told her.

She blinked. 'Really?'

He shrugged. 'Romantic mother. And I never liked Stan, but that's what most people call me.'

'Tristan,' Mandy said, trying it out, though she had a little hitch in her voice as she held in a giggle. 'Much better.'

He winked at her then strode away.

She watched him move down the sky bridge, and decided he had just as good a body as Dr O'Hottie, and a much better person-ality. Maybe Tristan Burrell would be the next hospital heartthrob. But what would his nickname be?

SEVENTEEN

Mandy felt cheerier on the drive home thanks to her conversation with Dr Burrell, but as she scooped up the day's mail, she felt her tear ducts spiking with hot moisture again.

Loud clomping noises from Vellum's favorite heavy boots made her straighten, clutching their unpaid bills to her chest.

'What are you doing home so early? Do you have a fever?' Vellum stepped up to her and put her palm on Mandy's forehead. Her skin felt warm against Mandy's February outdoor chill. 'You're freezing.'

'That's from outside,' Mandy said. 'I'm not sick.'

'Then what's wrong?'

'I went into work an hour early,' Mandy temporized.

'But you're home two hours early,' Vellum pointed out.

Mandy sighed. 'I'm temporarily laid off while the bar is disinfected.'

Vellum went rigid. 'Why?'

Mandy put her hand on her daughter's arm. She could feel the tension as her muscles quivered. 'Don't worry, sweetheart. Some nurses reported becoming ill half an hour after visiting the coffee bar.'

'That's terrible!' Vellum exclaimed.

'I talked to Doctor Burrell on the way out and it didn't make sense to him. He said foodborne illness usually takes longer to affect people. It will probably turn out to be something else.'

'What if soap got into the coffee or something?'

'It was the cookies, supposedly.'

Vellum worried at her lip. 'Let's sit down, Mom.'

'OK, but I'm fine.' She winced as she followed her daughter to the sofa. While she might be sort of coping, something was happening with Vellum, and the mere thought of her baby being troubled made her own muscles tense in both sympathy and fear. 'What's going on with you?'

Vellum sat, then leaned against the sofa back and crossed her legs underneath her. 'I want to move in with Dad for a while.'

Mandy felt a sudden sense of weightlessness, as if the sofa had vanished beneath her and she floated on air. She put her hand to her throat, fighting to make her voice sound normal. 'Why?'

Her daughter shrugged. 'Because.'

'I'm sure I'll be back to work in a couple of days. Well, maybe Monday, since tomorrow is Friday. Nothing odd happened with the cookies. I'd served tons of them and I'd used the same mix for two days. I'm sure Doctor Burrell is right.'

Vellum poked Mandy's arm. 'You're babbling, Mom.'

'Sorry,' she said automatically, her mind churning. Those tears pricked her eyes again.

Vellum sighed, but the tension didn't leave her body. 'Mom, you can't afford me between the layoff and Ryan dying. You say we're taking the business seriously, but you aren't. We should have been doing sticker orders last night.'

'All weekend,' Mandy promised.

'We need to do them now,' Vellum said. 'I don't want to put more pressure on you. Dad has plenty of money. His family is rich. They can support me without blinking an eye.'

'You think I don't know that? It's his fault,' Mandy said, fighting for control. 'But even so, we were doing fine.'

'I know, Mom. Until Ryan died. How much money did he owe you?'

'Just for February. He was good about paying me.'

'You're on the ragged edge. You couldn't even pay my allowance. I'll come over to work on our videos. I believe in the business. I'll keep doing my share.'

'I have custody of you,' Mandy said.

'He has weekends. And I'm old enough to decide.'

'We have to go to court.'

'Why spend the money on lawyers?' Vellum asked. 'Just let me go, Mom. It's for the best. I promise you'll see me at least a couple of days a week.'

'As my business partner,' Mandy said glumly, 'not as my daughter.'

'I'm fifteen,' Vellum pointed out.

Mandy knew this speech, her daughter asserting how grown up

she was. She cut Vellum off. 'I know you're a sophomore in high school. You have more than two years of dependence to go. You don't need to give me the "I'm practically an adult" speech. Trust me, you aren't. You can go stay with Cory.' Rattled, she added, 'He has ignored so many days that he was supposed to take you that I'm sure we could go three weeks before it is made up.'

Vellum went still as a car shut off its engine in front of her house.

'You called him before talking to me?' Mandy asked, fighting to keep the accusation from her voice. 'You were going to leave before I came home from work. You didn't know I'd been laid off.'

'I heard a voicemail from your boss, Mom. She must have called the house instead of your cell phone by accident when the hospital administrator showed up.'

'You knew all along?'

'Sorry,' Vellum said.

They both listened as steps, once so familiar, came up the concrete stairs outside. 'Did you pack?'

'Yes. I'll come over Saturday and help you with orders, OK?'

'If you can get a ride,' Mandy said.

'You'll come get me, right?'

Mandy forced down her anger. This was her daughter, and who knew how she'd been manipulated by the Moffats. While Cory didn't want the responsibility of his daughter underfoot, her ex-mother-in-law would be thrilled. She might have offered to loosen the purse strings or something. For instance, Cory was driving a three-year-old BMW and Mandy knew that would irritate him. He liked his cars to be two years old or less. And because of his careless ways, his cars didn't look new for long. 'Of course. Anytime, day or night. Really, since I'm obviously not working tomorrow.'

'Saturday,' Vellum said with an air of beleaguered patience. 'I'll call you Saturday morning for a ride.'

'Got it. We can even stop at the bakery on the way home and get treats before we start work.'

'Don't spend any money right now,' Vellum said, then smiled. 'Maybe Dad will give me some spending money and I can treat you.' She winked, not realizing she was driving a dagger into her mother's heart, and bounced up from the sofa to open the door.

Mandy, unwilling to see what expression would be on her ex-husband's face – triumph, despair, or something else – went the long way around to the basement door, unbolted it, and fled downstairs to check on the laundry situation.

It continually amazed her how an otherwise intelligent teenager couldn't recognize the irony of asking the father who wouldn't pay his child support for spending money. The sad truth was that Cory would likely give Vellum what she asked for. Maybe she should craft a plan to get a child-support-worthy amount of spending money from him each month through Vellum.

She stuck last week's sheets into the washer and turned it on, then quickly toured the basement, making sure nothing had been disturbed. When she hummed under her breath, trying to fill the air, she swore she could hear an echo. So strange to have no furnishings in the rooms. It had not been like this since the day they moved in.

She wandered upstairs as the silence and cold got to her. In the art studio, she set up her camera and flipped her planner to her collection of journal spread ideas. She compared it to her list of videos to film and decided to work on a pen test page. Some journals had a page in the back, but that didn't mean they were formatted with brand, color name, color number, wash of color and calligraphy sample.

She also checked when she had last done a giveaway, and decided to set up a new journal for one of her subscribers to win. The pen test spread could go in that. She grabbed a new planner that a manufacturer had sent her that week and flipped on the camera, wanting to talk about the unfamiliar brand and why a pen test page would be important to make sure that pens didn't bleed through its particular paper.

After that, with the camera still on, she stopped speaking and picked up a ruler so she could set up the page with boxes. 'Better make this a double spread,' she said. 'I never use just one brand of pens. I like to have a set of pens I use for each month. My lettering pen, a pen for lines, and two or three colored pens to suit my theme.'

Her voice sounded thick, and when a drop fell on the page she realized it was a tear. She blotted the page with a tissue. 'It's been a rough day, guys,' she said. 'And I don't want to waste this spread.'

Realizing how idiotic she sounded, she shut off the camera and leaned back on her chair before she ruined the page. As it was, she'd buckled it with her tear and couldn't possibly send the journal to a contest winner now.

She grabbed her own journal. When she pulled off the elastic, it opened to her mood-tracker page. For February, she'd set up twenty-eight cactuses on shelves, and had chosen five different shades of green to color in based on her mood. On the sixteenth cactus of the month, she used a dark forest green. The moods she'd listed were 'Best Day Ever', 'Getting Stuff Done', 'Functional', 'Falling Behind' and 'Sad Face'.

She considered her spread. Way too much dark forest green. It had been a Sad Face month. Thinking back to the origins of the mood spread, how different journalers had tied them to sleep spreads, productivity spreads, recovery spreads, exercise spreads and the like, she realized a lot of her fellow journalers worried about mood disorders. Many had problems with depression and documented their lives in order to help themselves. 'A well-organized, proactive, group of depressives,' she muttered. Had she found her sisterhood without meaning to?

It didn't matter if she had. When in doubt, she made a quote page, something she needed to remember. She found a blank page after her most recent weekly spread and then searched on the internet until she found something that spoke to her. When she found the perfect quote, she penciled it in, alternating lines with faux calligraphy and block lettering. Then, she went over it all in black pen.

She sat back and looked at the wise words of Charles Dickens. 'The most important thing in life is to stop saying "I wish" and start saying "I will".'

She smiled. 'Thanks, Mister Dickens.' Of course, she had to do extra, so she chose orange and yellow Tombow dual brush pens and drew sunrays around the quote. Finally, she scanned the page into her computer just in case she wanted to make a sticker out of it at some point.

For now, she needed to listen to these words and get to work. Resolutely, she flipped to her list of sticker ideas and decided to do pastel sets of number strips in various colorways for spring. She could also do matching weekly headers, too. They would sell. Not the most exciting product, but the basics were important.

She spent the rest of the day on that, then, as the sky darkened, she put on her camera makeup and filmed an intro for her pen test video. She added teasers for her new pastel stickers and edited the video until her eyes blurred long after the moon had risen.

Now, she could sleep. Who needed fresh air to wear yourself out when you could stare at a screen half the night? Bedtime didn't matter during a layoff.

The next morning, Mandy rolled over when something disturbed her. 'C'mon, Zac, I'm sleeping,' she muttered, then her eyes shot open when she registered the sound of her own voice. Had she really spoken out loud to Zac Efron? 'I'm losing it.'

Her phone rang. Again. That had been what woke her up. She glanced at the time as she accepted the call. Ten-thirty in the morning. Exactly how late had she stayed up? She didn't usually sleep in like this.

'Hello?' she quavered.

'Good news,' Fannah said.

Mandy blinked. 'Aren't you laid off like us?'

'I was called in an hour ago and just left a meeting.'

Mandy heard excitement in her supervisor's voice. 'A good meeting?'

'Yes. You've been exonerated, along with the coffee bar.'

'We didn't get anyone sick?'

'No.' Fannah's voice had gone all high-pitched, then calmed. 'When I went to Mister Cho's office, he said all three nurses were put on the spot when they arrived for their shifts today. I'd certainly have been suspicious if they were all perfectly well again so soon after vomiting.'

'What happened?'

'They were taken into a conference room and told they were being sent to mandatory drug testing.'

'Like a pee test?'

'Exactly. Employees are subject to them at will. Right then and there, one of them fessed up. The weak link, I suppose.'

'They took some kind of drug that got them sick?'

'You bet.' Mandy heard Fannah smack her lips. 'When faced with drug tests, all three nurses admitted they took Adderall.'

'Wow. Just like Doctor O'Halloran.'

'Mister Cho was smart enough to ask them where they got it, and it wasn't from you or me.'

'Who from, then?'

'He didn't say, but we're cleared to work. I'm in the prep room now and it's been thoroughly wiped down. Everything perishable was thrown out but I'll have all of our non-dairy and dairy milks replenished by noon and we'll have smoothie ingredients on Monday. Can you be here at noon? Then we can reopen.'

'What about Kit?'

'I can't reach her.'

Mandy wondered if she'd picked up an extra shift at her new job. 'I guess if we don't open until noon it's no trouble for us both to work until six.'

'That's my plan. Can you stay?'

'Yes,' Mandy said. 'That's fine. I'll be there at noon.' She disconnected from the call and wiped sleep from her eyes. Her neck ached from her long night of video work. In her layoff frenzy, she'd done what was normally two days of work in one half day and reached the upload process before her eyes had blurred. The video was only eight minutes, half her usual length. She hoped she hadn't brought down the quality of her vlogging.

Mandy was blinking hard, trying to stay alert, when Dr Burrell appeared at her counter later that day. She stared at him. 'Did you appear out of nowhere? I didn't see you coming.'

He chuckled. 'Late night? I saw you loaded a video in the wee hours.'

She goggled at him. 'How do you know that?'

He mimicked hitting buttons on his phone. 'Like and subscribe, right? Remember to hit the bell so you'll get notifications?'

She put her hands to her face and then smoothed curls back behind her ears. 'You really have watched at least one of my videos.'

'You bet,' he said lightly. 'What are you doing back here? Yesterday you were cruising for a breakdown due to your layoff.'

'Exonerated.'

His blue eyes brightened. Maybe they'd just caught the light, but that Chris Pine resemblance intensified. 'Excellent. I knew your cookies couldn't be poison.'

'Very funny, Doctor.' She made a face at him. 'The Adderall problem is getting worse. First Doctor O'Halloran, and now all three of those nurses.'

'Ah, so that's what was going on.' He winced.

She nodded. 'When faced with a drug test, they admitted it.'

'I hope you ban them from the coffee shop for life. Assuming they still have jobs here.'

'I hope not. Abusing drugs, lying about it, and threatening the coffee bar and the livelihoods of the employees?'

'Your co-worker was assaulted not too long ago, right?' Dr Burrell asked. He stretched out his hand and she gave him a paper coffee cup, then followed him around the inside ring of the counter while he moved to the urns.

'Monday night. It's been a horrible week.'

He loaded his cup with dark roast. 'I wonder if that's related somehow. A couple of years ago, a nurse who worked with me in the NICU unit was assaulted at the bottom level of the parking garage.'

'What does that have to do with what happened?'

He opened a shelf-stable creamer and splashed it on top of his coffee, barely changing the dark color, then snapped a lid on. She handed him a cup guard.

'She had a personal alarm and was able to turn it on. Security reached her quickly and the assailant was still in the garage. They found Adderall when they searched him.'

'He was her dealer?'

'No, at least I don't think so. She had her third child about six months later and quit to stay home with her family after that.'

She shuddered. 'Pregnant and assaulted.'

He winced. 'She told me that's why her husband had given her the personal alarm. Because of her job she was out late at night.'

'I'm glad she could afford to stay home after that.' She walked back to the cash register and rang him up. 'We should have real milk and cookies again on Monday. The weekend team isn't going to have much to work with.'

Fannah bustled out of the back room, carrying a plastic tub of biscotti, individually packaged nuts, and stroopwafels. 'Don't mind me. Without the baked goods we have been selling out of the packaged goods.'

'Glad to see you back at work, Fannah,' Dr Burrell said.

She flashed the doctor a megawatt smile. 'Me too, Stan. Yesterday was not a good day.'

'No Kit?'

'Still haven't been able to reach her.'

Mandy considered Fannah's unusual friendliness. Was she watching a love connection develop between her boss and the increasingly handsome neonatologist?

Dr Burrell paid for his coffee, nodded in Mandy's direction, then strode off toward the elevators.

'He works too hard,' Fannah said. 'Needs a good woman.'

Mandy leaned over the counter. 'You, maybe?'

'Eh? I'm older than he is.'

'I wasn't aware that we knew the actual ages of the doctors,' Mandy teased.

Fannah slotted in the biscotti. 'Only the nice ones. He would be a prize for the right woman.'

'And who is that?'

Fannah fit in all but one of the nut packages. 'Someone who can teach him that life is not all about work. Make a family with him. Unlike that Doctor O'Hottie, who is all about playtime.'

'He's gone, anyway,' Mandy said.

Fannah concentrated on sliding in the stroopwafels without bending the delicate caramel-filled concoctions. 'Oh, he'll be back.'

'Really? After using drugs on the job?'

'Doctors get special treatment.' Fannah picked up her empty tub. 'They have rehab programs that have up to a ninety-five percent success rate, close to double the success rate of less specialized programs.'

'I guess it's good to be a doctor.'

Fannah curled her lip and walked back behind the coffee bar. 'I wouldn't want to be an addict and be around drugs all day.'

'If rehab works they must figure out how to cope with it.' Mandy turned, but Fannah had already disappeared from view into the back room. So much for their conversation. She sighed and pulled out her phone, ready to text Detective Ahola with the information

Dr Burrell had recalled. But then a trio of surgical nurses approached and she had to shove her phone back into her pocket.

When Mandy and Vellum checked statistics on Saturday morning while digging into the lattes and cinnamon chip scones that Cory had unwittingly provided with Vellum's spending money, they discovered wonderful news. The March 'Plan with Me' video, with its minimalist snowdrop theme, was a huge success.

'I'll start up the printers and cutters,' Vellum said.

Mandy wiped her hands on a napkin. 'I have a bunch of snowdrop stickers ready, but I'm guessing we need at least double what I prepped. It's going to be a long, loud day.'

Vellum snapped her fingers. 'That's what I like. Vellum wants a car someday.'

'Vellum had better stop speaking about herself in the third person, like her father,' Mandy said. 'Terrible habit.'

'It's very insincere,' Vellum agreed. 'Why did you marry him again?'

'I was pregnant,' Mandy said, gathering their garbage.

'How did that happen?'

Mandy turned in the doorway, the crumbs, cup and napkin-filled sack still in her hands. 'You've never asked me that before.'

'I'm getting older.'

Mandy looked, really looked, at Vellum. When had she grown so big? She must be a couple of inches taller than Mandy now, even without those boots she loved. And her hair framed her lovely, heart-shaped face with heartbreaking grace. Vellum didn't like praise about her appearance, since she only saw her dusting of teenage acne when she looked in the mirror, but she was a stunner. Were boys already trying to take her to bed?

'I know you are,' Mandy agreed. 'I was dating your father. On and off for two years. He never took anything or anyone very seriously, but he seemed charming in those days.'

'He married you.'

Mandy nodded. 'Surprisingly. I think his family wanted their heir born into wedlock. Your grandmother is very old-fashioned.'

Vellum sniffed. 'She never talks about my future career, just my future husband. At least she expects me to find him in college.'

'You're in a rare position of having college completely funded.'

'As long as I don't mess anything up with them,' Vellum said in a small voice.

Mandy gave her a moment to gather her thoughts while she dumped the trash and washed her hands. 'What's up?' she asked when she returned.

Vellum cleared her throat and pulled a freshly printed sticker page from the printer and loaded it to the cutting board. 'Just that Grandma is really critical. She wants to buy me a new wardrobe and a really expensive and time-consuming skincare line.'

'Ah,' Mandy said. 'Free stuff.'

Vellum glared. 'It's not like that. It's not anything I want and she wants to throw out what I love, like my boots. And Dad hates her.'

'Hate is a strong word.'

'He's capable of it. You should have heard what he said about you last year, and then about Ryan when he moved in.'

Mandy's nerves sent painful pinpricks into her hands. 'What did he say about Ryan?'

'He didn't think the two of you would survive living together,' Vellum explained.

Mandy's jaw tightened. 'Was it a comment or a threat?'

'He said he thought he and Ryan would come to blows. Remember all that drama over those bar glasses? And that was only what we saw.' Vellum set the sticker sheet into the cutter then met Mandy's eyes. 'You don't think Dad killed Ryan, do you?'

EIGHTEEN

'Of course not,' Mandy said automatically. 'Your father wouldn't kill Ryan.'

'Are you sure? I know you want to believe Reese did it, but what are the chances? I mean, business is great,' Vellum said, pointing at the clattering machines, 'but it's not that big of a deal.'

Mandy sighed. 'I have no idea who killed Ryan. I feel like I'm failing him, like I'm missing something.'

'You already work two jobs,' Vellum said. 'Give yourself a break.'

'I don't want a break. Most certainly not one from you.' She hoped Cory never learned that his daughter considered him capable of murder.

'I'm sorry, Mom.'

'I only lost a couple of hours of pay,' Mandy told her. 'I'm already back at the coffee counter. You don't need to worry about my finances.'

Vellum nodded. 'That's great, but like you said, I need to stay in Grandma's good graces. If I come back here after one day, I'm not going to look very responsible.'

'You aren't coming back?'

Vellum closed her eyes. Mandy could tell she was prepping for a negotiation. She knew this precious young woman so well.

'I'll come back when Ryan's killer is found,' Vellum said. 'You should talk to the police.'

'Oh no!' Mandy exclaimed.

'What?'

'I forgot to call Detective Ahola about the drug dealer.' She quickly explained what Dr Burrell had told her, then called and left a message on the detective's phone. 'OK, let's get back to making money.'

They worked until dinner time on Saturday, then Mandy drove Vellum back to the Moffats and returned home. That evening, when Mandy needed a break from her own thoughts, she busied herself with liking and responding to comments on her video page about March, and taking suggestions for the April video, which of course she'd already filmed. However, lots of people were asking for tulips, and she'd done cherry blossoms.

She ignored it all and went to bed. Vellum had to be picked up at eight so they could put in another full day before Sunday dinner with her grandmother.

Early on Sunday afternoon, Mandy took a break and returned to the video comments. By the fortieth comment begging for tulips, she dropped her head into her hands and moaned.

'What's wrong?' Vellum asked, as she used a sponge to close a set of twenty envelopes stuffed with the snowdrop kit.

'Everyone wants tulips, not cherry blossoms. Even Reese wants me to do a tulip theme for April.'

'The April video is entirely finished.'

'I could do a second one. The question is, would that bring more income for more work, or just double the work and split the business?'

Vellum shrugged. 'You won't know until you try. I can handle the orders we have left. Why don't you find some reference photos and do some sketching?'

On Monday, Mandy's coffee bar customers were in a chatty mood. She welcomed the distraction, rubbing at her aching arms while they gossiped about the shutdown, the disgraced nurses, the extra shifts others would have to work as a result. The maintenance department was busy replacing lightbulbs all over the hospital, which always went out in waves.

Scott, minion-free for once, appeared just after Mandy's lunch break. 'How's it going?'

'Can't complain,' Mandy said, wishing she'd taken a painkiller at lunch to counteract the hours of sketching she'd done yesterday. She still hadn't decided whether she'd release the tulip kit after nailing down a color scheme, or just do a cute sticker sheet matched with her new pastel weekly headers and number sets.

'Well, I can. Give me your largest coffee.'

Mandy pointed to the bucket of bulbs in his hand. 'Bucket of coffee?'

'Got that much in your urns?'

'I can check,' Mandy said. 'If you're serious.'

'Nah. Just give me a twenty-ounce cup. It will get cold eventually, anyway.'

Mandy nodded and rang him up, then handed him the cup.

'So what's going on with you? Why so down in the dumps?' he asked.

'I'm not down.'

Scott narrowed his eyes at her. 'I walk by you a dozen times a day, Mandy. That isn't your happy face.'

She shrugged. 'Vellum went to stay with her dad for a while. I hate it.'

'That sucks,' Scott agreed, setting his bulb bucket on the counter. He held up his cup. 'Do you have fresher coffee than what's in the urns?'

'I can make you an Americano instead? Fresh espresso with hot water?'

'Deal.'

She took the cup back and went to the machine.

'I miss my kids, too,' Scott said as she worked. 'I got divorced about a year before you started working here.'

'I didn't realize it was that recent,' Mandy said.

'Oh yeah. I hated not being able to see my kids every day after that.' He wiped his forehead with a rag he kept tucked into his back pocket. 'I mean, you work hard to earn money to take care of them, and then you can't even see them? Not fair.'

'Life isn't,' Mandy agreed, inserting the espresso filter holder into the machine.

'How are you going to get her back?' Scott asked.

'Patience,' Mandy said. 'Cory will screw up eventually. He always does.'

'Kind of a loose cannon that guy, right?'

'You know my ex?'

'Ryan bitched about him a lot. I think they had words a few times behind your back.'

Mandy finished Scott's drink and capped it. 'You're the second person to mention tensions between Ryan and Cory recently. I don't know what to do about that.'

'Tell the police.'

'He's my daughter's father,' Mandy said.

'You have to let them do their job.' Scott lifted his cup and sauntered away with his bulb bucket.

Mandy sighed and tried to visualize her lazy ex as a killer. Wouldn't murder be too much work? Ryan hadn't just been pushed down a flight of stairs. He'd been hit with a hammer.

As she considered the facts, she realized she just might not want to believe that her own ex-husband would try to set her up as a suspect by putting a planner under Ryan's body. Could he really be that evil? Did he really want custody of his daughter that much?

'Earth to Mandy . . .'

Mandy startled. She glanced up. It took her a second to recognize Detective Ahola. 'Sorry. Woolgathering.' She forced a smile. 'What brings you to the USea coffee bar?'

He held up his phone. 'You called?'

'I didn't mean for you to come over here. I just thought you should know there really was a drug dealer in the hospital. The story I heard was from two years ago, at least, but obviously the nurses are getting drugs now.'

He sighed. 'Yeah. Let me know who it is as soon as you figure it out. I'll pass the information along to the right department.'

She handed him a cup. 'Coffee?'

'Sure. But I need lunch. What have you got?'

She gestured to the refrigerator case. 'There are a few sandwiches down there.' He grabbed an egg salad on whole wheat, and she rang him up.

'Anything else?' he asked.

She hesitated, but after he narrowed his eyes at her, she spoke. 'Does my ex-husband have an alibi?'

'Why do you ask?'

'My daughter and Ryan's supervisor both mentioned tensions,' Mandy admitted. 'Nothing I really knew about.'

'Head in the sand?'

She shrugged and took the cash he offered her. 'I don't know. Maybe.'

He took his change. 'I'll look into it. Thanks.'

She hesitated. 'I was hoping you could tell me he had an alibi.'

He smiled at her. 'The protective type? I admire that, but I'm sorry, I can't discuss it.'

Her lips trembled. 'I wouldn't want the father of my daughter to be that bad of a person.'

He dropped coins into the 'take a penny, leave a penny' dish. 'Of course not. But it's tough to get an alibi for someone who doesn't work and who claims to have been home with his mother at the time of a death. You see my problem?' He winked and strode away.

Mandy took a deep breath, realizing she'd been starving herself of air. Cory had been investigated, and he did have an alibi. Sort of. She didn't think his mother was the most intelligent of women, so it would be rather easy to catch her in a lie if the police tried. But had they?

Mandy checked her phone at the end of her shift and discovered a text from her mother, asking her to drop by. With nothing better to do, she texted back saying she'd be there as soon as traffic permitted.

She clocked out and went through the main hospital door. A gust of wind hit her hard, right outside of the sliding glass doors. The tall buildings of the hospital and other large structures nearby created their own weather systems.

She shivered and reached for her gloves, balled up in her coat pockets. As she fumbled to pull them on with icy fingers, a woman walked up the sidewalk toward the main entrance. She looked familiar.

Faux fur coat, skinny legs in motorcycle leggings and scuffed boots. What was Alexis Ivanova doing here at the hospital?

On the other side of the street, a classic sports car came out of the parking garage and turned into the passenger drop-off lane. Alexis, not noticing Mandy, trotted up to the car as it pulled to a stop.

Mandy's eyes widened as Scott opened the door and climbed out. She'd never heard the maintenance supervisor talk about being a car aficionado, but the cherry red paint and perfect exterior spoke of hours of loving maintenance.

Alexis put her arms around Scott's neck. He gave her an awkward one-armed hug, walked her around the car, then shut the door after she climbed in.

The gentlemanly gesture, if not the hug, gave the appearance of a date. What was that about? How had they even met? Here, probably. Maybe Alexis had met Ryan during his lunch breaks or picked him up after work. Still, she seemed a poor choice for Scott.

'There's no accounting for attraction,' Mandy said aloud, startling a man pushing his post-partum wife in a wheelchair.

'What?'

'Sorry.' She smiled. 'Congratulations.'

He grinned at her as a sedan pulled up next to them. 'It's a boy.'

She congratulated him again and headed toward the parking garage and her own car. The rain held off long enough to keep traffic snarls from forming and she made good time to her mother's house, parking there instead of driving across the street to her own house.

Her mother, looking chic in a sweater dress and dark hose, embraced her warmly when Mandy arrived at her front door. 'Back to work so soon? I walked over to your house before I texted you and was surprised to find it empty.'

'If only the entire work drama hadn't happened.' Mandy's eyes welled up. 'Vellum went to the Moffats after the layoff news.'

'I know, sweetie. She texted me.' Her mother hugged her again, then led her into the kitchen, where a fat-bellied turquoise pot of tea waited in the center of the small table. Mandy took a seat and her mother set a plate with two frosted brownies next to the cream pitcher.

'Linda?' Mandy asked, nodding at the plate.

Her mother sat and leaned forward, as if to confide. 'I freeze most of them. She delivers here when you aren't home.'

Mandy chuckled and put one on a delicate porcelain plate rimmed in silver. 'Using your wedding service?'

'Life is too short. I never used these because I was too scared of breaking them, but what's the point of worrying now?' She lifted the teapot and filled both of their glasses with oolong.

Mandy considered her mother's change of heart. 'Birthday woes?'

Her mother wiggled her shoulders. 'Sixty-seven in a few days. I have to tell you that sixty-seven does not feel like the new forty.'

Mandy stared at the delicate plate, knowing each one was imbued with the hopes and well wishes of everyone who'd chosen them off the wedding registry for her parents back in the early 1980s. 'I know, Mom. We've found ourselves single again at the same time, and I hate that.'

Her mother rolled her eyes. 'I'm happy to remain single. Are the men your age as disgusting as those my age?'

'Why?'

'That George Lowry hit on me at the grocery store on Sunday. I thought he was with Linda?' Her upper lip curled as she picked up her teacup.

'Did you ask him about her?'

'Rather pointedly. He had the gall to tell me they were just hooking up. Sixty years old and he suggested he could bring over a bottle of wine at dusk.' She snorted. 'Dusk!'

Mandy blew steam off her tea. 'Poor Linda. I guess George must be back from Hawaii.'

'Only just. He was stocking up. Beer and sausages, that sort of thing. I'm sure he needs a woman, but she's not me.'

'More than one,' Mandy chuckled. 'Are you going to tell Linda? I wonder if he took another woman on his Valentine's vacation.'

'What do you think?' Her mother looked troubled. 'I'm not sure what to do.'

'I don't think Linda took the fling too seriously, but she was hurt about him ignoring her on Valentine's Day.'

'Then she knows he's not serious.' Her mother sighed. 'If he didn't send flowers or anything. I'll tell her about yesterday, so she doesn't get her hopes up again.'

'You could invite her to dinner with us,' Mandy suggested.

Her mother nodded. 'But not until we finish our brownies. She hasn't brought any over for a couple of weeks and I don't want her feelings to be hurt.'

Linda arrived just in time for homemade chicken pot pie. 'Ooh, Barbara, you've outdone yourself,' she cooed, breathing in the heady cheese-laced sauce that was the family trademark. She set a wrapped platter on the counter.

'Brownies?' Mandy asked, feeling mischievous. She winked at her mother.

'Chocolate is never wrong,' Linda said, flattening her sweater over her hips. 'How are you? I saw you leaving at an odd time this morning.'

Mandy recounted her horrible week as they dished out salad, poured wine, then spooned the pot pie into their dishes.

'It wasn't all bad,' her mother said. 'Doctor Tristan Burrell sounds promising.'

'I agree,' Linda said. 'Though I've missed the sight of that attractive Detective Ahola around here. Any news about Ryan's death, Mandy?'

'Cory,' Mandy said, then gulped down half her wine.

Her mother looked concerned. 'Cory?'

She nodded. 'Both Vellum and Ryan's hospital supervisor said there were issues between Ryan and Cory. They never saw eye to eye, but I didn't think anything of it. It was rare for Ryan to get along with functional people.'

Her mother snorted. 'Of course there was tension. Ryan replaced Cory in many ways. And Cory's immature enough to have a problem with that.'

'Only because I couldn't pay my mortgage, thanks to Cory.'

'Cory is one of those people who, despite the evidence, have things done to him rather than by him,' her mother opined. 'I wouldn't call him functional now.'

'He's just trying to hurt me by not working.' Mandy changed the subject. 'I saw Detective Ahola today. He was awfully nice, and managed to tell me that Cory's mother claims Cory was with her at the time of Ryan's death, though he isn't supposed to tell me anything.'

'Elaine Moffat,' her mother muttered, nose wrinkling as if she'd just smelled a stinky cheese. 'Not really a liar, for all her faults.'

'Not that bright,' Mandy agreed.

'Which means Cory could have fooled her,' Linda added. 'Claimed he was in the bathroom or something when he'd actually sneaked out.'

Mandy turned to her. 'You want Vellum's father to have killed my cousin?'

'Not on purpose,' Linda said slowly.

'Someone bashed him on the head with a hammer.' Mandy

picked up the wine bottle and emptied it into her glass. 'You want that person to have been my ex-husband?'

Linda shuddered. 'You need something nicer to think of. A man, perhaps. Sex? With this Burrell, or even the detective?'

'They are both very attractive.' Mandy sighed. 'But look at what happened the last time a doctor asked me out. And if Detective Ahola moves in he'll be my housemate. Awkward.'

'Not with Vellum out of the house.' Linda winced at Barbara's glare. 'Sorry.'

'I advise against dating right now,' her mother said, picking up Mandy's full glass and neatly dumping a third of it into her own. 'You need to focus on talking Vellum into coming back home and securing a new tenant, in that order.'

Mandy needed to reconsider her friendships as well. Why was Linda being so cold about Cory? Had she always disliked him, or was something else going on?

Mandy arrived at the coffee bar at nine-thirty the next morning for her shift. Kit had the earlier shift and Mandy saw her at the counter as she walked by. Her bruises had faded, but she hadn't been at work on Monday. Still, her reappearance proved she'd had nothing to do with the Adderall drama of the week before.

Mandy dropped off her personal possessions, then clocked in. When she poked her head into the counter area to see what she was supposed to do next, she saw Scott on his knees, his hand over his heart.

Was he OK?

Nervously, she asked, 'What's going on?'

Scott grunted and Kit stepped away from him, alarm in her shaded eyes. Mandy saw no sign of Fannah anywhere. Probably on her morning break. She edged through the door and grabbed for the phone. 'I'll call for help.'

NINETEEN

'What's wrong?' Kit asked, frowning at Mandy.

'Screwdriver?' Scott asked, his hand reaching out.

Kit raised her eyebrows.

'Oh.' Mandy blushed. 'The way your hand was on your chest, I thought something terrible was going on.' She realized she was standing next to an open toolbox, balanced on the rear counter next to the microwave. 'Umm, flat head?'

'That'll do.'

Mandy selected a medium-sized one from the molded plastic tray set inside the open toolbox and handed it to Scott, who grunted again when he shifted. 'You sound like you're hurting.'

'Two of my guys called out sick today so I have to do the minor repairs.'

'The shelf underneath was wobbly,' Kit said.

'I didn't notice it,' Mandy said.

'Fannah complained that a notepad slid out and dropped on her foot.'

'Huh.' Mandy took a deep breath and tried to release the adrenaline that had coursed through her system. 'I thought he was having a heart attack or something.'

'Just overdid it this weekend, Mandy,' Scott said, hauling himself up. 'I don't have teenaged knees anymore.'

'Too many dates?' she asked.

He frowned, then cut his eyes to the counter. Dr Garcia was heading toward them, followed by a row of duckling-like residents.

Mandy handed him his toolbox and followed him into the back room, knowing she only had a second. 'Alexis Ivanova? Don't you have better taste than that?'

'I don't know what you're talking about,' he said as he dropped in his screwdriver and closed his toolbox.

'I saw you with her last night. She dated Ryan, you know.'

He blinked at her.

'Fine. What about our security camera?' she pressed.

'They're out of parts in Hong Kong and it's going to be a while due to the component shortage.'

'Did you tell that to Fannah?'

'We don't talk,' he said. 'Back off, Mandy. I'm having a bad enough day without you chattering at me.' He snapped his thumb and forefinger together several times, imitating a talking mouth.

She wanted to tell him off, but Fannah came through the back door and she didn't want to be written up for rude behavior.

'Gotta go,' Scott said, and pushed past Fannah.

'What was that about?' she asked, looking disgusted as the door shut behind him.

'He was fixing the wobbly shelf that bothered you.' At Fannah's look of confusion, Mandy added, 'Under the cash register? You know, the junk shelf?'

The backroom phone rang. 'Whatever,' Fannah said, reaching for it. 'Get back to work.'

Mandy went home to her empty house after work. No Vellum, no Vellum's music, no dishes in the sink, no laundry to sort. It was suddenly as if she had unlimited time to do her second job. But it wasn't the same without Vellum.

They had cleared the online shop orders over the weekend. She fulfilled the orders that had come in during the past forty-eight hours, then went into her art studio.

When she turned on the light, she felt as if she'd entered a meditative space. Rain dropped steadily on the roof, creating a background melody. The bright white paint woke up her eyes, and the sight of her boxes of art supplies, lined up around a pristine cream-colored workspace, created a blank canvas sure to please any artist.

She flipped her planner to her collection of ideas for future projects. Nothing excited or stimulated her. One of the big events in a vlogger's planner year was finishing one journal and starting another. She usually fit about six months in her journals, which meant she was a long way away from starting another one. Still, she found herself flipping through January and February, and saw the murder spread she'd created.

As she studied the names, she compared them to Ryan himself, in the center of the page. Ryan Meadows. Age forty-two. Single. No kids. Janitor. Alcoholic.

Would Linda, at fifty-seven, have had a fling with him before George? She hadn't liked how Linda had commented on Cory at dinner last night. Steeling herself, she grabbed her phone and dashed off a quick text to Linda and asked about her remarks at dinner. She had to solve this if she ever wanted Vellum to move back home.

Given the recent comments, she added Cory to the family list, writing ex-cousin-in-law to represent his relationship to Ryan. She didn't like it, but he belonged there.

Her eyes moved down the lovers list. First Dylan, who she hadn't seen for days. But she knew Linda had spoken to Dylan and Alexis on occasion. Was there more to that story?

And Alexis. Alexis was dating Scott. Mandy moved her finger to the co-worker list on the left side of the page. She'd never written down Scott's name at all. After she wrote it in a bubble, she added the word 'boss' and considered his similarities to Ryan. Maybe Alexis had a type.

A rapping noise scattered her attention. She lifted her head from her journal page, then heard the noise again. Someone was at the back door.

That made her realize how stupid she'd been. What if Linda was Ryan's killer? And her text had lured her here?

Mandy shut her eyes tightly. Linda. Could she really visualize her brownie-loving friend hitting Ryan on the head with a hammer? Why? Even if she had been with Ryan, she'd moved on to George Lowry. And he wasn't dead.

She pushed herself back from her desk, stuck a pair of scissors into her pocket, and set her phone to make an emergency call easily. Then she went to the back door, where, as predicted, Linda stood in the rain.

Mandy opened the door, leaving the screen closed. 'What's up?'

'What's up?' Linda echoed, water dripping down her face.

'Where is your umbrella? Or at least a hat.'

'I don't even own an umbrella. This is Seattle,' Linda scoffed. 'Are you going to let me in?'

'Why did you want Cory to be Ryan's killer?' Mandy countered.

'Because he's a jerk,' Linda growled. 'He hurt my friend.'

Mandy teared up. Her hand shaking, she unlocked the door. Linda grabbed her, pulling her into a showery hug.

'Please tell me you don't still have feelings for that louse,' she said into Mandy's ear.

'It's just that he's Vellum's father.'

'I know, honey, I know.' Linda pulled back and looked her right in the eye. 'I did not sleep with Ryan. I did not kill Ryan. We need to figure out who really did before you lose your mind.'

Mandy nodded. 'What about Reese?'

Linda rolled her eyes. 'That persnickety child did not sleep with Ryan either. Can you imagine?'

'She offered to buy my business.'

'Because she wants to be you,' Linda said. 'She had nothing to do with Ryan. It makes no sense.'

'OK.' Mandy paced the kitchen floor. 'Here's one big new thing.'

'What's that?' Linda grabbed a dishtowel and wrung out her hair.

'Alexis knows Scott. Ryan's boss? I saw him picking her up at the hospital. And he was in a car that probably cost a ton of money.'

'More than he makes?'

'Yeah, and he's one-year divorced with kids. He should be living in a ratty apartment and driving something old and crappy.'

Linda looked at the ceiling with a thoughtful expression. 'Something is off.'

Mandy nodded. 'Now what?'

Linda worried her lower lip. 'Could we search his office or something?'

'Something,' Mandy echoed. She paced again, then brightened. 'Something strange was going on with Kit and Scott at work today. Scott was fixing a shelf in the coffee bar and Kit lied about it. Or Fannah did.'

Linda balled up the wet towel. 'One suspicion at a time. Let's focus on Scott.'

Mandy took the towel and dropped it into the sink. 'Should I get a look at that shelf?'

'When?'

'Now,' Mandy said. 'The coffee bar closes at six. I closed today, in fact. The lights are turned off but it isn't really dark. One little pen light would do.'

'It isn't really dangerous because it's a hospital. There are always people around.' Linda lifted her eyebrows.

'Right,' Mandy agreed. 'I'll get a flashlight.'

'Let's do it,' Linda said. She glanced at her watch. 'Then we can go out for dessert. I heard about a cupcake place on Pike that's open until ten.'

'Solve a murder, eat a cupcake,' Mandy said. 'Easy peasy.'

'We'll deserve a reward.' Linda felt her hair. 'Can I borrow a decent rain jacket?'

'Here goes nothing,' Mandy said, as she and Linda went down the escalator to the USea coffee bar area from the parking garage.

Linda squeezed her arm. 'I do enjoy being your partner in crime.'

'I shouldn't be spooked.' Mandy stepped off the escalator. 'I was just here a few hours ago.'

'It's pitch-dark outside,' Linda pointed out.

'It was when I left, too. The joy of February. It is staying light longer, though.'

Linda stopped in front of the coffee bar. 'Do you know that I've never been here?'

'Really?'

'It feels kind of famous to me. Like a movie set or something.'

'It doesn't really come to life until the lights are on. Your ex-husband never worked here?'

Linda shook her head. 'No. He's always been at Swedish Hospital since we lived in Seattle. There was a time when hospitals were no big deal to me, but it's been a few years.'

'I honestly kind of like it,' Mandy said. 'Even with an at-home business, it's nice to get out to talk to people.'

'It must be like watching a soap opera at times.'

Mandy nodded. 'Or lately, we've been the soap opera.'

'I can just imagine Doctor O'Hottie strutting up for a quad shot,' Linda said dreamily, her gloved finger trailing through the air.

Mandy snorted. 'He didn't turn out to be such a figure of fantasy after all.'

'OK then.' Linda struck a pose. 'Doctor Tristan, hands over his heart as he asks you out.'

Mandy giggled. 'No, no, it's Doctor Burrell. Tristan is his first name.'

'He'll always be Doctor Tristan to me,' Linda said in a wistful tone.

'OK, crazy lady, let's get on with this before Security gets concerned.' She led Linda behind the counter. 'Let's crouch down here.'

'This is where the wobbly shelf is?'

Mandy lowered her voice to a whisper. 'Yep.'

Linda wrapped her fingers around the edge of the shelf. 'It isn't wobbling now. I guess he fixed it.'

Mandy reached for a tray, stacked on its side in a crack between the counter units. They kept a few from the cafeteria for larger orders. She started pulling out notepaper and pens and set them on the tray. When she reached in again, she found a few sandwich baggies and – gross! – a used tissue. Next was a stack of napkins.

'Not an exciting haul,' Linda observed. 'Good thing we don't have our own reality show.'

'Ha,' Mandy said. 'Going in.' Her fingers reached around. She swept out a pile of crumbs. 'Hand me that garbage can.'

Linda picked up the small plastic basket and Mandy slid the crumbs into it. 'Is that it?'

Mandy pulled the flashlight out of her pocket and turned it on. She moved into a kneeling position and peered into the shelf.

'It's pretty deep,' Linda said.

'Yeah. I do see more stuff far back. Let's see if my arm is skinny enough to reach all the way.' Mandy handed the flashlight to Linda and maneuvered herself so her arm could go underneath the counter. 'Oooh, awkward.'

'Feeling anything?'

Mandy rotated her shoulder and spread out her fingers. 'Oh yeah. A whole set of round things.' She swept them together, then rolled them out as she pulled her arm back.

'Coin rolls,' Linda exclaimed as they dropped into the tray. 'Shouldn't they be in the cash register?'

'Maybe they didn't fit one day and someone stuck them there,' Mandy said. 'Oh, crap.'

'What?'

'I bet this is the missing money! They didn't get into the drawer, or fell out of it, and then Kit and I had to pay the money back. How much is in a quarter roll?'

'Umm,' Linda said, her eyes moving back and forth as she calculated. 'Ten bucks.'

'Huh.' Mandy stared at them. 'Four rolls. This is forty bucks.'

'Then unless you have some sort of regular problem, the missing money doesn't add up.'

'No.' Mandy poked at the roll. 'Hey, wait a minute. This isn't stuffed with quarters. Something a little smaller is in here.'

'Like what?'

'I don't know.' Increasingly concerned, Mandy ripped open the tough paper covering, revealing a white plastic bottle like those used by hotels for complimentary lotion. 'Weird.'

'I think I know where this is going,' Linda whispered. 'Unscrew the bottle.'

Mandy did as she suggested, pouring the contents into her shaking hand. Yellow gold capsules came out. 'Adderall XR 30 MG,' she read off one of them.

'The Adderall,' they said together.

'It was coming from the coffee bar all along,' Mandy gasped. 'I can't believe it. People have been taking pills with their drinks. We haven't just been selling coffee and snacks, we've been selling drugs!'

'It wasn't your fault.'

'No. It's Fannah or Kit, or one of the weekend staff.'

Linda winced. 'The problems have been happening on weekdays, right?'

Mandy nodded. 'It's Fannah or Kit then.'

'Which one?'

Mandy thought. 'Kit's the one who was beaten up recently. She's been planning to quit, though.'

'Maybe that's why she was hurt? Her drug boss doesn't want her to quit?'

'It makes sense. Unfortunately.' She pulled out her phone. 'Given that there is security here, there is no safer place to have this conversation.' She found Kit in her contacts and dialed.

Kit answered with a distracted, 'Why are you calling so late?'

'You go to your other job on Wednesdays, right?' Mandy asked.

'Yeah, but my shift just ended.'

Mandy heard Kit yawn. She decided to get to the point. 'Were you beaten up and forced to sell drugs at our coffee bar?'

Kit let out a breath. The harsh sound whistled in Mandy's ear. She flinched but kept the phone to her ear.

'How did you find out?' she whispered.

'I discovered the drugs, Kit.'

'Please don't tell anyone,' Kit begged. 'Just put them back, like you never saw them. Hopefully you won't be approached if I can ever quit.'

'Did my cousin have something to do with this?'

Kit didn't respond.

'Ryan had so many coin rolls. He must have been involved.'

After a long pause, Kit said, 'He was my supplier.'

'Did you ever actually date him?'

'Yeah. I can't believe I dated my dealer. He knew I was hard up and offered to discount my supply if I sold through the coffee bar.'

'Is Fannah involved?'

'No,' Kit said.

'OK.' Mandy squeezed her eyes closed. 'Are the four rolls here still from Ryan?'

Kit said nothing.

'Kit?'

'No,' she finally said.

'Who is supplying you now that Ryan is dead? Why didn't you stop selling?'

'Right,' Kit said in a bitter voice. 'Think, Mandy. Why would I have gotten beat up?'

'Because you tried to stop?'

'Ding ding ding.'

Linda, wide-eyed, shook her head. It wobbled a little as she glanced at the coin rolls, then her gaze shot away as if they were too dangerous to look at.

'Who is supplying you? Who took over from Ryan?' Mandy demanded.

'I don't know who took over for him in general. His upline is dealing directly with me now. There's a whole network but I don't know the details. Addicts just kind of find each other, you know? The drugs go out the back door of the office building pharmacy, then into the Maintenance Department, since the janitorial staff move around the complex.'

'They approached you after he died?'

'Yeah. I need to stop before I get caught and fired. Obviously, word is getting out, with those stupid nurses and dumb Doctor O'Hottie.'

Like Kit wasn't the dumb one for getting involved in the first place. 'How could you leave this stuff on an open shelf where anyone could find it?'

'It wasn't my idea, Mandy.' Kit's voice had grown huffy. 'Someone put it there after close for me to sell in the morning.'

Mandy stared at the four small containers of pills. 'You sell this much every day?'

'How much is there?'

'Four containers.'

'Sure.'

Quickly, Mandy used the edge of her sleeve to wipe them clean. What if she'd left fingerprints or something? 'I opened one of the coin rolls. Should I tape it back together?'

'Do what you can,' Kit said. 'Hopefully the person I sell it to won't complain.'

Mandy's stomach contracted. She was getting in too deep, but she had to know. 'Did your supplier kill my cousin?'

'Why would he do that?' Kit asked. 'Ryan was doing what he was told. Look, I have to go.'

Her phone beeped and the call vanished. Mandy huffed. 'She's a drug dealer but she hardly has a minute to take my questions.'

'What are you going to do?' Linda asked.

Mandy shook her head. 'Let Detective Ahola know. I'm sure it's important for him to be told that my cousin dealt drugs.'

'It's a good way to shorten a person's lifespan,' Linda agreed.

She held the flashlight so Mandy could see to put everything back as close to how she had found it as possible. Finally, Mandy slid the tray back into its slot.

'I can't believe I have to be back here at five-thirty. We're so behind because of everything being thrown out last week that I have to bake cookies before I open at six-thirty.' She yawned.

'But you still have the energy for that cupcake, right?'

Mandy turned over Linda's arm and looked at her watch. 'It's too late for that.'

Linda pouted. 'Darn it.'

Mandy used the counter to pull herself up, then helped Linda to her feet. 'We can stop at the grocery store. The bakery will be closed, but we can buy one of the four-packs of the upscale cupcakes.'

'Now you're talking my language. Call the detective from my house when we get home. I don't really want to stay here anymore. It's creepy.'

Mandy switched off the flashlight and shrugged. 'It's just my workplace.'

They held hands as they went up the escalator. Mandy knew her friend was spooked. When they reached the parking garage, Mandy felt the same way. Kit had been hurt here. Bad people were roaming the hospital. They moved quickly to the car and got in.

Mandy drove them out of the garage, then pulled to the side of the road. 'I'm calling Detective Ahola right now. I don't want to wait.'

TWENTY

Linda nodded as Mandy pulled out her phone. 'Just pay attention to the cars, OK? Let's not get rear-ended while you're calling.'

'At least I'd be talking to the police,' Mandy joked, but she got the hint. The call could wait. She set her phone down and pulled back onto the road.

They went to the grocery store, then to Linda's home. Mandy pulled out her phone again and called while Linda made tea.

'Detective Ahola.' The deep voice on the line was instantly reassuring.

'Oh good, you answered,' Mandy said.

'Hello, Ms Meadows. Have you solved the case?'

'It's not funny,' she countered.

'The murder, definitely not. Your exciting phone calls, though, they can be amusing.'

'This isn't one of those calls, Detective,' she said, injecting steel into her voice.

'Do tell.'

'You told me to let you know when I figured out who the drug dealer was,' Mandy said in her most professional tone. 'I found out that my cousin was the drug dealer.'

'I see.' His voice lost all humor. 'What is the basis of your conclusion?'

She wilted. 'I was told, by someone he supplied drugs to.'

'I see.'

His tone was level, but she still didn't like it. She'd stuck her arm into a gross shelf space and pulled out actual illicit drugs, for crying out loud. 'That's important, right? I mean, people kill drug dealers. Honestly, I remember joking about him being the drug dealer, because of all the women that seem to have been around him, but I never believed it until tonight.' She paused. 'Am I babbling? I sound like I'm babbling.'

His voice lowered, became more intimate. 'What's going on, Mandy? You don't sound like yourself.'

'I don't like any of this. And I'm going to get people in trouble if I tell you,' she explained. Linda gave her a sympathetic glance and squeezed her shoulder. How had she ever doubted Linda's innocence?

'Tell me what?'

Mandy lowered her voice. 'I know where some drugs are, right now.'

'Where?'

'In the hospital.'

'A hospital dispenses drugs.'

'I'm well aware of that. I found a cache of pills.'

'Are they accessible to all employees?'

'Technically, yes. They are in the coffee bar area, but in a part of it that is accessible to anyone, in the sense that they aren't behind locked doors or anything.'

'Then we don't need a warrant.' He cleared his throat. 'We will need to take these items into evidence and take a formal statement from you, Mandy.'

'That's fine.'

A pause. 'Where are the drugs, Mandy?'

'Oh, sorry. You know where the cash register is?'

'Yes.'

'There is a shelf underneath it. Way in the back of that shelf are four quarter-sized coin rolls, full of drugs.'

'I'm going to send someone to pick them up. Meanwhile, I'll come take your statement. Are you at home?'

'I'm at my neighbor's, but I can go home.'

'Have you created any new danger for yourself?'

'I confronted someone about the drugs.'

'Who?'

'The person who is selling them now.'

'Mandy,' Detective Ahola said, a note of frustration and irritation evident.

Seeing it from his perspective, Mandy understood. 'If I hadn't called her I wouldn't have known what was going on. I know she didn't kill Ryan. She has an alibi.'

'All right.' She heard him release a breath. 'Kit, I take it.'

'Do I have to tell you?'

'I'm a homicide detective, remember?'

'Right. Yes, but I'm telling you with extreme reluctance. Remember, she was beat up, right? And she dated Ryan. Maybe she got sucked in by accident.'

'Not your problem.' His voice took on an authoritarian tone. 'Stay at your neighbor's house for now. What's the address? I'll be there as soon as I can.'

Mandy hung up after giving Linda's address to him.

'Should we save him a cupcake?' Linda inquired.

'No. I'm pretty sure he wouldn't accept it while officially questioning us. You're part of this too, now.' Mandy paused. 'I guess we know what Dylan and Alexis were after all along. They wanted the coin rolls because they had drugs in them. I'd better warn Jasmine to inspect them.'

Detective Ahola didn't arrive for a full hour. By then, Mandy and Linda had polished off all four cupcakes and were drinking peppermint tea in the hopes of staving off indigestion.

'I hate to say it, but I'm glad Vellum is with the Moffats. I'd hate to have left her alone all evening.'

'I'd rather she was with your mom,' Linda said loyally. The doorbell rang and she went to open it.

Detective Ahola, looking both gorgeous and irritated, was accompanied by Detective Rideout. They questioned Linda and Mandy separately.

Finally, when they were done with Mandy, Detective Rideout said, 'While we can't assume your assessment of the implications and connections to your cousin's death are valid, we will investigate that angle.'

'Thank you,' Mandy said. 'I'm supposed to be at work at five-thirty. Is the coffee bar going to be open?'

'We searched the entire publicly accessible area,' Detective Ahola said. 'We also notified the hospital administrator, who discussed it with your coffee bar manager. They asked us to allow them to open up if at all possible.'

'I'm the first in tomorrow,' Mandy explained. 'I have baking to do in the prep room. We're still recovering from last week.

Aren't you going to get a warrant for the back area and search that too?'

'In the course of interviews, we determined that the drugs are not coming through the back rooms of the coffee bar. We're still researching how they are supplied to the shelf,' Detective Ahola said.

'So we go on as if nothing happened?' Mandy asked. 'Didn't Kit's information give you enough to go on?'

'Not without names. The hospital administrator convinced our higher-ups that closing the bar yet again would be fatal to the operation, which is important to the hospital.'

'We can't have anyone losing out on their espresso drinks,' Mandy said sourly. 'Especially with everyone's favorite amphetamine out of supply.'

Detective Ahola narrowed his eyes at her. 'Why don't you get some sleep, Mandy? You aren't part of the drug problem and you have to work in a few hours.'

'I know I have an alibi for Ryan's death,' Mandy said. 'Because I was on camera. But what about the drug issue? I just don't understand.'

'The hospital already cleared you of involvement. They investigated you after a doctor accused you of selling drugs to him.'

'How do they know I'm innocent?' Mandy asked. 'Not to belabor the issue, but as many times as I've asked for a security camera near us, a working one has never been installed.'

'We've made an arrest,' Detective Rideout explained. 'We have the seller.'

'But not the upline?' Mandy asked.

'We'll probably offer a plea bargain to get the name,' the detective explained.

'What happens if she doesn't know the chain of command?' Mandy asked. 'She told me she didn't.'

'The hospital administrator will increase security on the main floor starting tomorrow. You'll be fine.'

Mandy put her hand over her mouth to hide a yawn. 'OK, then. I need to get home or I'll be worthless tomorrow.'

The detectives glanced between each other. Detective Ahola nodded. 'We'll walk you home, Mandy.'

'OK.' She went to tell Linda her interview was over and they were all departing, then pulled on her coat and left with the detectives.

'Cold night,' Detective Rideout observed.

'Watch out for the sidewalks, they can be really slippery,' Mandy said as they walked alongside Linda's fence. The detectives followed her down her driveway and through her back gate, then stopped at her steps. 'Thank you for following up on this.'

'Just doing our job,' Detective Rideout said. 'Thank you for being a responsible member of the public.'

'I want my cousin's killer found and punished,' Mandy told him. 'That's what I care about. I hate that I've cost Kit everything.'

'She isn't your responsibility,' Detective Ahola said.

She raised one hand in a wave, then walked up her wood steps, holding on to the railing so she wouldn't slip on the slick surface.

Inside, she tried to take a deep belly breath, but didn't seem to have it in her. When she went into her room, she climbed onto her bed and just lay there, falling asleep in her clothes.

Mandy's alarm went off at four-thirty. She lay in a daze, hardly recognizing the sound for what it was. Eventually, she forced herself up, the number 'five-thirty' ringing in her head.

Oh, that's right. She had an hour and a half of overtime today. Usually someone from the weekend shifts covered the first hours of Wednesdays so they could open on time, but the weekend people weren't trained to bake. Yawning, she texted Fannah to make sure someone else would be working with her until Fannah arrived at nine-thirty for her Wednesday late shift. Otherwise she'd be alone.

Mandy walked into the bathroom and turned on the shower, wishing she still had Vellum to fight her for space. But Vellum wouldn't have been up now anyway.

She showered and decided to skip breakfast, since she could eat the imperfect cookies, and probably would whether she'd had breakfast or not. Instead, she dumped a coffee pod into her machine to brew while she did her makeup, then found slacks and a coffee bar T-shirt, threw a plush hoodie over it, and grabbed her coffee.

Automatic lights flashed on when she went out, fighting the winter morning darkness. Frost crystals sparkled on the grass as she trudged past. No one else seemed to be moving in her neighborhood and very few lights were on in the houses. *Lucky them.*

The hospital felt eerie when she arrived on the main floor. She never worked this early. In the back and prep rooms, she flipped on all the lights and set to work. She only had an hour before she had to turn on the coffee bar lights and start taking orders.

Before she washed her hands, she checked her phone but Fannah hadn't replied. No doubt she usually slept in on Wednesdays, but Mandy would have appreciated an update. Maybe someone from administration would come by at six-thirty. She mixed up batter for chocolate chip cookies and ginger thins, thinking it was time for a change, or at least an addition. Lemon cookies with crusty edges, dusted with powdered sugar? Something with luscious butterscotch or jam thumbprints?

She pulled out the first batch of chocolate chip, set them on a wire rack, and inserted the ginger thins. By the time she had the first cookies in their waxed bags, the ginger thins were cooling. She watched for color on the second set of chocolate chip cookies anxiously, because the clock was moving closer to six-thirty.

The cookies were done at six-ten. She opened the door into the coffee bar, hoping a line hadn't formed yet because she'd had no time to prep drinks. No one was there so she slipped her cookies from the tray into the glass case, then started brewing coffee for the urns. She should have done it first, but she had hoped someone else would come in, and besides, she was a coffee snob. The fresher the better, even for the urn drinkers. Stupid of her, since she'd pay the price now in crabby staff.

As the clock reached six-fifteen, she realized she didn't have a cash register drawer. She dashed into the back and unlocked the cabinet where Fannah kept the first drawer of the day on Wednesdays, since no one but her had access to the safe.

She had to turn on the coffee bar lights in order to see well enough to open the cash register and slide in the drawer. Anxious now that no one else had shown up for work, she decided to keep her phone in her slacks, even though it was against the rules.

Moving fast, even with just one cup of coffee and two broken cookies in her belly, she loaded the dark roast urn, then filled the hot water urn. 'Only two left to go.' She glanced out at the floor. A lone man walked from the elevator bay through the front entrance. Surgical patients had probably come and gone for morning surgeries while she'd been baking in the back.

She had just finished pouring light roast into the coffee urn when the coffee bar lights flickered and went out. Mandy turned around. The coffee bar was in shadow but the rest of the hospital still had light. She locked down the urn lid and set the empty carafe next to the brewing station before going to the light switches.

When she jiggled them up and down, nothing happened. This wasn't good. All her fumbling efforts to prep and now she couldn't open. She went to the cash register. If people used their phone flashlight apps, she could see well enough to ring them up for cookies and coffee. When she looked at the register, however, she could see it wasn't working either. She turned back to the brewing station and it had lost power too.

Muttering, she ran into the back room and called Scott. He didn't work until seven, but he must have a minion on duty at all times. She knew little about the workings of the hospital outside of her shift hours.

She left a message on his office phone, an extension she knew by heart, and his cell phone, then fumbled through Fannah's desk and looked up the general number for maintenance in Fannah's hospital reference. She was just dialing it when the back door opened and Scott appeared in the doorway, holding his toolbox.

'You're here,' she greeted him, surprised. 'I didn't think you came in this early.'

'You're never here now.' He rubbed his unshaven upper lip.

'I had to come in unusually early. We're still catching up from last week's shutdown.' She set down the phone receiver. 'I was about to call the main number for your department.'

'It's not the average day,' he said, holding his toolbox in front of him.

'No kidding. I need to open up the coffee bar, but the lights are out.'

Scott stepped through the doorway into the coffee bar, glanced out, then turned and shut the door behind him. 'So they are.'

Mandy felt a prickle of unease. 'Can you fix the problem? It's just the coffee bar, but all the power is off out there. No coffee, no cash register. Fannah is going to kill me.'

'Fannah's no killer.'

'You know what I mean, Scott,' she said, exasperated. 'I don't want to be blamed for not opening on time.'

'You look like you're having an anxiety attack.' He said it flatly.

'Exhaustion attack, more like. I just wanted to do a good job, you know? But I was hoping someone else would turn up to work with me. It's far too much for one person, even starting early.' She stopped when he didn't banter back. 'What's wrong?' she asked uncertainly.

'It's been hard for you, all this getting-in-other-people's-business drama,' he said. 'It's got to stop, Mandy.'

'What do you mean?'

'Kit's arrest? All your fault.' He took a step toward her. 'My business turmoil? All your fault.'

'What? I didn't want her to be arrested. But I couldn't lie to the police.'

'Did you really have to turn Ryan into a goody two-shoes? All that harassing him to lead a different life?' He moved again.

'I didn't know he did drugs, Scott,' Mandy said. 'I didn't harass him.' She put her hands behind her, hoping to find the desk and the phone. If she hit the '0' hopefully someone would hear and help her.

'That's not what he told me, when he said he was getting clean and going straight. This is your fault.'

'I had no idea what he was up to,' Mandy cried.

'He said you were back on your feet and didn't need the extra cash anymore.'

'What extra cash? He only paid me rent.'

'Are you that stupid? Really?' He lifted his toolbox.

'He didn't give me money. This has nothing to do with me. I think he was subsidizing Kit's habit.' And from what Kit said, his entire department was involved. Had moving into Mandy's house changed Ryan's perspective? Shown him another way to live?

'He never should have found you a job here. Everything was fine until you started creating problems!' He threw his toolbox at her.

She hopped to the side, easily avoiding the heavy box despite her shock. Her hands shook as adrenaline took over her body. Scott lifted his arm, clad in a black long-sleeved shirt instead of the usual maintenance jumpsuit. Time seemed to slow as she saw long white cat hairs clustered along his sleeve.

Scott owned a cat. A cat owner had visited Ryan right before he died.

'You killed him!' she yelled as his arm flashed through the air.

She cowered back, knocking the phone off the hook. Before she could reach for it, Scott grabbed her by the arm and hauled her through the doorway into the prep room, then pushed her hard.

'Hell, yes I did. He threatened to tell the police about my operation!' Scott shouted.

She skidded on the floor and collapsed in a heap on the pantry floor, hitting her head on a metal rack. It rocked, sending sacks cascading to the floor. One thumped her on the head. She hit the rack again and blinked, dazed by the sudden pain of ten pounds of baking mix knocking on her skull. Scott slammed the door, leaving her in darkness.

TWENTY-ONE

M andy heard the snick of the pantry door locking through her haze of pain. Alone in the dark, she had a moment of panic, then reason surged through the battering and fall she'd endured. Instinctively, her hands pushed ten-pound sacks out of her way. A cloud of flour floated into the air, making her cough as she tried to find a safe path to the door.

How had he locked the door? Then she remembered. The hospital's maintenance supervisor would of course have the master key. Her chest contracted painfully.

'What are you planning to do to me?' she called out. 'This is ridiculous, Scott!'

She heard footsteps move away. He'd actually left the prep room. What was he doing? She forced herself to focus on immediate concerns. Carefully, she crawled toward the door then stood, putting her palms against it for support.

It went without saying that Scott had killed her cousin. Tender pain flashed through her as she went through what Scott had said. Ryan had been trying to quit dealing, because of her. He was going to go to the police. And he'd died. Kit had tried to quit. She'd wanted to leave the hospital for her other job. She'd been beaten up.

And herself? Mandy was worth exactly nothing to Scott, just like Ryan had been once he'd quit. Scott wasn't going to try to bring her into his dealer club. He was just going to kill her.

Her mind went blank. In times of crisis, she always turned to her journal for clues, but it was in her purse. Mentally, she scanned the pages. Finally, she hit the spread with that Charles Dickens quote she'd found during a previous crisis.

The most important thing in life is to stop saying "I wish" and start saying "I will".

'That's it,' she said. 'No more wishes for me. I *will* get out of here.'

She tightened her hands into fists, then raised them into the air, opening them as if she was doing a Sun Salutation in yoga class. She had to calm down, had to focus. *Confidence, Mandy. You have to think! He's wrong about you having anxiety attacks.*

With a blaze of clarity, she realized what a fool he'd been. She still had her cell phone.

She lifted her apron and fumbled in her pockets. Scott would have assumed she'd left it in her cubby, but she hadn't today.

The door rattled. She froze for a millisecond, phone in hand, then fumbled to call nine-one-one. At least they'd hear what was going on even if she couldn't talk. She shoved the phone back into her slacks. Then, she bent down and came up with a twenty-pound sack of flour that hadn't exploded. As she staggered back, she promised herself that if she survived this, she would start lifting weights. Or doing yoga handstands. Anything to make this easier.

The door opened and light filled the pantry. Her pupils fought to make sense of the dark shape surrounded by the fluorescent glow. She rushed forward, using her flour sack as a battering ram. Scott's arm went up. What was in it? A long tube? A syringe?

Oh, no. He was trying to inject her with something. But he wouldn't win.

She shoved the flour sack up, desperate to keep the syringe away from her skin. The shape grunted. The arm came down in her direction. She tilted the sack and pushed it away, grimacing with effort.

He turned and hit a metal rack. Cans rattled and fell around them. Mandy stumbled and hefted the sack again as the syringe came at her. The thick brown paper bag ripped on the needle.

They danced in a half circle. Mandy's hip banged against a cooling rack and cookies slid onto the floor. When she shoved her torn sack, Scott fell through the door. His legs tangled in hers as he fell into the back room.

She slipped and collapsed over him, the scent of ginger and chocolate filling the space. The ripped bag poured flour over everything, misting into the air. She saw Scott's intent face through the white haze, still trying to get to her with the syringe.

'No,' she said in a gargled kind of exhalation, and wrapped the half empty sack around his arm, trying to get leverage.

'Die, damn it!' he screamed. His hair moved through the flour, sending more into the air. She sneezed. He grabbed her hair with his free hand, legs bucking, trying to throw her off. His floury fingers slid through the strands, catching on her curls, as she snapped her head back.

She scrambled up his protuberant belly, eyes watering from the pain of pulled hair, fighting to wrap the sack around the syringe. Running feet outside pounded on the tiles.

'Stop, Police! Drop the syringe!' a commanding voice ordered.

Before Mandy could react, she saw a hard-soled shoe slam down on Scott's wrist. His arm clunked against the tile. The syringe went flying. She scrambled off Scott, various squishy body parts squelching underneath her as her legs kicked into him. He squealed.

Detective Ahola stood over them. He flipped Scott over and pulled his arms behind his back. Mandy pulled herself into a fetal position, then stood, noting where the syringe was. She backed against the cubbies, as far away from it as she could get in the crowded room. The beached whale shape of Scott's body took up most of the floor space. Detective Ahola secured Scott's arms with handcuffs, then read him his rights.

Mandy heard squawking from her phone. 'Oh, right.' She pulled it from her slacks and started explaining what was going on.

The homicide detective pulled Scott to his feet as two hospital security guards came in through the door from the coffee bar.

'We've had reports of a disturbance?' one of them said, his hand on his radio.

'Just attempted murder,' Mandy said. 'Scott Nelson is the Maintenance Department drug kingpin.'

Scott spat on the floor. 'Hospital work is hard on the body. Normal people can't stay alert for twelve hours without a break. You think this place can run without Adderall? I'm just the smart guy who decided to profit from the misery of this place. My department roams the complex freely. We were perfect for the job.'

'You killed my cousin!' Mandy yelled. 'You beat up Kit!'

Scott curled his upper lip. 'That's how it works. There's no backing out once you start. You think my suppliers would let me? Once in, always in.'

Detective Ahola told the security guards to hold onto Scott while he called for backup. But Mandy could already hear police cars coming up the hospital drive, sirens blaring, from her nine-one-one call.

'Why did Ryan have a journal under him?' Mandy asked. 'Why did you have to make me feel responsible for killing him?'

Scott snorted. 'I used those freebie journals to keep track of orders. But you have that journaling business. I thought it might throw the police off the scent.'

Mandy gasped. 'You were trying to pin the murder on me?'

'No one was around. I walked right out your back door and down the street to my car.' He shrugged. 'It could have been anyone. It will be anyone next time. Drugs and hospitals go together.'

Before he could say more, they were overrun by police securing the scene and taking statements. Mandy felt dazed. Flour hung heavy in the air. Eventually the hospital administrators came and put up a closed sign at the coffee bar, then told Mandy she could take the rest of the week off with pay after the police were done with her. They'd need the time to have the coffee bar suite cleaned and sterilized again.

After she left the hospital, Mandy didn't go home. Adrenaline still coursed through her. Shaking, she went to her car, flour drifting off her legs the entire walk to the garage.

Too upset over her brush with death to cope with real life, she decided she needed to spend some time in nature. She drove to the Arboretum and, without thinking, grabbed the watercolor sketchbook she always kept in her glove compartment. Along with it she had a small pocket sketch box and a water brush, filled with water.

While part of the extensive botanic garden was still closed in February, it did feature a winter garden, a stream that flowed all year, and plenty of interesting trees. Even better, no one was around. Solitude was exactly what she needed.

She wandered around, looking for peace and inspiration, until she found a stunning example of a paperbark maple, with shards of terra cotta bark peeling and catching the winter sun. When she found a semi-dry spot in the warm light, she sat down and sketched the tree, forcing herself to empty her thoughts. She could always come back to art to soothe herself, and she needed to let it work its magic on her.

Only when she'd finished sketching the tree and surrounding plantings did she allow herself to process what she'd been through.

How had she missed the flaws in Scott's character so completely? She'd known Kit had odd interactions with him, while Fannah had none at all. When she'd seen him with Alexis, that should have been some kind of giveaway. Who better to distribute Adderall through the hospital than the anonymous maintenance workers, who could go anywhere and talk to anyone?

While she might never know the full story of Ryan's involvement, at least he hadn't been a mastermind. Most importantly, he'd tried to quit. She bet all that stuff about him being about to be fired had nothing to do with his performance, or even alcohol abuse, and everything to do with him wanting to do the right thing. Hopefully the police could figure out how the drugs were leaving the pharmacy and shut the entire operation down.

She stared at her painting, warm in the light, and felt at peace, as if the universe was trying to hug her. But she didn't want a hug from the universe, she wanted one from Vellum. She needed to apologize and make things right.

She went back to her car and drove to the University Village. After she bought coffee and a box of cheese and fruit, she perched on a stool in the chain café and chose a color scheme for her tulip stickers. Using the water pen that Reese would revile due to its cheapness, she started sketching pages of tulips, so that she could do another monthly sticker kit to make Reese happy. It was the least she could do given that she'd suspected her friend of murder.

When school was out, Mandy drove to Laurelhurst, the quiet, upscale neighborhood nestled along Lake Washington, a trip that had become unfamiliar since her divorce. Some of her paintings, still drying, slid off the seat onto the floor of her car as she made the winding turns.

The Moffats' house, on a hill, had a gorgeous water view on one side and looked over a three-acre park on the other. The beach club was less than a mile away. Mandy liked her house, off a busy, mixed-use street and far from downscale, but she'd always felt she could breathe more deeply in this neighborhood, just off the beaten path. It smelled better.

She drove into the alley behind the Moffats' house and parked outside the garage. Light rain fell on her shoulders as she trudged past the garbage cans to the gate separating the backyard from the alley. Glad that it had held off until now, she reached over the gate and fought with the damp lever until it released and let her inside.

Elaine Moffat wasn't a back-door-visit person, even when Mandy was her daughter-in-law, so she walked alongside the house and up the steps to the front door. She rang the bell and waited.

When the door was opened, she didn't recognize the woman who stood there.

Mandy smiled. 'Hello. I'm Mandy, Vellum's mother. Is my daughter available, please?'

The woman looked at her, confusion registering, then said in a broken accent, 'I get Miz Moffat for you, OK?' She shut the door in Mandy's face.

Mandy jumped back, even though the closing door couldn't possibly have hit her. It felt like rejection. She turned and looked down to the street. Except for the evergreen bushes protecting various properties, the trees were still bare. But she knew spring was coming. Some trees would even be in full bloom in a couple of weeks, the cherry blossoms that flowered in mid-March. But today had descended into winter while she'd perched on her café stool. The air bit at her now and she huddled into her coat.

At least the weather matched her life. The peace she'd found in the Arboretum flowed away with her entrance onto the Moffat property. Words she'd likely hear from them spit invective into her thoughts. Her cousin had been exactly the kind of guy she would have wanted to keep her daughter away from, and she'd missed the signs, her vision obscured by old loyalties. Her trust in him had cost her in many small ways – now even the sight of her beautiful daughter on a daily basis.

'How do I forgive you, Ryan?' she whispered, just as the door opened again.

'Mandy.' The cold voice belonged to Elaine Moffat. Seventy-one now, she had always reminded Mandy of the repressed and judg-mental upper-class mother, Emily Gilmore, from the *Gilmore Girls* television show, but without the intelligence or charm.

'Mom,' Mandy said. She wasn't sure if she should still call Elaine that, but after all these years, what was the alternative?

Elaine frowned but didn't correct her.

'I'd like to see Vellum. Has she arrived home from school?'

'About ten minutes ago.' Elaine looked at her impassively, thanks to heavy Botox paralyzing her face. 'I hope you don't think it is acceptable for you to show up uninvited.'

Mandy stiffened. 'She's my daughter. I have the right to see her. I don't want to get my lawyer involved.'

'You made your choice, Mandy.' The superior tone again.

Mandy's response was flat. 'No, your son did.'

'He tried to save your marriage.'

'Oh, please.' Mandy put one hand on her hip. 'One night. One night he called me, drunk, after he'd moved out, after his affair, and said he was sorry and we could try again. I'm surprised he even remembered the conversation afterward.'

She could see the clockwork mechanism of Elaine's slow-moving brain, the exact moment she seemed to dismiss Mandy's words. 'Well, you must have said no, and therefore you forfeited any right to be a part of my family.'

The door started to close, but Mandy put her hand on it and stared into the old battleaxe's eyes. 'I would like to see my daughter. I can stand here in the rain and text her to come outside, but it would be a lot more dignified if you'd simply let me in.'

Elaine let Mandy hold the door open. She figured it was safe to step inside. Her sensible shoes squelched on the oriental rug. Elaine sighed at the damp spots, then held out her hand for Mandy's coat.

'She is in the guest room at the far end of the floor,' Elaine said, inclining her regal head at the curving mahogany banister surrounding the wide steps that led upstairs.

'Thank you,' Mandy said with dignity, slipping off her shoes at the edge of the rug. The upstairs was carpeted and no shoes were allowed.

Nerves carried her until she reached Vellum's door. She tried not to wonder which of the bedrooms housed Cory, but he had probably taken over the basement suite again. He had still used it on weekends when she met him in college.

The door was cracked open. 'Vellum?' she called.

Mandy heard springs squeak just out of sight. 'Mom?'

Vellum appeared in the doorway, her eyes slightly shadowed and her hair pulled into a messy ponytail. Mandy didn't recognize the beige slacks and sweater set.

'Good grief! Did your grandmother dress you?'

'Mom,' Vellum said, half-laughing and half-crying, then she wrapped her arms around Mandy's waist.

Mandy tucked her daughter against her and leaned from side to side, comforting her.

'It's Wednesday,' Vellum said, her voice muffled in Mandy's shirt. 'What are you doing here? And why does your hair smell funny?'

'I came to apologize. And I got flour in my hair. Sorry.'

'For what?' Vellum lifted her head. 'Baking accident?'

'For letting Ryan move into the basement in the first place. And yes, at work.'

Vellum frowned. 'Really?'

Mandy put her hand to her forehead. 'Really. I'll never let anyone with obvious problems stay with us again.'

'That's good. I mean, not that he ever caused problems.'

Poor Ryan. 'Not that we saw, until it was too late. I owe several people an apology for suspecting them of murder.'

'You know who killed Ryan?'

'Yes. It was someone at work, honey. Not connected to us.' Fifteen was far too young to hear about her mother's brush with a syringe holding who knew what.

'Maybe you do owe Linda an apology, but don't apologize to Crystal next door. She's such a jerk.'

Mandy held back her laughter. 'Duly noted. Listen, honey, you can stay here with Cory if you want. You're old enough to decide, and we can go back to court to change things.'

'That's a pain.'

Mandy pressed her hands together in front of her chin. 'True, but you ought to know that I want you home. And we should have a cop moving in downstairs, not a bad guy.' She smiled brightly. 'Roosevelt Way, safer than ever!'

Vellum nodded thoughtfully, not relieving the mood. 'I'll think about it.'

'That's all I can ask.' Mandy hesitated. 'You need to do what's best for you.'

'What are you going to do now?'

'I have the rest of the week off, so I'm going to take the sketches I've done and turn them into a second April monthly kit, and then film another 'Plan With Me' video in collaboration with Reese.'

'Cool!' Vellum exclaimed. 'How about Friday after school? You can do the kit tonight and sketch out the spreads tomorrow, and we can film on Friday?'

'Perfect,' Mandy said. 'Thanks. I'm so glad you want to be involved.'

'It's my part-time job.' Vellum shrugged. 'I didn't quit my job.'

'Very responsible of you,' Mandy praised. 'I guess I'll see you Friday.'

'Yeah, but message me the designs. I want to see them.'

Mandy nodded. 'I can't wait.'

'And keep Reese in the loop. You don't want to outshine her too much,' Vellum advised.

'Good point.' Mandy bit her lip. 'I guess I had better go. Elaine wasn't too excited to have me stop by.'

'She blames you for the divorce, but we both know that's ridiculous.'

'Yeah, but she does have a fancy security system and no druggie cousins in the basement.'

Vellum rolled her eyes. 'No, she just has Dad.'

Mandy raised her eyebrows, not sure how to take that, but Cory wasn't her problem anymore. 'He around?'

'I don't know. I just got home, but it's not like there's any point in you talking to him. I see Grandma like ten times more than I see him. He's not exactly parenting.'

'That's too bad. Just remember, no matter what, I'm a phone call away. I'll pick you up, listen to you, anything.'

'If you remember to keep your phone charged and in your pocket.'

Mandy saluted her. 'I'm getting better. Heading toward perfection.'

Vellum smiled. 'You can try, Mom. I'll see you Friday after school.'

'Did you dream about tulips last night?' Reese asked Mandy on Friday evening. They were perched on the iron chairs in Mandy's backyard, watching a trio of handsome police officers walk back and forth between the driveway and the back stairs. Detective Justin Ahola had signed the lease Mandy had printed off the internet and paid his first and last months' rent as well as a damage deposit. The Meadows household financial worries were a distant memory.

'So many tulips,' Mandy agreed. 'I'm glad I did some of the original sketches in watercolor so that I didn't have to do everything with my iPad.'

'I don't know how to do real sketching, just digital,' Reese said. 'But you're older than me.'

Mandy rolled her eyes. 'Everyone learns how to use art supplies in school, Reese. It's just a matter of whether you keep up your skills or not.'

Reese grabbed Mandy's arm and shushed her as the box-carrying cop went by. The other two were working together, hauling in furniture.

'I admit I lost my mind when the mattress went by,' Reese murmured, 'but do you think that one is single? He's adorable.'

'He's not Indian,' Mandy said, watching from the rear. The policeman wore jeans that fit his thick, athletic frame, and he'd lost the beanie that had covered his short, buzzed black hair a couple of trips ago. His jacket had come off next, exposing thick, weightlifter's arms covered in smooth, reddish-brown skin.

'No tattoos, and an officer of the law. My parents might be OK with that.'

'I assume he's a good friend of our Detective Ahola to help him move. We'll see him around again.'

'It just had to be February. You can't have a casual backyard barbeque in February,' Reese fretted. 'Football game party? Are there still football parties?'

'It's almost March. It's about baseball season, right?'

'We'll think of something,' Reese said, smiling flirtatiously at Detective Ahola and his other friend, who had a friendly face but a frame so large that he intimidated both women.

Mandy heard a squeak of fear and stood up from her chair. She saw Vellum at the fence, struggling with her backpack and suitcase, her eyes wide with shock at the sight of the oversized cop.

'Hello, Vellum,' Detective Ahola said, smiling at her. 'Remember me? Justin? I'm moving into the apartment now that your cousin's case is closed.'

Vellum stared at him. 'Umm, alone?'

'Sure. My buddies are just helping me move. This big lug is Detective Burns, and the other guy is Officer Frost.'

'He can frost my cookies any time,' Reese cooed, fluttering her eyelashes.

'He's single,' Justin said, humor dancing in his eyes.

Reese's eyes went wide and all of a sudden something on her phone seemed very important.

Mandy smiled at her daughter. 'Ready to film our "Plan With Me"?'

Vellum nodded as Mandy gave her a hug. 'Ummm, Detective? I've been wondering something.'

'What?' Justin asked.

'Mom was always worried that Ryan slipped on her journal and fell down the stairs. I know that's not what happened, but where did that teal journal come from?'

Justin took Vellum's suitcase from her hand. 'It was Scott's.'

'Scott Nelson had a fancy journal?' Vellum asked.

Reese colored. 'It was a teal journal?'

'Yes, why?' Mandy asked.

'Was it one of mine?' Reese asked the detective.

'One of yours?' Vellum asked.

'I gave them away when I started my video channel,' Reese said. 'To a lot of people around the hospital. Not to Mandy, of course. She is my business rival.'

Justin nodded. 'It had your information printed inside the cover, but most of the fingerprints were Scott's. All the notations inside were in code, however, and only a few pages were used, so it wasn't until he confessed that we understood the contents.'

'Oh,' Mandy said, remembering that cryptic piece of paper she'd found. It must have been in the journal. 'Scott admitted he left it there on purpose, since I have the journaling business.'

'By the way,' Justin said, 'the locks will have to be changed. Scott had a copy of your basement door key in his possession.'

'He must have taken Ryan's key.' She didn't want to think about when he had done that. 'Did he put the hammer in that cabinet?'

Justin worked his jaw from side to side. 'Yes, but he hasn't admitted when he put it there. I'll pay for the locks to be changed. It is in my best interest.' He smiled at them, then went up the back stairs with the suitcase as his friends crisscrossed the yard with boxes.

Mandy winced. She still didn't know if Scott had come up behind Vellum in the laundry room, or if her daughter had really seen a ghost. Maybe she'd better schedule that séance after all.

'That's a big suitcase,' Reese said to Vellum. 'Did you have a project at school?'

'No, it was stuff I took to my grandma's house,' Vellum explained.

Mandy tensed. Could Vellum be moving back home?

Reese seemed to sense they needed some private time. She smiled brightly and said, 'I'm so excited to be guest-starring in your "Plan With Me". I'll see you in your solarium!' Then sashayed up the stairs behind Justin.

'Guest-starring?' Vellum asked, wide-eyed and frowning.

Mandy winced. 'Marketing idea. I had to move the camera back, but I can get all three of us in the shot. Then I'll guest-star in her video tomorrow.'

'That's a new one. Three journalers in one video.' Vellum held out her hands.

Mandy chuckled and put her orange-tipped hands into her daughter's. 'With two journaling vloggers on the same block, we're sure to come up with some crazy ideas. We'll see if it works.'

'I see you had time to do a proper manicure for once.'

'Reese and I went to a salon at Northgate Mall last night. Hers are blue, exact opposite on the color wheel. Last I checked you had a French manicure.' She looked down. 'Still do. We should look good together.'

'Mom?'

'What, sweetie?'

'I had a crazy idea too, going to Laurelhurst,' Vellum confessed. 'I'm sorry I wanted to move out.'

Mandy squeezed her hands before letting go. 'I know you didn't feel safe here.'

'I was too safe there,' Vellum whined. 'Grandma drove me nuts, and Dad is totally self-absorbed. She orders him around too, but then he just disappears. It's not like having a dad over there, just a loser big brother. Not only that, the guest room is really stuffy but I couldn't open the window because they are painted shut and alarmed.'

'That's too bad.' Mandy sighed for Vellum's benefit.

'At least when I see him here, he acts like a father.' Vellum sighed too. 'Anyway, I know you would never let me get hurt. And you have a tenant again, so the money problem is solved.'

Mandy put her arm around Vellum's shoulders as the three policemen crossed paths, one with a box, the others heading back to the moving van.

'It looks as though life is settling into a new normal,' Mandy said, gazing at the moving men. When she looked up, Reese waved through the art room windows. 'It's going to be busy around here.'

Linda appeared in the driveway, bearing a plastic tub. She waved. 'I brought brownies. I saw all the activity when I looked out of the upstairs window.'

Vellum chuckled as Linda came toward them. 'I usually wouldn't like a bunch of strange men around, but I think we have the good kind.'

Mandy hooked her hand around Linda's arm and, laughing, the trio went up the back stairs together.

ACKNOWLEDGMENTS

I am so grateful for the community who assisted with this book! First and most importantly, I need to thank Cheryl Schy for her unending cheer in answering questions about the Maple Leaf neighborhood in Seattle. My time living on Roosevelt Way was much less recent than hers.

Thank you to Gary Blatter for answering insurance questions, to Kayla Mason from Planning With Kay for answering planner business questions, and to the Quora.com community for answering hospital questions. Thank you to 'J' – a police officer who prefers to remain anonymous, for answering my many procedural questions. Thank you to author J.M. Frey for facilitating the connection. Also, thank you to the WritersDetective – a Q&A group on Facebook, for answering my questions. All mistakes or dramatic license are my own.

Mandy's version of journaling involves art and I appreciate the support and feedback of Mary Jo Hiestand, Stand Hiestand, and Donielle Dickerson. I appreciate Ryder Carroll's leadership in the journaling community and how his book *The Bullet Journal Method* has fine-tuned many journaling practices.

A number of people read part of this book or the entire manuscript and offered their opinions. Thank you to Delle Jacobs, Marilyn Hull, Peggy Laurance, Judy DiCanio, Mary Keliikoa, Mary Jo Hiestand, Cheryl Schy, Donielle Dickerson, and Paula Hrankowski. My agent Laurie McLean was an invaluable part of this feedback process as well and her support has meant everything.